Old Poison

Old Poison

A Diana Hunter Thriller

Joan Francis

Lobathian Publishers

Old Poison

First Lobathian printing in July 2009

For information
Lobthian Publishers
LobathianPubs@aol.com

ISBN: 978-0-9821370-1-7

Printed in the United States of America

For Lucy, who taught me *nothing is ever what it appears to be* and Charlie who taught me *never assume*.

ONE

I opened the manila envelope and found a CD and a small bundle of hundred dollar bills. At our last meeting his envelope had contained only fifty dollars, the fee for one hour of my time as a private investigator.

Mr. Borson had first approached me at the courthouse after I had testified in a civil litigation case. He'd seemed to be a quiet, normal, little man, with the demeanor of a bookkeeper. He was about five nine, 145 pounds, with wavy dark brown hair, and a small round face. Wearing plain wire-frame glasses and an unremarkable business suit, he could fade into the woodwork almost anywhere. However, for such a normal appearing man, Mr. Borson was developing into one of my stranger clients. My first clue should have been the fact that he insisted on meeting in the park, but even this request had sounded reasonable when he explained he wanted to get away from the office and phones and have a pleasant lunch. My second clue should have been that he chose a park and a picnic table I often used myself.

I held up the wad of cash and looked at him for an explanation.

"That is an initial retainer for your first assignment."

"What's on the CD?"

He hesitated, studying my face, then in a matter-of-fact tone stated: "It is a diary, written on Mars. The information on that disc was carried to Earth by the last wave of colonists when Mars was a dying planet. It has been hidden and handed down from one generation to another by a secret society that is older than known human history."

Oh, damn! Worst suspicions confirmed.

"Right," I said. Noting the label on the CD, a comment just sort of slipped out before I censored myself: "Wow, Microsoft's on Mars too. Does the Attorney General know about this?" I put the cash back in the envelope and set it down on the picnic table.

He smiled, then chuckled.

I stood up to leave.

"Wait, Ms. Hunter, please. Let me explain."

I hesitated. Ripping off some lunatic who thinks the Martians are after him was outside my moral boundary, though I knew one private eye who did just that. My concern was, what would this guy do now? During our previous interview it had become clear that he had done quite a detailed background check on me. If I refused to work for him, would he decide I was one of *them*?

"Look, Mr. Borson, I'm sorry, but I don't think . . ."

"Ms. Hunter, I'm sorry I said it that way. It was just my little joke. It's actually a novel, a sci-fi novel. The writer wants a little research assistance, that's all."

Somehow this sudden shift was as unsettling as his first statement. "I still can't help. I'm a private investigator, not a research assistant."

"The writer wants to present hard-hitting, factual information to make a real statement regarding environmental dangers. As I'm sure you know, power and money can make it most difficult to obtain information regarding industrial and military pollution of our environment.

"Now your diary or novel sounds like an expose. If you're looking for some sort of industrial espionage, try one of the ex-CIA types invading my profession these days. They are not as deterred by illegality as I would be."

"You won't be asked to do anything illegal, but that doesn't mean you won't encounter powerful resistance that will require more investigative skill than an ordinary research assistant could deal with. It's not really such an unusual request. Other PIs help detective novelist all the time."

"I would like to meet with this novelist of yours."

He shook his head. "She wants to remain anonymous. That's why she hired me."

An anonymous writer? This is why I don't advertize in the yellow pages. I don't want layman clients. You have to investigate the client before you can investigate his case. I preferred to work for attorneys in the familiar framework of laws and forms and procedures.

Mr. Borson had been gathering up our picnic. When he spoke again, the only item still on the table was the envelope with the CD and money.

"Look, this is really a fairly simple assignment. On the CD is one chapter of the book which describes a fictional industrial waste product called Red 19. The author just dreamed up Red 19, but I think she is a little obsessed by her own fantasy. She wants to see if any of the new alternative fuels might behave in a manner similar to her fiction. You probably won't find anything, but I promised her we would do a search."

From his jacket pocket he took a white envelope and handed it to me. "If you find the work acceptable, we continue. If not, just send an email to me at the address on this assignment letter, and you'll never hear from me again."

TWO

As I walked home, I wondered why I had accepted the assignment. Admittedly, I was curious. Over the last three weeks, Borson had done an extensive background on me and had spent two lunch hours interviewing me for this project. No one had ever concentrated that much effort on selecting me for a job. I did want to find out what all the fuss was about.

I entered the lobby of my apartment building, on the corner of Eighth and Ocean, which is in a seedy little patch of the county known as Bluff Beach. After stepping into the ancient manually-operated elevator, I waited for Merle to put the thing in gear. She glared at me and said, "Floor".

Merle is about five feet four, thin, and has badly dyed red hair, which is also thin. Her small features are highlighted with lipstick and eyebrow pencil in the same shade of red as her hair. Every day she wears a shirtwaist dress with a white pillbox hat, white cotton gloves, and a yellow cotton jacket trimmed with white lapels and white buttons. This seems to be her own idea of a proper uniform for an elevator lady rather than anything specified by the management. I doubt the "management" whoever they are, ever enter the building, much less Merle's elevator.

"Eighth floor, Merle, same as it's been every day for the last year."

As she maneuvered the small box up to my floor, she mumbled something inaudible. She has been the elevator operator in this building for twenty-three years and seems to have had too many ups and downs, though I have never had the courage to pry into her personal life. She is not exactly friendly. In fact, I am absolutely certain that one day she will quit mumbling angrily to herself, pull a knife out of her pink plastic purse, and with her white-gloved hands madly butcher everyone in the elevator with her. I just hope it's not on a day I ride with her. She jarred the thing to a stop, approximately at the eighth floor. I stepped to the door ledge and down five inches. "Thanks, Merle," I said cheerily.

"Your phone's fixed."

I hesitated and turned to look at her. Was it more of her craziness or had she once again seen someone at my apartment? The last time she said something like that it was the first hint that someone had tried to break into my apartment. "What was that?" She looked at me as if the question had offended her, then shut the elevator door. I shrugged off the thought. Sam had great security on my apartment now.

My apartment is a long, narrow loft, with windows on the north wall. The kitchen and living room areas are defined solely by the arrangement of furniture, and the decor is early St. Vincent de Paul. The bedroom and bath are hidden behind a plywood wall that is completely substandard. But, the place is cheap and it has location. I'm six blocks from the Pacific.

I opened the blind over my desk and sat down at my computer. Borson's written instructions supplied a password but said I was allowed to read only one chapter. Telling a PI not to look at the whole file is like putting a T-bone in front of a hound and telling him to play dead. I slipped the disc into my PC and tried to pull up the directory. "Access Denied." That exhausted my computer hacking skills, so I gave up and typed the password, *rdskblu.* The screen opened silently.

15643-9-23

(47th language translation-English(Copy 2,783) (Caretaker-Nosha)

ESCAPE FROM THE BURROCITY

Squinted my eyes almost closed, did I. Harsh red sunlight almost blinding, and blowing sand stinging exposed skin on me. This sand, this thin oxygen, barely breathe, could I. My lungs like drying Marto skin, did feel. Stopping running, must I, slow to a walk, then stopping for rest. Never outrun them, would I, without a Breather.

I have recently decided I must stop talking to myself before I am mistaken for one of the nuts on the street, but it's a hard habit to break. I mumbled to the computer, "If this writer keeps up this dialect I won't even get through one chapter." The screen blinked, I read the next line, then I blinked.

Syntax adjusted to 20th century English

Though my skin prickled slightly, I concluded that it was coincidence, not an interactive computer program. Reading became much easier.

Would they simply confirm that I had gone Nomad or would they follow my track in the sand? If I could make it to the Great Drain the Enforcers would not follow because no one ever knows when Red

19 residue will be released.

I tried to hold my breath so I could hear something besides my own rasping gasps. At first I could hear nothing but the wind, then I heard the high whine of their Breathers, like a harmonic hum above the wail of the wind.

I adjusted the sand screen over my nose and pulled my hood far down over my eyes. Running westward toward the Great Drain, I prayed the wind would obliterate my tracks.

When I reached the edge of drain, I saw it was at least a hundred feet straight down, no slope, no hand holds. Shaka had said that it had been at least two centuries since there had been any real bridges on the surface. Anything not salvaged by the Protectors was salvaged by the Nomads or eroded by the elements. Construction was now done with rock block and anti-gravity lifters, and that was restricted to the underground burrocities. To cross the drain and find the Nomads, I would have to find a plastibag.

Legend said that the Great Drain had once held rushing waters, but that was probably born of wishful thinking and myths taught to gullible children. If our planet had ever really had such treasure, where would it have gone? Not even the greedy Protectors could have used so much water.

Feeling dizzy now, I could only manage a stumbling walk, but I could see the shape of a plastibag a few yards farther south. As I struggled toward it, the Enforcers' combox voices sounded closer.

Having never seen a giant plastibag, I was dismayed when I got close enough to see what it was really like. It was nothing but a giant bag of sand encased in indestructible Plastiform and placed at a slant against the rim of the drain. Granted, this steep ramp did offer easier access than the straight sides of the drain, but in my condition it looked daunting. The Enforcers were within twenty yards. No choice. I stepped onto the bag.

The Plastiform was covered with fine loose sand, and instead of walking down the slope I found myself skidding faster and faster toward the bottom. With no way to stop or slow my pace, I concentrated on maintaining my balance. I tried to hit the bottom running but landed too stiffly on my left leg, jammed my knee socket, and fell in a heap on the rocky bottom.

Holding my knee, I looked to see if the Enforcers were following. They laughed, pointed up the wash, then turned to jog back to the burrocity. Looking where they pointed, I saw a bright red circle that stained the eastern rim of the drain. The burrocity was dumping Red 19 waste!

I watched in horror as the slick, oily red liquid seeped out of the flotube, spilled down the side of the drain, and began sluggishly rolling south. The leading edge seemed to stretch into a skin-like dam, allowing the thick liquid behind it to build into a wall of swirling, iridescent red ooze.

It's almost pretty, I thought as I sat momentarily mesmerized by a sight I had only heard of and never seen. But it would not make a pretty death.

Ignoring the pain in my knee, I scrambled up and hobbled across the drain to the plastibag on the far side. On hands and knees I tried to climb the slippery slope, a few feet up, then slide back, a few feet more, slide back. Each time I looked, the Red 19 was looming larger.

At first I believed I could climb high enough to be above the flow, but halfway up I saw the wall of red ooze had expanded to the height of the canyon rim. As the flow expanded, it also moved faster down the channel of the drain. Exhausted and without hope, I stopped struggling and waited for the red death to engulf me.

As I watched, the leading edge changed both color and texture. Losing its deep red iridescence and its swirling viscous texture, it began to look more like a gas than a liquid . It was rising slowly off the ground and floating toward me like a heavy red cloud. Suddenly, as it reached some point in its transition, the entire mass lifted rapidly toward the sky.

I sat there watching as the red cloud continued to rise and dissipate until it became indistinguishable from the rest of the thin red atmosphere. Huddled alone on the plastibag, I listened to the wind roar across the desolate wastes of our land.

I hit the down arrow to go to the next page and the entire text first dissolved into meaningless symbols, then disappeared from the screen. I tried repeatedly to restore the text but got nothing but a blank screen. The program had self-destructed.

THREE

I wasted an hour trying to get something to come up on that disc, but once I had read the file, the data had simply disappeared. I decided to call the expert.

"Yeabot."

"Yes, Mother." He rolled over to my desk on his little wheels.

"I have a new problem for you."

Yeabot is a one-of-a-kind, computer robot that was designed and given to me, in lieu of fee, by my friend and mentor, Sam Dehany. I had originally named him Yeibichai for the Navajo talking god, but Sam could never remember that and called him Yeabot. It stuck. Yeabot is three and a half feet high with a body of white plastic and looks like a cross between R2D2 and the Pillsbury Dough Boy. Not only does he gratify my penchant for fantasy, but he is also a very useful tool.

In addition to fun things like keeping me company while I talk to myself, and pouring me a scotch at night, he understands the spoken word better than any voice responsive system on the market. He takes dictation, types my correspondence, searches the Internet and my database sources, and is a full-time guard with phone contact to his creator, Sam. Best of all, like a living, breathing partner, I can simply assign him a problem and he can work out a solution.

I slid the CD into Yeabot's slot. "Check this CD and see if you can open the files or if all the files have been erased."

"Yes, Mother."

Yeabot whirred and beeped and hummed along while I went back to my computer to finish a report for another client. Suddenly, Yeabot made a squawk and ejected the CD so forcefully that it flew out and landed with a clatter on the floor. He was turning from side to side, repeating, "Access Denied, Access Denied, Access Denied."

"Yeabot, end program!" He immediately quieted to his normal unflappable self. "Yeabot, what's the matter with that CD?"

"That CD is protected by a destructive device. If accessed, it will release a virus which will destroy all programs and data on the disc as well as programs and data on any computer operating the disc."

"I see. Mr. Borson seems to have hidden talents." I picked up the disc and considered this new mystery. Deciding what to do was going to take some serious thought. I tossed the disc into my Out basket and turned to my case files.

There were several cases in the file drawer that were screaming for my attention. I pulled out the Carpenter file. I had only a few days left to serve this turkey. A lot of PIs won't fool with process service, but I had developed a reputation for doing *hard serves*. Of course, no one pays me fifty dollars an hour to serve process unless they have already tried regular servers or marshals who do the job for much less. So when I get an assignment, I know before I ask that the recipient either could not be found or could not be caught.

In the case of Mr. Carpenter, the server had broken my number one rule: *Never door-knock anyone*. He'd knocked on the door and was told that Carpenter had moved a year ago. The server accepted this and raced on to his next delivery. The subpoena was handed back to the attorney marked, "Moved, no forwarding address." That's where I come in.

I turned back to my computer and ran the name of my quarry through all of my database accounts, checking for property, vehicle, employment, and consumer public filings. When finished, I concluded that the guy most likely lived right where the server had tried to serve him. In fact, the server had probably been talking with him. Early tomorrow morning I would do a little field reconnaissance and see if I could verify this assumption.

I stretched and looked at the file cabinet and then at my watch. Yeah, 5:15, sun was over the yardarm. I picked up the phone and dialed Sam. His J.Edgar, Yeabot's technological father, answered.

"Sam, you there? It's Diana. How 'bout dinner at the Ocean Way Grill?"
Sam picked up. "Who's buying?"
"Me. Got a fat retainer today."
"I'll see you there."

I turned off the computer, slipped my wallet into my jeans pocket, and the CD in my jacket pocket. I needed Sam's take on this CD.

For twenty-five years Sam had given his heart, soul, and body to the U.S. intelligence service, and high-tech toys and deceptions were his area of expertise. When disillusionment and disgust had replaced duty and patriotism, Sam had looked for a way out. He'd spent his last four years in the service developing advanced robotics technology but had decided he didn't want this technology put to the uses the military had planned for it. With my own brand of deception, I'd helped Sam leave the service and take his robotics knowledge with him. But that's another story, one I don't tell.

Sam now lives quietly in San Pedro. He has no wife, no children, few friends, and no hobbies other than his computer and robotics skills, which he can never use openly. I'm lucky to be his friend and recipient of his genius. However, it is painful to watch such genius and decency wasted and see a dear man grow old in boredom and disappointment.

"I'm going out, Yeabot. You have the security watch."

"Yes, Mother. Security on."

This old building I live in was once an office building. When Bluff Beach slipped into decay a couple decades ago, the office suites were haphazardly converted to low-rent apartments. When crazy Merle goes home at five p.m., the elevator is left on the first floor and there is no auto-call button for the old relic, so tonight I walked down eight flights. It's a toss up as to which is worse, getting in the elevator with Merle or walking the stairs.

Despite its drawbacks, I am enjoying my funky little place, and nowhere else in Los Angeles or Orange County could I find a place so close to the water and so cheap. With the town now redeveloping rapidly, it probably won't stay cheap for long.

The six blocks between my apartment and the grill used to be an area one did not venture into without an armed guard. Now it is a lively, exuberant mix of shiny urban renewal buildings and upscale supper clubs set among the pawn shops, used bookstores, antique shops, tattoo parlors, and seamy bars. The sidewalks are filled with yuppies in evening dress, city kids on their way to the sixteen-screen theater, and panhandlers. As I walked to the restaurant, Dixieland and progressive jazz emanated from two of the clubs, while three street entertainers tried vainly to compete.

I sat at the bar, nursed a Grant's scotch, and waited for Sam to drive over from San Pedro. As soon as he arrived and we were seated at our regular table, I began the tale of my new client, our strange meetings, and the seriously protected CD. Through cocktails and salads, Sam listened silently to my whole story and then looked briefly at the CD.

"Well, Diana, if Yeabot says he can't break this thing, I sure can't do any better."

"Oh, no, I didn't want you to try. I just want you to help me figure out who the heck I'm dealing with here and if I should be. At first I put Borson down as just a curiosity, then as a nut, and then as a crusader with both money and a cause. But this CD puts a new icon on his head. I mean, what writer would go to this length to protect a sci fi manuscript? And, who the heck could do this stuff?"

Sam picked up the CD again and turned it over in his hands as he considered his answer. I noticed how much puffier and softer his hands looked, and noticed the liver spots that had formed on his skin.. He had put on at least twenty pounds. His once handsome face had become round and double chinned, and his bright blue eyes looked tired and dull. I looked back down at my salad plate, hating myself for noticing how much he had aged in the last year. It somehow seemed disloyal.

"Well, you see, just about any able programmer could booby-trap the thing with a virus. To do it so well that Yeabot couldn't find his way around it, that took someone special. Could be someone from the community, all right."

"You mean intelligence community? Maybe I should decline the assignment."

"I don't see why, unless researching this Red 19 leads you to classified information."

"Yeah, but in his assignment letter Borson said to check up on all the latest developments in experimental fuels. What if this is some sort of industrial espionage?"

Sam shrugged. "That's possible, I guess."

"So you think I should drop it and return the retainer?"

He thought a minute. "Not at this point. You know how to evaluate his requests for information. If they stop sounding like science fiction and start sounding like Leavenworth, get out. I think you can handle this, Diana."

At that moment the waiter walked up with two plates of steaming lobster. "Besides," he added, "you're going to need that retainer to pay for my dinner."

FOUR

I was up at five a.m. and by six was settled in on a discreet surveillance near Carpenter's house. My second rule of process service is: *Never let them see you coming*. No matter how many lead-footed, inept servers have tipped them off, I can still surprise them if I handle it right. A corollary to this rule is my sexist rule of thumb: *Never hire a man for the job*. Most of the men in this business are too puffed up with macho images of themselves to use stealth. They have to pound on the doors, kick the trash cans, and announce, "I am a PI!" It's the Sam Spade syndrom.

My subject left his home about eight, driving a Toyota pickup with a plate that matched his vehicle ownership records. His physical description matched the one on his driver's license and I was ninety-nine percent certain that this was Carpenter. However, as all young PIs and police officers are taught, *never assume*. Once I found a guy living in the subject's house and matching his description, but he turned out to be the wife's live-in boy friend.

I followed Carpenter to work and watched as he parked the Toyota. His work place also matched my research, but I didn't try to jump out and run him down. Rule number three: *Never chase after the subject*. Breaking this rule not only caused one of my few failures, but also a broken high-heel, a sprained ankle, and the loss of a client. I watched Carpenter walk into the building, then drove back to Bluff Beach.

It was time to do some research on Red 19. My first job out of college was as a librarian, and I carry a reverence for the wonderful resources of the reference desk. Not in my wildest imagination, however, did I ever envision the amazing, living, breathing, growing leviathan of information that would be born on the Internet. With information being loaded from all over the world and growing exponentially, it seems that any subject you search for can be found. Everything, that is, except for Red 19. Try as I might, I found no fuel or fuel byproduct that begins as a viscous red liquid and transforms into a gas when it hits the atmosphere.

However, I did learn a great deal about the R and D of alternative fuels and identified a couple California firms working in this field. I gave them each a call, but I never made it past the PR desk in either firm. The responses I got made it abundantly clear that my inquiries were considered suspect. Next I tried three chemistry professors to see if anything in basic science could behave like Red 19. No luck.

Next I tried Mike Shelley, a friend of mine who works as a tech writer at Space Delivery Systems, Inc. SDS, Inc., is a well-funded, low-profile, private company working on exploration and colonization of the planet Mars. This is not a governmental operation nor a bunch of science fiction dreamers, but a private corporation that is dead serious about showing a profit, someday. I knew that among other subjects, Mike was well read on the development of fuels for space flight. He wasn't in, so I sent him an email and asked him to check on my mystery fuel.

Finally I called the Wedgeworth Clear Sky Foundation. I am not usually shy about asking questions, but then I normally feel comfortable with my reason for asking them. By the time I dialed Wedgeworth, I was beginning to feel both foolish and frustrated.

Steven W. Wedgeworth had been one of the first chemists to accept and verify the work of Nobel Prize winners Rowland and Molina. Their research had determined chlorinated chemicals were eating a hole in the ozone shield.

Wedgeworth had not waited for the idea to gain acceptance and the prize to be awarded. Though he was at the time a junior chemist for GarlChem, Inc., he had boldly gone where no industrial establishment chemist had gone before. He'd conducted research which damned products manufactured by his employer. When he couldn't get them to make changes in the polluting products, he had the study published in a respected peer-reviewed journal. He was promptly fired and blacklisted. What else? That's the American way. Wedgeworth might have found a position in academia but chose instead to devote his life to the cause of saving the planet. He lived like a church mouse and used every bit of his resources to set up a foundation. On the Internet that morning I had learned that this foundation had the world's largest database for atmospheric studies. If they didn't know about Red 19, no one did.

I expected to get a secretary or receptionist and at least three lines of defense between me and the Man. When Wedgewood answered the phone himself, I felt guilty for taking his time to ask him about a fictional substance.

He hesitated a long time before answering. Then in slow, carefully measured words he replied, "What you describe to me does not sound like anything currently known to science."

I thanked him and was about to hang up when he added, "Of course, the entire idea of ozone depletion was unknown to science a very short time ago, so one does not wish to make absolute statements. But at this time, no." Embarrassed at taking the man's time for this fiction, I thanked him and quickly hung up the phone.

I was studying my notes to see if there was any other useful place to check when the phone rang. It was Mike Shelley at SDS, Inc. Without even the preamble of a hello, he shouted at me: "Hunter, don't you ever pull shit like that on me again. I haven't had a dressing down like that since boot camp. I don't know what sort of fringe element freaks you're dealing with these days, but don't ever use me as the patsy again. Hear?" He slammed down the receiver before I could respond.

I listened to the dial tone a while, depressed the button a moment, and called him back. His phone just rang. He did not want to talk with me.

"Yeabot, send this note to Mike Shelley's email: 'Dear Mike, whatever happened, I am sorry it put you in a bad spot. We've known each other a lot of years, and I hope you know I wouldn't do such a thing on purpose. Maybe I don't know what sort of fringe element freaks I've gotten into either. It would really help me if you could enlighten me on that subject. Diana."

The damned *Martian Diary* CD lay on my desk, taunting me while I debated what to do next. The answers I had gotten so far indicated that establishment scientists had no knowledge of anything looking or acting like Red 19, at least nothing accepted and proven. But someone, somewhere, must have been talking about it or Mike wouldn't have gotten the response he did. Some "fringe element freaks" must have tried to tell the tale of the *Martian Diary* to the team planning the exploration of Mars.

Enough! It was time I found out who the hell I was really working for. I instructed Yeabot to scan my description of Red 19 and search for any information on any persons or organizations associated with such a substance. His search brought up thousands of hits, so I helped him define the search a little better.

Eventually we got the results down to three articles reported in a community weekly in Paso Nuevo, California, a small mountain community about forty miles outside of Bakersfield. These three chronicled a protest attempt by a young woman named Professor Evelyn Lilac. It crossed my mind that with that name she might have escaped from a game of *Clue*. She had chained herself to the gate of the Blue Morpho Petroleum research laboratory and refused to leave until press and television reported her statement. She wanted the world to know that Blue

Morpho was experimenting with a new red-colored fuel that she called *Red 19*. She claimed it would be disastrous to the environment. It appeared that the only press she got was the local weekly, and even there she was written up as a total nut case.

"Hell, Yeabot. I think we just identified the mysterious author of the *Martian Diary*. It seems Mr. Borson has us working for a crackpot . . . I think."

"Crackpot is unknown reference."

"Means she's crazy. Yeabot, this article says she got full television and press coverage. Check for other stories on this event."

He whirred and clicked and reported, "Zero hits."

"Zero? No one else wrote anything about this event. Scan these stories and check every name, date, fact, and location."

"Zero hits on this event. Twenty-two stories from Costa Rica on Evelyn Lilac, environmentalist, president of the Lilac Environmental Institute. One article from the Long Beach Press Telegram on the environmental expo."

"No other paper even covered the story. That is strange. The Paso Nuevo paper even ran a picture of the reporters surrounding her. Maybe she's not a nut. Maybe it's Mr. Jordon time."

"Mr. Jordon reference unknown."

"Movie reference, Yeabot. *Heaven Can Wait.* Mr. Jordon said, 'The probability of a person being right increases in direct ratio to the number of people trying to prove him wrong.' Think I need to talk with this lady."

Yeabot translated the Spanish articles and I read through the rest of the clippings. In addition to picking up bits and pieces of information on Evelyn Lilac and the Costa Rican environmental movement, I learned one very interesting fact. Professor Lilac was in the United States for appearances at public conferences on global warming. The first was held two days ago in Chicago, Washington, D.C. would host the last and largest event at the end of the week, but one was scheduled in Long Beach in two days. Bingo! I would meet this lady before I filed any report or spent any more of that retainer.

FIVE

I turned my bike over and popped off the front wheel with its flat tire. Nine years of riding this trail and never a flat. Murphy's corollary I guess. If it's going to go wrong it will be at the worst possible time.

Professor Evelyn Lilac had graciously granted me an interview, but her only available time was during her morning bike ride. I was to meet her at the beach entrance to the river bike trail at precisely eight a.m., and if I was late by one minute, she would leave without me. Even getting this concession out of her had taken hours of calls and call-backs from myriad intermediates associated with the upcoming environmental conference.

After chaining my bike to the nature center fence, I picked up the tire and took off at a run down Fall Avenue. As I ran, I tried to figure my chances of making it. At my normal cruising speed of ten to twelve miles an hour, it took me twenty-five minutes to ride down the trail from Fall Avenue to Seal Beach. It was 7:30. That gave me five minutes to fix the tire. It took four of those minutes just to get to the station.

I ran up to the lone attendant and plunked down the tire and a twenty-dollar bill. He was a very young, good-looking kid, with brown eyes and long naturally blond hair tied back in a pony tail. Breathlessly I said, "There's a ten-buck tip in it if you can do me a rapid pit stop and change this tube in two minutes."

He eyed my twenty and with a smile replied, "Cool." With no wasted motion he pulled the old tube, popped in a new one and pumped it up to seventy psi. As he finished, he put his hands in the air like a rodeo cowboy after tying off a calf. With a beautiful, good-natured grin, he called, "Time! Did I make it?"

I actually hadn't even looked at my watch, but I replied, "With twelve seconds to spare." I thanked him, handed him the extra ten bucks, and ran toward the river.

By the time I had the wheel back on, I had lost fifteen minutes. That meant I had to make up ten minutes on my usual time. I had recently replaced my beach cruiser with a ten-speed and today I pushed my speed to eighteen miles per hour. I was feeling smug until a voice behind me said, "On your left." With that, two tall lean bikers in matching "real" biking attire swept past me like I was standing still. I wondered if I could go faster if I changed my blue jeans for a pair of those brightly striped spandex pants.

Just before the Cathedral Street overpass, I heard a noise that was closer and different from the steady traffic sounds on the overpass above. The trail at this spot dips sharply downhill, so that when you go through the underpass, you are within two feet of the river. Then the trail climbs up again on the far side and angles to the left. Because of this configuration you can't see the bottom of the underpass until you ride into it.

The noise, which I realized was the thrum of an idling boat engine, grew louder, and as I rode into the underpass I saw a shallow draft motorboat sitting at the edge of the water.

Cathedral Street is supported by several cement columns, which are two or three feet thick and run the full width of the roadway. The first of these is about ten or fifteen feet into the river, and from the bike trail it looks like a cement wall. The boat was about eighteen feet long and wide enough that it did not have a lot of leeway between the edge of the trail and the cement support.

The man at the wheel turned his face from view as I rode by. As I pumped up the far side of the underpass, I looked back at the boat and he again turned his face.

As I rode out of the underpass, my peripheral vision caught a biker, dressed in sweats and a stocking cap, sitting at the edge of the northbound lane, huddled over the handlebars of an old bike. He looked like he was poised to lunge into motion, like a participant waiting for the start of a bike race. As I did a double take and looked directly at him, he too averted his face from my view and pulled the cap a little lower.

My mind tried to go in about three directions at once. At such times I like to imagine that there are different personalities on my internal board of directors. Though my friend Jenny thinks this is bordering on a serious mental disorder, I have a shrink friend who actually uses this as a method of therapy. For me it is a way to bring order out of chaos.

For instance, as I considered the guy hunched over his bike, and the boat strangely parked under the overpass, one member of my board wanted to play though a number of scenarios and speculate on what they were doing there. This member is always suspicious and is capable of finding possible villains and conspiracies everywhere. The investigator on my board suggested stopping to chat them up and see if there seemed to be any real problem here. My ever vigilant manager, however, reminded me that it was now eight a.m., I was still five minutes from the beach, and my bike speed had slowed to nine miles per hour. Concentrating on my bike pedals, I was soon picking up speed.

A short way down the trail I saw a woman riding toward me. I had passed several people on the busy bike trail, but this one caught my attention because of her clothing. Though it was a clear, sunny fall day, she wore a broad-brimmed, plastic-coated rain hat and a rain jacket brightly emblazoned with a flag. I had ridden several yards past her before the inspiration hit me. *I'll bet a dollar to a doughnut that was a Costa Rican flag on that jacket.*

As I attempted to execute a sudden stop and U-turn, I lost my balance and almost landed on the huge rocks that made up the riprap at the edge of the trail. By the time I got turned around, Professor Evelyn Lilac was well on her way north and going like a bat. I pumped hard and was gaining on her when she rode into the turn and descended into the underpass. The biker sitting at the edge of the trail lunged after her, his front tire inches from her back tire. "I told you so," gloated my suspicious board member.

The professor's scream echoed out from the underpass, rising over the constant noise of the traffic on Cathedral Street. By the time I could see down the trail, I had more speed than I'd dreamed I could muster. As my eyes adjusted to the shadow of the underpass, I saw two bikes lying in a pile blocking the northbound lane. Lilac and her assailant were locked together in the southbound lane as he struggled to pull her toward the river and the waiting boat.

There was no way around them. I started to hit the brakes, though I knew I would never be able to stop in time. Then Lilac landed a fairly well-placed knee, dropping her assailant to the rocks at the water's edge. She tried to turn and run but tripped and tangled herself in the fallen bikes. Her assailant was getting up slowly from the side of the path. The guy in the boat was yelling something in Spanish.

Seeing a narrow opening between Evelyn and her assailant, I let go of the brakes. Hunching down over the handlebars, I lowered my head, keeping the back of the helmet toward the assailant, and peddled like hell. I know I was going thirty miles per hour when I hit the sucker because my nose was only about two inches from the computer on the handlebars. Fortunately for me, he stepped backward when he saw me almost on top of him, so I only hit him a glancing blow. His own loss of balance and the rocky bank did the rest. He stumbled backward, falling with his upper body in the boat and his legs in the water.

I struggled to keep myself and the bike upright, but about halfway up the far side of the underpass, I tipped over and landed heavily on my right side. I lay there a moment, legs still wrapped around the fallen bike, the breath knocked out of me, my head stunned, my ribs in pain.

Both men were cursing. The guy who had fallen was pulling himself into the boat but wasn't moving very fast. The driver was starting to climb out of the boat and head for the bike path.

With my left hand I unzipped the handlebar bag. With my right I reached into the bag and pulled out my Walther .32 semiautomatic. Still lying there tangled in my bike, I pulled the slide on the Walther, chambered a round, and took aim. The driver was out of the boat, making his way though the riprap when he heard the sound of the slide. He looked up to see the muzzle aimed at his chest, and without a word turned back to the boat, climbed into the pilot seat, slammed the boat in gear, roared out of the underpass, and headed down-river.

SIX

As I watched the boat speed toward the open ocean, I pushed the release on the Walther and dropped the clip into my bike bag. Pulling the slide, I popped out the chambered round, pushed the loose bullet back into the clip, and returned the clip to the handle of the Walther.

All the time I was doing this mechanical routine, I was chanting the CF number on the boat. As a Sherlock Holmes I have one great handicap: poor visual memory. If I want to remember what a subject looks like, I must turn what my eyes see into words and remember those words, because the minute I look away, the mental picture is gone. It's like a camcorder with no video tape in it.

I put the Walther away and hunted for a pen and paper to write down the number. During this process, Professor Lilac was trying to ask me a question. By the time I got that number on paper, the volume of her voice had increased and her tone expressed either annoyance or alarm. "Are you all right?" she almost yelled.

The line was irresistible. "Professor Lilac, I presume?"

If she caught my reference she was not amused. "Are you that detective who was supposed to meet me this morning?"

Her tone was what my great-aunt Leah would have called "snippy." I tried to disentangle my legs from the bike and stand up. My ribs hurt, a lot. I reached down gingerly for my bike. "That's private investigator."

"What?"

"I'm a private investigator, not a detective."

"What's the difference?"

"A detective is either a rank in the police department or a character in bad fiction."

"Whatever you call yourself, I do wish you could have been on time and protected me from this assault."

Now my voice got a bit testy. "If you want protection, look up 'body guard,' or perhaps 'executive protection specialist,' not private investigator. And in case you didn't notice, despite the fact that it is not in my job description, I did rescue you from this assault at the cost of ribs which are either broken or badly bent."

Her facial expression and voice changed. "I guess you did, Ms., ah, Ms. Hunter, isn't it? I guess I'm a little rattled. When he grabbed me–I thought– three of my associates in Costa Rica were murdered and–thank you, Ms. Hunter. I am quite sure you saved my life today."

She had gone from snippy to a quivering damsel in distress in thirty seconds, and my suspicion quotient went up with equal speed. If I had busted myself and my bike over some staged incident, I would toss this broad in the river myself. With great control I said, "Well, we were lucky. If they had gotten you into that boat they could have had you out to open sea quite quickly. Why do you think they want to kill you?"

She gave me an appraising look. Her personality did another shift. "It's a long story. Do you think you could make it back down to my motel in Seal Beach or should we call an ambulance and get you to a hospital?"

"I'm okay," I lied. "But I thought you had this tight schedule and couldn't talk to me anywhere but the bike trail."

"This morning's attack changes things."

"I see." I hoped my voice didn't reveal the skepticism I was feeling.

Dramatically she looked around the underpass and down the river. "Let's get out of here. We're only five blocks away from the place I am staying."

"Does your room have a coffee pot?"

She looked blank for a moment, then smiled and said, "Yes, and good Costa Rican coffee." Her smile changed her looks completely, and in a strange way revealed that she was older than I had first thought, maybe in her late forties.

Ms. Lilac didn't want to talk until we got back to her room, and that was fine with me because every breath I took sent pain through my rib cage. This was definitely going to require an x-ray.

Her rental bike and my ten-speed were both a bit bent and dented but serviceable. However, as I listened to the bent fender rub against the tire on my bike, I decided this was a perfect excuse to trade up.

Her "motel" turned out to be a wonderful B&B composed of many small cottages. I had always wanted to try it, but the price tag was out of my reach. We parked our beat-up bikes in front of her cottage, and Prof. Lilac welcomed me into her two-bedroom suite. I looked around the adorably decorated rooms with envy. Money must not be a problem for her. I avoided the soft overstuffed furniture and sat carefully in a straight-back chair that would support my back and put less stress on my ribs.

The professor dug into her suitcase and pulled out a plastic bag with coffee. She placed a small wooden stand on the counter, hung a cloth filter from the top, and put a coffee cup on the round wooden tray beneath the filter. As she opened the sack and measured coffee into the cloth bag, that wonderful aroma of fresh ground coffee filled the room. We made small talk while she boiled water and poured it through the coffee bag, distilling two steaming cups of aromatic coffee. When she handed me a coffee and a sweet roll, my attitude toward her softened. What a pushover I would be. They wouldn't have to torture me, just hold a cup of coffee under my nose.

As she sat across from me I said, "Okay, Professor Lilac, let's talk about what's going on with you."

She looked down and sipped her coffee and her hair fell forward, partially covering her face. She had light brown hair with reddish highlights, naturally curly and very thick. Her ebullient halo of hair contrasted with the slightly anemic look of her pale white skin. Freckles, of the same reddish brown as her hair, covered her face and seemed to diminish her small features. Her lashes and brows were so light they almost disappeared against her skin.

I waited for her to answer, but the silence lasted a full minute. "Okay Professor, let's start with an easier one. Who were those guys in the boat?"

As she looked up at me with eyes of washed-out blue, the pain in those eyes was so real I abandoned my momentary suspicion of her. Then in a flash, the pain turned to anger and she snapped: "Stop calling me Professor. My name is Evelyn."

"Okay, Evelyn, who were those men in the boat

"I don't know who they were, but I can guess how they found me. When you were calling all those people at the conference yesterday, did it ever occur to you that I might have reasons I didn't want my location known?"

Her rebuke was a complete surprise. "No, it didn't. You're the keynote speaker. That didn't sound exactly like you were hiding out."

"Why were you so determined to find me?"

"Because your pal Borson hired me to do research on your Mars novel. I needed to talk with you directly."

Her eyes widened and her mouth opened as new fear registered on her pale features. "Borson? What does this Borson look like?"

The vague apprehension I'd had about Borson's motives suddenly grew and formed a cold knot in my gut. "White, male, about five feet ten, wavy dark hair, medium build, neatly dressed. Sort of bookkeeperish."

Her expression changed subtly, and she seemed to relax somewhat. "I see. Borson told you I was writing a novel and told you to talk with me?"

"Not exactly. Your name turned up while I was researching your red stuff. Evelyn, you didn't tell him to hire me, did you?"

Ignoring my question, she countered with one of her own. "What, exactly, was the assignment he gave you?"

"To see if any real substance behaves like Red 19 does in your book."

"He showed you the diary? When?"

"Just one chapter."

"One chapter."

"Yeah, then the thing self-destructed like a *Mission Impossible* tape. What the hell is going on here? Who is Borson?"

She studied me a minute, breathed a deep sigh, then avoided my gaze by burying her face in her hands. With the heels of her hands covering her eyes, she sat silent for several moments. When she looked up at me again, there was a finality, a deadness, in her expression. She stood up. "No, I didn't tell him to hire you. I am grateful you were around this morning, but I won't be needing any further assistance."

I was dismissed. "Just like that? What about your life being in danger and people in Costa Rica being murdered?"

"I believe you pointed out that 'body guard' is not in your job description."

"Yes, but, I just meant I'm not skilled in physically protecting people. If you tell me what's going on, maybe I can help. If we need muscle, I sure as hell know who to call. Who were those thugs? Who has threatened your life? What does that have to do with your novel?"

She walked to the door and opened it. "I don't have time for you, Ms. Hunter. Please leave. Can you make it home, or do I need to call you a taxi?"

Not only dismissed, but patronized to boot. "Yeah, I can make it home just fine, Evelyn. How about you? Can you make it wherever you 're going?"

"Yes, thank you, Ms. Hunter. Goodbye."

That was that. I took a last swallow of coffee, stood up and pulled out my wallet. As I left, I handed her a business card. "If you change your mind, give me a call."

She took the card, studied it a moment, then without a word, stuffed it into her bra.

I smiled. "There was a character in an old WWII movie who did that. Her code name was High Pockets."

"I'll treasure that bit of trivia," she said with heavy sarcasm and shut the door in my face.

I glared at the closed door for a moment and then carefully mounted my bike, testing the effect on my ribs. Finding the pain tolerable, I headed north but only got as far as the entrance to the river trail. I had to go back.

I was a block away when she came out of the cottage, carrying a large backpack, and climbed into a cab. I pedaled after her, yelling her name. She turned around and looked at me out of the back window of the cab. She looked frightened and sad but simply turned her back on me as the cabby hit the gas. That was the last time I saw her alive.

SEVEN

I considered the open cottage door. Despite the fictional stereotypes, most real PI's do not gather evidence by breaking and entering. In fact, most of us take great pains to ensure that nothing we do violates privacy or evidence statutes, because judges tend to frown on illegally obtained evidence. Not only can illegal acts cause the loss of the case, but it can cost you your license, your freedom, and leave you open to a liability suit that could put you in the poor house forever.

On the other hand, Professor Lilac had not only left her door unlocked, she had left it slightly ajar. Entering was not a B and E under any interpretation of the law. It might be considered trespass, but after all, I had been a guest less than fifteen minutes earlier. Finding a door ajar any responsible person would naturally feel obligated to make sure the room was secured. With this justifying logic, I stepped inside.

All the lights in the place were on. Evelyn had left the suitcase open on the bed and briefcase open on the table but each looked as if it had been rapidly ransacked.

I looked through the briefcase but found only material on the three conferences she had come to attend. Lilac was a featured speaker, talking about the destruction of the rain forest in Costa Rica and elsewhere. There was a copy of her speech carefully written in longhand.

Her suitcase contained nothing but clothing and the LAX luggage tags. Closet and dresser were empty. There were no toilet items, not even a toothbrush, no hidden diary or address book or other wonderful, convenient clues left for me to find.

"The lady travels light," I said aloud. With that thought expressed, my brain finally settled on what I had missed seeing and why it bothered me.

I searched the kitchen, checking all the cupboards and the fridge. Her Costa Rican coffee and coffee maker were gone. All that remained were some of the coffee grounds in the sink where she had rinsed out the cloth. The professor was not coming back. Whatever was left in this room, she had jettisoned. Anything she needed was in the backpack she'd loaded into the taxi.

In the silence of that room a depression settled over me, and I thought about the sad, lonely look in her eyes as the taxi sped away. I now had no doubt that she was in real danger and that my angry response this morning had pushed her into facing it alone. Whatever drove her was too urgent or too complex for her to take time to explain. "Damn!"

With this insight, I searched the briefcase again. Her airline itinerary showed a flight to the DC area in two days and a flight from LAX to San Jose, Costa Rica, a week later. No tickets, just the itinerary. How had she planned to get back to LA from D.C. and what had she planned to do during that week? None of this would help now. All this was abandoned . . . all plans changed.

There was a Long Beach Environmental Expo schedule and Evelyn's conference identity badge. I pocketed these and her speech, took one last look around the room, and headed home.

After a slow, careful ride back up the river trail, I swapped my bike for my baby blue 1957 T-Bird with the vanity plate "PRE10D" and headed to urgent care. No, the ribs showed no break; and yes, they would probably hurt for three or four months. I filled my pain pill prescription, picked up Chinese take-out, and headed home.

After an early dinner and a steaming hot shower, I took two pain pills and climbed into bed with Evenly Lilac's speech. By the second page the pills hit and my eyes closed.

It was eight a.m. the following day when I opened my eyes again. After that many hours in dreamland, I woke up with that wonderful blank memory you develop while you sleep. The first movement, however, sent pain through the ribs and brought back yesterday's events. With a groan I climbed out of the sack.

Sipping coffee, I stared out the window as my mind kept replaying my meeting with Evelyn Lilac. What could I or should I do about her? She was not my client and had made it clear she wanted nothing to do with me. She had left with nothing but a backpack, and I had no idea where she was or how to contact her. I could go to the conference and see if she showed, but I didn't expect her to. There was nothing I could do. So why did I feel so guilty?

I shook it off and filled the morning with breakfast and the newspaper. About 1:30 I sat down at the computer and typed a brief report for Borson, telling him about the incident on the river trail and that I would not continue the case. In figuring out how much of his retainer could be legitimately billed and how much had to be returned, I toyed with the idea of including the hours spent in the emergency room but couldn't bring myself to do it. Bill attached, I sent his report via email and asked for a physical address to return the retainer.

I spent about fifteen minutes checking my case log and was about to shut down when the little voice on my computer told me I had mail.

Mysteriously, the Borson report had been returned as undeliverable. I checked the address–it was the one he had given me. "Damn! Now what?" I sat and stared at the screen a moment. With a rising awareness of professional incompetence, I realized that I had no other means of contacting him. How had I let that happen? I lectured everyone I knew on the need to get full information on their business contacts.

"Well, just peachy keen! If he wants his report and his retainer, he will have to contact me."

I slapped a hand over my mouth. I had to quit talking to myself. Listening to Merle mumble angrily as she delivers me to my floor is like seeing the Ghost of Christmas Future. I turned to my only residential companion and added, "Right, Yeabot?" Maybe that's why my great-aunt Leah talked to her little Chihuahua all the time.

At the sound of his name, Yeabot rolled over to my desk and said, "Good afternoon, Mother. Today's calendar has one deadline. You must serve Terrence Carpenter."

"Thank you, my little friend." I shut down my computer, pulled the subpoena out of the file, grabbed the essentials, and headed out the door. "You have security, Yeabot."

"Security on," he replied.

My background investigation complete, it was time to nail Terrence Carpenter in a way that would leave no question about his identity or the legality of the service. That's what my clients pay me fifty bucks an hour for.

At 4:30 I arrived at his work parking lot, found his pickup, and parked close by. Rule number four: *Never let them see papers*. Since I had no pockets, I folded the subpoena and stuffed it into my bra. As I stashed it there, I thought of Evelyn and wished I knew where she was.

I busied myself with rearranging the mess in my trunk until Carpenter's shift was off at five. As he walked out to his car, I looked up and smiled.

"Hi, Terry."

His face registered a blank as he tried to figure out who I was. Like most people, he didn't want to let me know he didn't recognize me.

"Hi there. How's it going?" he replied.

"Not bad. Did Marge get that folder to you today?"

Now he really looked blank. He stopped right in front of me and asked, "What folder?"

That is how it works. I don't chase after or door-knock anyone. I do my homework and let them walk right up to me and practically ask me to hand them the service.

I reached into my blouse and pulled out the subpoena. "I have a subpoena for you, Mr. Carpenter, in the case of Solco versus Marvin. The attorney's name is on the top, right here. If you have any questions, you may call him at this number."

"Hey, lady, you got the wrong guy. My name's not Carpenter." He tried to hand the document back and when I did not take it, he tossed it to the ground.

"Yes, you are Mr. Carpenter. I have already identified you, your truck right over there, your fifteen-year residence on Hermosa Street, and your job as a foreman in the metal shop here. If necessary, I will testify in court that I served you. I suggest you call the attorney before he has the judge issue a bench warrant for you for failure to appear. Goodbye, Terry."

I shut the trunk, climbed into my car, and drove away. In the rearview mirror I watched Carpenter bend over and pick up the subpoena.

There is always a slight adrenaline rush after a service, and I didn't want to sit around the apartment. I had several other cases to work, but Carpenter had been the only deadline, and I could not get Evelyn Lilac out of my brain. She was a mystery, she was in danger, and she had looked so scared as she drove away in that cab. I dressed in a business suit, pinned her conference badge on my lapel, and headed for the Long Beach Convention Center.

EIGHT

The banner read, "FIRST INTERNATIONAL ENVIRONMENTAL EXPO," not "Conference." Looking around the convention hall, I understood the difference. This was an expo for the public, not for the environmental professional. It had that home-show atmosphere, with mind-boggling rows of exhibitors displaying their causes, organizations and products.

I presented Evelyn Lilac's badge and waited to see if the fresh-faced young brunette would call the gendarme and have me tossed out. She processed me with a smile and rote phrase, "Enjoy the expo."

On the back wall of the convention center was a huge screen flashing images of exotic places, interspersed with adorable animal pictures and colorful flora. I stood mesmerized until the pictures cycled into a presentation of death and destruction: clear-cut forests, dead animals, and barren land peopled with starving, emaciated children.

I looked away. Since I was old enough to make a conscious choice, I have rejected any form of entertainment or information that graphically displays the inhumanity, cruelty, and stupidity of the human race. I understand that some people feel compelled to display such horrors in order to protest against them. I even concede that occasionally it works. Graphic news of the Vietnam War certainly helped bring that atrocity to an end. I, however, do not need pictures to feel the pain, and I cannot bear to watch. It is one of the ironies of my life that, both as a reporter and as an investigator, I have worked in cases of human tragedy that I would never allow on my television, either as news or entertainment.

When I turned away from the pitiful scenes on the screen, I caught a man staring at me. He was a slender fellow, of medium height, with a thin bony face and eyebrows so heavy and dark that they seemed to hold up his brown leather hat. When I first looked his way, his brown eyes were fixed on the badge attached to my jacket.

I pointedly returned his stare to gage his response. Most people caught staring will turn away. Not this guy. First his face registered surprise at my challenge, then assessment, and finally, a professional control. With real or feigned amusement, his mouth formed a smile, but his eyes remained coldly appraising. He saluted me with a slight tip of his brimmed hat and a nod of his head. His easy use of such Old World gallantry confirmed my suspicion that he was not from the U.S. With that salute, he turned and walked into the milling crowd.

Good. The badge was doing its job. Now I needed to know who this guy was and how he was connected to Lilac? If his interest was more than recognition of the keynote speaker's name he would be back.

A musical fanfare interrupted my thoughts, and I looked up to find the big screen dark and doors opening on each side of the huge room. A strange looking little two-passenger car rolled in through the door on the right, and climbed almost silently up a ramp and came to a stop on a circular stage. As the stage began to revolve, the loud speaker introduced this model as a clean, quiet, electric car, and said that in some cities you could ride the train to town and rent the little electric to run around town. Maybe Tweetie Bird's little old Grannie was really ahead of her time.

There followed an entire parade of cars, carts, bikes and scooters, powered by batteries, solar panels, hybrid engines, and experimental fuels. Major car manufacturers as well as smaller companies were displaying their versions of the future. Finally, a troop of four policemen mounted on electric bicycles, put on a little show of synchronized riding, complete with wheelies. When the bike chorus line rolled off stage left, the show ended.

I began my tour of the exhibits and found there were environmental groups from almost every country in the world, most states, and many for-profit companies. The amazing array of products and services included environmentally safe packaging, outdoor clothing and gear, eco-tourist trips, solar heating and cooling, alternatively fueled vehicles of every sort, ecologically safe batteries, and maps of electric recharging stations. Many companies offered technologies to clean the Earth, air, and water; and dozens of universities displayed their research projects covering myriad environmental issues.

I turned toward the booths on the north wall and saw a man in a brown leather hat turn quickly and disappear into the crowd. The hat was made with a hard waterproof leather finish and styled as a cross between a standard slouch hat and an Indiana Jones hat. Both its style and its timeworn patina made me certain there could not be two in this crowd. Had he been watching me again, or was it coincidence that we were at the same place in this crowd?

With my antenna up, I continued a leisurely tour of the expo. Everywhere I turned there were earnest, passionate people, young and old, asking for my support for some place, plant, or animal that was about to disappear from this Earth. In their fervor, they reminded me of Evelyn Lilac. Overwhelmed by problems I couldn't solve, I decided it was time to get to work on the problem that had brought me here.

There is some kind of energy transmitted when you are being watched. I am positive of this, though no science can yet prove it. I turned around quickly, certain that my friend in the leather hat would be there. The slight widening of his eyes showed he was startled by the sudden confrontation. I held him with my gaze as if to say, "Game's up."

NINE

His response was to give me a charming smile as he walked over and removed his hat. It occurred to me that if he really hadn't wanted me to notice him, he could have taken off that hat before following me around the hall.

"Please allow me to present myself. I am Guillermo Jesus Montegro y Monteblan." With the hint of a bow he added, "*A sus ordines*, that is, at your service, Senora."

The Old World charm was so natural I was sure he had been raised with it. He must come from a little patch of twentieth-century culture that had not yet given up the graciousness of its past.

"*Con much gusto, Senor . . .*" His name had rolled off his tongue like music, but I found myself at a loss to repeat it.

"My American friends call me Gill. I would be honored if you would also." His voice was soft, resonant, and mellifluous. He had a slight Spanish accent overlaid with a cultured, almost aristocratic English. That he had chosen to accept a personal confrontation rather than disappear again displayed the assurance and audacity of a professional. Now to learn what type of professional.

"I'm Diana Hunter. Pleased to meet you, Gill. Are you an exhibitor at the expo?"

"You are Diana Hunter? Then, please tell me, Miss Hunter, why does your name tag say Professor Lilac?" A half mocking smile played on his features, but his eyes warned me that his question was no joke.

"Evelyn and I had a passing acquaintance. She couldn't be here, so I borrowed her pass."

"I see."

"Now your turn, Senor. Why were you so interested in Evelyn's badge that you followed me around the hall?"

"The professor is also an acquaintance of mine. It was natural for me to wonder who was masquerading under her identity and why."

"I see." I studied his face, wondering what kind of acquaintance, friend or foe? Had he sent those two men to the bike path? "Why don't we sit over there and order a couple of the Amazon coolers and talk about our mutual acquaintance?"

He smiled. "I know something better. This way." He held out an arm, graciously allowing me to go first. That also put him behind me where I couldn't watch him.

"Why don't you break a trail for me though this mob?" I said.

"My pleasure," he replied. I followed him across the room to a booth I had visited earlier. The exhibitor was an institute called Enviro-Medic Research, which was based in Costa Rica. Running it were the Hoffmans, a husband and wife team: Judith, a medical doctor; and, Ken, a botanist. Together they had set up a foundation to protect a small patch of forest near their medical clinic. They provided modern medical aid to the local citizens and researched tropical plants used in traditional medicine.

Ken Hoffman walked over to us, and guarded looks passed between the two men. Ken was not really handsome but was large and athletic, with a strong masculine presence. From my first glance at his broad shoulders and thick neck, I pegged him as a college football hero and big-man-on-campus.

With forced casualness Gill said, "Mr. Hoffman, allow me to present Diana Hunter, an acquaintance of Professor Lilac's. It seems that Evelyn loaned Miss. Hunter her pass for the expo. I think maybe this solves the mystery of why it was said that Evelyn was here."

Ken tried to control his facial reaction but was artlessly transparent, revealing first relief then confusion and concern. His lack of skill in the fine art of duplicity seemed like a good opening.

Shaking his hand, I said, "I stopped by your booth earlier, Ken, but I had no idea we had a mutual acquaintance. How is it that you know Evelyn?"

His expression warmed immediately. "Oh, Ev lives in a small cottage at our institute. It's somewhat of a symbiotic relationship. In fact, she says she is like one of the air plants that cling to trees. We give her free rent to help with her work. Then she stays there year round and keeps an eye on the place during the months we have to come back to the States and beg for money."

"Oh, that's great," I said. "So does Gill work with your institute too?"

He started to answer in his same happy-puppy openness, but Gill interrupted before Ken could speak.

"No, I just live in the same village."

"Don't you believe him," said Ken. "If it wasn't for–"

"Whoa, whoa, my friend. Before you begin telling lies about me, I promised Miss Hunter a glass of our wonderful homemade fruit juice." The look that passed between them was sufficient to stop Ken's open discourse.

"Oh, ah, sure. Come on in the back here," he said, inviting me into a small canvas enclosure at the back of the exhibit booth.

It did not escape my notice that I was now out of sight of the people in the hall, and had lost what safety there had been in that crowd.

Ken stuck his head through the curtain to the front of the booth and asked, "Judy, we still have some Number Ten on ice?"

"Yes."

"Where?"

"In the ice chest, of course."

"Ah, which one?"

Through the opening I could see Judy's face and almost laughed out loud. Her expression was one of both exasperation and resignation. "You want me to come and do it?"

Ken gave her a little boy grin. "Please."

She came into the back to find the juice, and I was again introduced as Evelyn's "acquaintance," this time to Dr. Judith Hoffman, M.D. She was a tall woman who radiated an intelligent, calm control. The football hero had not married the cheerleader but the valedictorian. As she started rummaging around through the ice chest, Gill turned on his inquisitor voice and asked, "Miss Hunter, how exactly is it that you are acquainted with Professor Lilac?"

I hesitated as I considered truth or lie. My people-reader pegged Gill as an investigative professional of some sort. Revealing information to another professional when you have no idea whether he is a good guy or bad guy is dangerous. Sometimes, however, it's helpful to reveal some of your information in order to see what sort of response it draws. Here I had three people I could watch for reactions, and I already knew that one of them had a hard time with a poker face.

"We met on the river bike trail yesterday. Some guy had pulled her off her bike and was trying to shove her into a waiting boat. I sort of ran over the guy with my bike and knocked him into the boat instead."

I had hoped for a reaction and got both more and less than I had hoped for. All the color drained from Judith's face and air hissed past her teeth as she drew a sudden startled breath. She lost her grip on the bottle of green-colored juice and it dropped to the cement floor. The glass exploded like shrapnel, and the fragrant green juice splashed in a 360-degree radius. Ken cursed and all of us instinctively jumped away from the disaster. For the next few minutes all conversation about Evelyn Lilac ceased. We busied ourselves sopping up the liquid and picking dozens of sharp little diamonds of glass from the floor and our clothing. Judy was apologizing, Ken was reassuring, and Gill was very, very quiet.

As we were finishing the cleanup, Gill said, "Judith, Ken, it's almost time for you two to make your presentation to the pharmaceutical committee." For a split second I thought they both looked at him a little confused, but as he issued instructions, they checked their watches and seemed to catch his sense of urgency.

"Judith, you show Miss. Hunter to the exhibitor's powder room so she can get all the glass and juice stains out of her clothing. Work quickly, Miss Hunter, because that will stain if it dries. Ken, you and Judith go to the trailer and change into your presentation clothes, and I'll clean up the rest of the mess here.

"Miss Hunter, we all want very much to know more about this incident on the bike trail. If you have time, we would be grateful if you could meet us at the Costa Rican restaurant in the food court in about one hour. If you will be so kind as to be my guest at dinner, we can have time to talk."

I was hustled off to a spacious and well-equipped powder room and spent almost thirty minutes shaking my clothes, rinsing the spots out of my skirt, and drying it under the hand dryer.

Once finished, I still had a half hour to kill, so I ambled slowly toward the food court, looking at some of the exhibits I had missed earlier. When I passed the booth where I had bought a video of one of Evelyn's speeches, it occurred to me that I no longer had it and assumed I must have set it down in the Enviro-Medic booth.

I circumnavigated the food court twice, and though there was a wide selection of food, no booth said Costa Rica. I then sought out an employee and asked for directions to the Costa Rican restaurant. He told me flatly that there was no such thing. All the food was supplied by convention center catering.

Feeling unbelievably foolish, I fought my way back through the crowd to the Enviro-Medic Research booth. At the spot on the convention floor where the booth had been, there was nothing left but a large green stain on the floor and the sack with my video of Professor Evelyn Lilac.

TEN

Monday morning I had bits and pieces of eleven cases pending. By Friday, I had mailed nine final reports, with invoices attached. This burst of energy and efficiency was my way of ignoring the one case that had me stumped. Mr. Borson, Professor Evelyn Lilac, Guillermo Jesus Montegro Y Monteblan, and Ken and Judith Hoffman had all flat-out disappeared. I was left with part of a retainer and a very unpleasant question. What had been Borson's real agenda?

I had broken my own basic rule: Only work for attorneys where cases are filed and everything done through legal procedures. With a layman client you can get blind-sided by your client's hidden agenda. Private investigators who ignore this end up in the wrong kind of newspaper headline: "MAN KILLS ESTRANGED GIRLFRIEND. ADDRESS SUPPLIED BY PRIVATE EYE."

The fact is, if Borson had just tried to hire me that first day, I would have turned him down. He had played me expertly, introducing himself inside the courthouse, baiting me with my own curiosity, and sucking me in with two seemingly innocent meetings. "Just try the first assignment," he had said. "If you don't like the work, you will never hear from me again." Dumb, dumb, dumb.

Hard work on other cases allowed me to ignore the question until Friday night, when Sam and I were having dinner at the Ocean Way Grill. A young man walked up to me and asked, "Are you Ms. Diana Hunter?"

"Yes."

"I was supposed to deliver this package to you here at seven p.m. Sorry, I'm a little late."

The kid turned to leave and did not respond when I said, "Wait, who told you I would be here? Where did this package come from?" He kept right on going and was out the door in a dozen running steps.

I looked at Sam. He put his napkin on the table and lumbered his big body out the door. He returned in about five minutes. His only comment was a shake of his head. The kid had disappeared.

Eyeing the unopened package he asked, "You want to have a demolitions guy look at it before you open it?"

I smiled. "No, I know what's in it. A CD and a wad of cash. I just don't know how in the hell Borson knew I would be here at seven o'clock."

Sam shrugged. "We can check your phone and apartment for bugs, but with the equipment today, he could eavesdrop on you with no hardware in place. Chances are we won't find anything. Let's just go to your place and see what we got."

Neither of us spoke as Sam drove us the eight blocks to my building. As we climbed eight flights of stairs, however, he did mumble something unflattering about my choice of residence.

I pressed my thumb to the security button Sam had installed on my door. After reading my print, the system unlocked the dead bolts and I opened the door.

Yeabot rolled over to the entry and greeted us with, "Hello, Mother. Hello, Uncle Sam. Mother, you have two messages. Would you like to hear your messages now?"

Sam studied his handiwork for a moment, then said, "You know, Diana, if you keep living in this dump, you're gonna get hit. It's a bad part of town."

"Sam, I already have Yeabot to protect me, as well as the security system you put in. No, thank you, Yeabot. I'll hear messages later."

"Would Mother and Uncle Sam like a scotch?"

"No thanks, Yeabot. Just rest. We'll call you if we need anything."

Still frowning at his own thoughts, Sam said, "Yeah, well, you know what trouble I'd have if anyone knew about Yeabot. I think I better upgrade its security system a little. Maybe I could also work on some sensors that would pick up on anyone listening in on you."

We pulled chairs up to my desk; I turned on the computer and put in the new CD. I typed in my password, "rdskblu," and the screen filled with words. Above the diary text was a note.

"You will soon have news of Evelyn. You need to read this. B"

15665-6-3 MY LAST DAY (47th language translation–English 20th century)

Syntax adjusted

Copy 2,783 (Caretaker–Nosha)

I do not know if the dreams we Nomads have lived and died for have any hope of ever coming true. But hopeful or hopeless, I have lived for those dreams for twenty-two years. Now, I am ready to die for them.

The day the nomads rescued me was the real beginning of life.

That day is still vivid in my memory. I sat on the plastibag after the Red 19 dissipated and cried with relief, then crawled to the rim of the Great Drain. Looking around at the vast expanse of sand and sky, I was overwhelmed by the immensity of the world. Born and raised in a subterranean burrocity, I had never seen a ceiling of more than one man-height nor a habitat space larger than one cordat. This much sky and this much space was terrifying. How could I hope to find the Nomads or even survive.

Like a frightened nimwat who curls into a ball and becomes as still as death, I curled up, pulled my windrobe over my head, and gave up hope.

I awoke to rough hands picking me up and wrapping me tightly in great coils of cloth. I did not even care to resist for I had already accepted death. Then a man with kind blue eyes and a huge red-blond beard took my face in his hands. He made me look into his face and said, "My friend, you are in need of water and you have the open land sickness. I cover your eyes so you will not fear. Go to sleep now. We will take you to safety." Then he gave me water to drink and bound cloth around my eyes.

I was tied to some hard surface that moved roughly across the land, but I could not guess what propelled it. There was no sound or smell of motors, only the wind overhead and the thumps against the uneven sand.

I slept fitfully and awoke to chilling cold. We had stopped and I was on the ground again. Quiet voices murmured around me, soft footsteps patted about, and occasionally there was a muted tinkle of pots and dishes. Someone touched my shoulder gently and I heard the voice of the Red Beard say, "Here, Antia, let me unbind you. It is night now and the world will not look so fearsome."

I was surprised to hear my name and see the welcome roof of a low rock cave. An open fire blazed a few feet away, powered by small black lumps of fuel. I had never seen such a thing. Only Red 19 stoves were allowed in the burrocity.

Red Beard bade me move closer and warm myself and gave me a large cup of hot drink. It was a strange drink with many flavors vying for my tongue's attention, first bitter, then herbal, then sweet and satisfying.

Four men and two women moved about the cave in quiet efficient movements, revealing long familiarity with their routine. Soon a camp was set, a meal cooked, and security zones established. As we all ate our meal, Red Beard introduced himself as Ober, leader of this group sent to search for me.

Seven people risking their lives to rescue me seemed such an obvious fabrication that it insulted my intelligence and I said so. The group responded in anger that I should call their Ober a liar, but he calmed them, telling them that I was burrocity raised and knew no better.

"Antia, there are two things you must know. First you must open your mind to a totally different society. We Nomads care about one another and often give our lives to save others. Prepare yourself for a new world which you must learn about very quickly."

I knew what he said was true no matter how incredible it might sound.

"The other thing you must know is that you are a very valuable person to our movement."

"But my only skill is numbers."

"Numbers are one of the skills you bring us, but you also can make stories."

Again, I thought he was making a fool of me but knew better than to say so.

He laughed as he read my expression. "You make stories that can be remembered and retold generation after generation. Within those stories can be buried memories and history for our children's children.

And as strange as it seemed then, creating stories is what I have done now, for twenty-two years. But today is the end of my story. The memory coils that carry the stories of our people and our destruction are now complete. We hope that they will tell someone, someday, where and how our geneticists have hidden the cell patterns of many of the plants and animals that have disappeared from our world. Will anyone ever find these frozen treasures and learn the secrets of restoring our lost world? No one knows. I know only that like my dying planet, I must carry out my last task, and die with hope.

I will deliver this diary and the last of the memory coils to a safe drop. They will be given to the Hidden Ones who will carry our coded stories to the new home on Atland. A second set of coils is hidden in the great pyramid, and a third is interred with the ice crystals and genetic codes. It is my private joke that the safe drop is in the old astrological gardens at Nautical University. In the burrocity scientific knowledge has been withheld from the people, so my pursuers will not understand the significance of the great granite spheres that chart the stars and planets. But someone among the Hidden Ones may know enough to get my joke. I leave my last information buried beneath the sphere that represents Atland. Thus, in a way I am the first to get to the new planet.

A totally different set of memory coils are embedded in my scalp where the Enforcers can easily detect them, and be misguided by them. I can hear their combox voices behind me. It is time to bury the history coils and this diary, and give my pursuers a lively chase. If I tire them, they will act in hasty, thoughtless rage and slice off the top of my head to get the memory coils. It will be a merciful and instant death and give me no chance for betrayal. Dear Red Beard, dearest Ober, I carry my love for you to whatever may lie beyond. Antia

---

From my last experience, I knew better than to hit the down arrow, so I tried to save the file. Once again the letters dissolved into meaningless symbols and the damn screen went blank. Nothing we did could get it back.

ELEVEN

Before Sam left that night we brain stormed two complex searches for Yeabot to work on. In the first search we incorporated every fact, opinion, date and description I could remember from my talks with Borson. Then we asked Yeabot to search for a true identity and location. In the second search, we fed Yeabot everything I had found on Evelyn Lilac, including her video, and asked him to see if he could find her current location.

The next morning I opened a second client trust account to keep Borson's money separate from the rest of my client funds. I then put an ad in the *Los Angeles Times* personals that read, "Mr. Borson, assignment declined. Please contact me for return of retainer. DH." I doubted that Borson would respond, but at least I could prove my legal attempt to reject the assignment and return his retainer. I had an awful feeling I was going to need it, either for a criminal trial or a Bureau of Security and Investigative Services inquiry regarding my license. As it turned out, what I would need it for was an FBI murder investigation on the Navajo Reservation.

Yeabot's searches produced nothing useful on Borson, and all the information he found on Lilac was old. I had no funds of my own to chase a wild goose to Costa Rica and had no client to pay me to do so. The case went into the dead file.

For the rest of the week I worked hard and tried to forget all about Red 19, polluting Martians, and Evelyn Lilac. It was amazing how many reminders would pop up: I couldn't pick up a newspaper or magazine or listen to television or radio without hearing something about Mars or environmental issues. Pictures from JPL showed what scientists believed was evidence of water on Mars, and an international conference was predicting a disastrous rise in global warming. I started avoiding the papers, and turned to reading historical novels and watching old movies. My avoidance therapy was beginning to work. Then the call came.

"May I speak to Diana Hunter, please?"

"Speaking."

"Ms. Hunter, this is Neal Camas. I am a Special Agent with the Federal Bureau of Investigation in Flagstaff, Arizona. Are you a licensed private investigator in the state of California?"

"Yes, ah, could you hold just a moment, Agent Camas." I try never to answer questions over the phone unless I'm sure who is on the other end of the line. "Agent Camas, I have an urgent call on the other line. Could I call you back in about five minutes?"

Most professionals understand the need to verify a caller's ID, and after a pause he supplied me with a number and extension. After verifying that the number was, in fact, the FBI office, I dialed him back and waited while the receptionist put me through to his line.

"Agent Camas, this is Diana Hunter. How may I help you?"

"Ms. Hunter, we need your assistance in identifying a woman found dead on the Navajo Reservation."

Stunned by this request, I took a moment before answering. "Is there some reason I should know her? I don't believe I'm acquainted with any Navajo women."

"She's not Navajo, and your business card was found in her bra. It was the only ID on the body."

To myself, I mouthed the name "High Pockets."

Hearing my whisper, he asked, "What was that?"

I needed think time. Why did they need me? With Evelyn's arrest record from her protest days, her prints must be in the system. "I really don't know how someone in Arizona could get my card. Did her fingerprints give you any possible ID?"

There was a long pause, then he said, "With the condition of the body, there were no prints."

The vision of a totally decayed body I had once found came to mind unbidden. Memory of the sight and its unforgettable stench made my stomach turn. "Will there be anything recognizable for me to ID?"

"Oh, yes. Her face is undamaged."

"Then what happened to her prints?"

Another pause. "We won't speculate about that now, Ms. Hunter. The bureau is requesting that you fly down here. I can authorize something toward your expenses."

His tone made the request sound a bit more compelling than a simple invitation, so naturally, I agreed. I didn't need to piss off the FBI. Finishing my call

with Agent Camas, I turned on the computer and was about to search for airline
tickets when a message appeared on my blank screen:

> IT'S TOO LATE FOR EVELYN, BUT YOU CAN STILL BE
> OF HELP. THE FBI HAS WASTED TIME IN NOTIFYING
> YOU. MORE MONEY HAS BEEN DEPOSITED TO YOUR
> CLIENT TRUST FUND. PLEASE INVESTIGATE HER
> MURDER AND FIND THE *MARTIAN DIARY*. THE
> BUREAU DOES NOT HAVE IT. B

This was not an email. It was just waiting to come up on the screen the minute I
booted up. How the hell did he do that? The computer hadn't even been on. How
did he know about my client fund? Scared and mystified, I reached for the phone
and dialed Sam.

TWELVE

As I looked down at her lifeless body, I couldn't help pondering the big question. Where had the life gone? Was the real Professor Evelyn Lilac out there? Was her spirit floating somewhere around this room, glaring down at me for my failure, or was this inanimate organic form all there was? I like to believe that life is an energy and that, as Einstein said, energy can be neither created nor destroyed, only transformed. I like to believe birth and death are only transformations of that energy form, and that it remains a unique soul. I like to believe it, but I know it could be wishful thinking.

Agent Camas was watching my face closely, reading my response. "I take it you did know her."

"We met once."

"Was she your client?"

I thought about the question a moment, then shook my head, "No. There don't seem to be any marks on her body. How did she die?"

Camas nodded to Mr. Sanchez, the coroner's assistant. Sanchez pulled back a covering from her forehead revealing that the entire top of her head had been severed. Unable to control my reaction, I gasped and raised a hand to my mouth to shut off further sound. A small moan escaped my lips as I shut my eyes to block the shocking sight.

"Sorry you had to see that," said Camas.

Nothing on Evelyn's body had been covered but that gaping skull. Sorry, my eye. He had deliberately set up this little revelation to see what reaction he could get out of me.

"Sure you are. Please don't confirm all my worst first impressions, Agent Camas."

It was very dumb of me to let my anger out in such a direct verbal assault on a federal investigator. I knew the minute I did it that I would pay for it. Anger flashed briefly in his cold blue eyes, but he had sense enough to control it. The tone of his reply was wonderfully balanced between the apology he voiced and the sarcastic condescension he implied.

"Sorry to shock you, Ms. Hunter, but since you're a professional investigator, I naturally assumed you were up to this."

To complete his show and tell, he turned Evelyn's hands, palms up, so I could see that all the skin had been sliced from the tips of her thumbs and fingers.

"Here's why we got no prints."

Getting my anger under control, I realized I was lucky he thought it was the gore that had upset me. What had really shocked me was seeing that Evelyn had been murdered in precisely the same fashion as Antia in the *Martian Diary*. My suspicion of Borson jumped to the red zone. I prayed that the search Sam was doing would turn up some useful information that I could turn over to the FBI. That last mysterious message from Borson had really lit a fire under Sam. He had taken it as a personal affront to his skill as an intelligence professional, and he had turned on all his old skills to figure out how Borson was tapping into my apartment, my phone, and my computer. At this moment, however, I had nothing to give Agent Camas.

I decided to play the role his prejudice had cast me in. I feigned illness and left the room suddenly. It gave me a moment to be out from under his scrutiny and go over the amount of truth I should tell him.

I had gotten into Flagstaff late Friday, but Camas couldn't be bothered with me until today, so I had spent Friday night at a motel. That wasn't included in his expense reimbursement. From the moment we met this morning, he had pulled one obnoxious, bigoted, sexist thing after another. Brilliant he wasn't, but dogged and arrogant he was, and he would be capable of making my life miserable if I wasn't very careful.

He walked up to me outside, stuck a piece of chewing gum in his mouth, and offered me one. I declined. His lopsided, sarcastic grin revealed large teeth with protruding canines. There is no way anyone would mistake that smile for friendliness. It radiated smart-ass arrogance.

"Yeah, it takes a while to get used to that sort of thing, especially if it's someone you know. Who was she?"

"Her name is Evelyn Lilac. She is . . . was some sort of biology or ecology professor from Costa Rica."

"Costa Rica, huh. How did you meet her?"

"Someone asked me to interview with her because she needed a research assistant for a novel she was going to write."

"Research assistant? Is that the level of work you do?"

His voice was so derisive he almost taunted me into another angry outburst, but I had learned my lesson.

"No, and I ended up rejecting the assignment."

"When and where was this interview?"

"Late October, I don't recall the date. We met on the San Gabriel River bike trail."

"You mean, like, bicycle? Is this how you usually meet prospective clients?"

"No, Evelyn was in Los Angeles to speak at an environmental conference and was booked solid. Meeting her during her morning bike ride was the only way to see her."

He stopped chewing the gum and stared at me, open mouthed. I couldn't decide whether he thought I was lying or was just incredibly stupid. Holding me in a long appraising gaze, he resumed chomping on his gum. Finally, he pulled out a small notebook and pen.

"What's her address and phone number in Costa Rica?"

"I don't know."

"How did she contact you?"

Now there was a tricky question to answer. "She had some associate contact me and arrange the meeting." That might not be strictly true, but there was no way I was going to tell this sneering, arrogant man anything about Martians and Red 19. Even if I had been dealing with a more reasonable investigator, that story could be career suicide.

"What was the associate's name and address?"

I knew the questions would eventually come down to this, but I dreaded having to answer. "His name was Borson. I don't have an address for him."

He looked up from his pad. "Where did you meet him, the Disneyland Autopia?"

I blushed as I confessed, "No, a city park in Bluff Beach."

"A city park? Let me guess. You're one of those hand-to-mouth PIs with an office that's a typewriter and filing cabinet in the bedroom. Did we maybe think to get this Borson's phone number?"

I shook my head. "Just an email address, and it's no longer a valid address."

"Jesus! Let's recap here. You meet your clients on bicycle trails, city parks, and chat rooms, and you get no addresses and no phones. Hunter, if you're bullshitting me, I'll have you up on obstruction charges so fast it will make your friggin' head swim. So what great PI job did you do for these unidentifiable clients?"

"None. I met with Evelyn; we agreed I didn't know enough about the environmental movement to help with her book, and I left."

"You got any notes of this meeting, any letter rejecting the work? Oh, I'm forgetting. You'd have to mail it to the bike trail. Do you know how flimsy that sounds? I could have a subpoena this afternoon to turn your 'office' and any other private property that got in the way of our search, so don't hold out on me, Hunter."

In my most contrite and humble tone I answered, "I do realize how unprofessional it must look to have no more information on these people than I do, and I am thoroughly embarrassed by it, but you must understand, I never took them seriously. As you surmised, researching novels is not exactly my stock-in-trade."

I reached into my purse and pulled out a page from the *Times* documenting my message to Borson. "You see, Borson had someone deliver a cash retainer, and I don't even know how to get it back to him. But I am being perfectly legal. I even opened a separate client trust account to keep his money separate from my other client funds."

Camas read it and handed it back. "He ever get in touch?"

"He hasn't sent me any address for the return of his retainer, but I promise you, when he does, I will call you with the address immediately."

If Agent Camas figured out the difference between the question he asked and the carefully worded answer I gave, I'd be dead meat. To distract him from that fine detail, I kept talking.

"Look, all the guy asked me to do was some research that I didn't think I would do anyway. I only obliged him in meeting with Evelyn because he said if it didn't work out, he would go away and leave me alone. It was a way of getting rid of an unwanted client. It didn't seem like a real case, so I didn't take him seriously or check references. How was I to know this would happen?"

He studied me and he studied his notebook. He needed a little redirection.

"If you want more information on Evelyn, why don't you check the organizers of the First International Environmental Expo in Long Beach. She was a keynote speaker or something. They ought to have lots of stuff on her."

He took a breath, gave me his toothy, lopsided smile and said, "Right. I'll do that. It's been a real pleasure dealing with such a pro, Hunter."

THIRTEEN

Her body had been found a hundred miles northeast of Flagstaff. The dry wash wasn't on the map, but with the instruction I had gotten at the library in Tuba City, it wasn't hard to find. I left the highway a few miles out of Tuba City and followed a good dirt road north to the foot of the butte. Parking my rented jeep at the first spot where the road bent close to the wash, I walked up the dry riverbed looking for some sign that would indicate the exact location.

The temperature was right on my comfort cusp, a little too cool in the shade, making the sun feel deliciously soothing and warm. Despite my unhappy purpose for being here, the happy memories of childhood seemed to materialize in the clear air of the open desert, like ghosts, unexpected and unbidden.

The mines my dad had run were always two hundred miles from anywhere, so I'd spent my free time searching those open, wild lands for neat rocks, trap door-spiders, lizards, coyotes, rabbits, birds, wind-carved caves and other secret places, known only to me and the critters.

With habit engendered by early training, I placed my feet carefully, making only a whisper of sound in the sand and giving a wide berth to any brush or rock that might conceal a rattlesnake soaking up a last bit of the early winter sun before hibernation.

The crime scene wasn't hard to spot. There were several sets of tire tracks on the west bank, just before the wash made a wide turn past a red sandstone cliff. As I walked from the sunny wash into the cold shadow of the cliff, a shiver ran down my spine. It wasn't due entirely to the change in temperature. If Evelyn's spirit had survived, she was here in the desert, not in the morgue.

At the library in town I had looked up the newspaper report on her death. It didn't tell me much, but as I looked around, neither did this dry wash. I found month-old tire tracks, rounded spots in the sand that may have once been footprints, and a bit of rabbit fur caught on a creosote bush. Nearby coyote tracks finished the rabbit's tale, but what of Evelyn? Was she dead when she was dumped here, or was this cliff the last thing she saw before she died? Etched in my memory was the look on her face as she left in that taxi, sad, frightened, resigned. Had she known her fate in advance? Why then would she run to it? Was her death due to that damned diary or her protests or some tragic accident of being in the wrong place at the wrong time?

"Damn you, Evelyn! Why didn't you let me help you?" The sound of my own voice breaking the silence of this empty place was a shock. More surprising was the pain I heard in my own cry. I sat on an outcropping at the edge of the cliff, studied the sand, and wondered what on earth I thought I would accomplish by coming to this spot.

I stood and began a careful foot-by-foot search. I worked my way slowly upstream for about two hundred yards until the path became choked with rocks, cactus, and brush, then I turned around and headed back, searching the same ground from another perspective.

By the time I retraced my steps the sun was setting and the clouds to the west were blocking what little daylight remained. Streaks of gray streamed down from the ragged edges of the clouds, and the winds carried the sweet perfume of wet earth, creosote and sage. Some lucky folks were getting rain, and I was getting cold.

Standing there blithely considering the blessing of rain in the dry lands, it dawned on me that those heavy rain clouds were upstream, and it would be wise to head for higher ground. It is a bleak irony that every year a few folks die in the middle of the desert by drowning. You don't get much warning. The water begins as a hard rain in the highlands. Drops collect one by one, forming many tiny rivulets that converge into fewer but larger dry stream beds until finally a wall of water of awesome power fills the main channel. Moving brush, boulders, and debris down the wash, the flood fills the silent desert with a monstrous roar. When I was a young girl I would go out and wait beside a wash, hoping to see a flash flood. Twice I was lucky enough to be in the right place at the right time. I stood mesmerized, taking guilty pleasure in the exhilaration of being so close to such thrilling power, and knowing my dad would kill me if he found out.

Thinking of childhood adventure, I climbed out of the wash and was brought abruptly back to present time. A man stood on the bank watching me. I thought briefly about the gun I had left in my suitcase in the car and hoped I wouldn't need it.

"Good evening," he said.

"Hello."

"I saw your jeep down there. You having any trouble?"

"No, no trouble. You, ah, just passing by this far off the highway?"

He smiled and his thin features lit with a warmth and shy charm. "No. Sorry if I startled you."

As he walked a little closer, I could see he wore a police uniform, but the identifying shoulder patch was hidden under his blue denim jacket. He was about five-foot-ten, slender, with wide shoulders, slim hips, and looked to be in his late twenties or early thirties. He introduced himself, but my brain was so busy wondering if this could be Evelyn's killer that I didn't catch his full name, just Jim somebody.

I responded automatically with my own self-introduction and saw his face change completely. His smile was replaced with a look of startled recognition. In that first telltale moment, I saw a candor I usually associate with persons totally lacking in the stony-faced artifice of law enforcement. In the following moments, however, his quiet, slow appraisal of me showed the control and self-assurance of an experienced police officer. The measured tone of his voice told me he had carefully constructed his next question.

"Diana Hunter. What brings you here, Ms. Hunter?"

I decided to give no information until I got a little. "I was rock hunting. What brings you here?"

He considered the question, and probably read my apprehension. His voice took on that quiet, relaxed, conversational tone a good police officer can use to reassure a nervous witness.

"I'm on my way home. My house is just a little way on down this road. Out here if we see a car off-road, like your jeep, we check to make sure the driver isn't lost or sick or injured. A few weeks ago I met another woman here when I was on my way to the office. I stopped to see if she needed any help and she assured me she didn't. Basically told me to mind my own business. So I did, or thought I did. About a week later I saw her here again, but that time she had been murdered. So you see why I would be reluctant to leave another woman out here in the same place." Though he tried to keep his voice even, I could hear an echo of my own regrets. Evelyn had gotten to him too.

"You actually spoke to her a week before she was killed?"

A hint of angry defensiveness slipped into his voice. "I tried to get her to let me help her, but she flat-out refused and she wasn't doing anything to arrest her for or–

"I'm sorry," I interrupted. "I didn't mean to imply criticism. Believe me, I understand. Evelyn did the same thing to me, refused my help and left in a taxi. I never heard from her again until the FBI called me yesterday to identify her body."

"Yesterday! Camas just got around to calling you yesterday?"

A clap of thunder rolled through the clouds above us, and large drops of rain started making quarter-sized rings on the ground.

"It was your PI card we found in her, her clothing?"

It was more a statement than a question, but I nodded.

"So you did know her. You called her Evelyn. Look, this case isn't my jurisdiction. It's FBI, and you aren't legally obligated to talk with me; but I really need to know what that woman was doing and why she was murdered practically at my door step."

"Actually I was hoping you could tell me what she was doing. I don't think I can help you much, but I would like to talk to you about it."

He looked at the sky. "We're gonna get soaked if we stand here. Would you like to have a cup of coffee or something at my place?"

All my instincts told me he offered no threat, but the cautious one on my internal committee still caused a momentary hesitation. He picked up on it immediately.

"If we talked at the police station that would sort of make it official business, which it isn't; but if you like, we could drive back to town and talk over dinner at a restaurant."

"No," I answered. "A coffee at your house sounds fine."

His small trailer home was orderly except for the large number of books stuffed into every available corner. He offered me a seat at a table and began assembling the coffee-making equipment. With a shy apology he explained, "This won't take too long. I just use this cone and make it right in the cup. Almost as fast as instant, but it tastes better."

I smiled and nodded.

He looked in the refrigerator and then at me and said somewhat hesitantly, "I don't have much in here but some leftover lamb stew."

"If that's an offer, I accept. I just realized that I haven't eaten today. After an unpleasant interview with Agent Camas at the morgue this morning, I went straight to the rental car agency and drove from Flagstaff to Tuba City."

As he put the stew on to heat he said, "Well, he's enough to ruin your appetite, all right."

He said it in such a quiet, straight-faced manner that it caught me by surprise, and I laughed a little too loudly. His appearance at the wash had startled me, and my cackling outburst was partly an emotional release as my adrenaline began to subside.

He served the coffee and sat down across from me. I was about to admit that I hadn't caught his last name, but his first question distracted me.

"You know, he had that business card of yours from the time the body was found. I know because I found the body. Why do you think he took so long to contact you?"

"I don't know, but the way he talked to me made it obvious that he has a low opinion of both private investigators and women. I'm afraid what I had to tell him pretty much confirmed his prejudice."

"What did you tell him?"

His question was direct but did not have the coldness of interrogation. Taking a good look at my new friend in the light of his home, I found his brown eyes reassuring, observant and honest. Though there was tension in his face, he seemed to need to know about Evelyn on the same level I did. I kept my story simple and close to what I had told Camas. He listened quietly, without interruption.

When I had finished, he went to the stove and dished up two bowls of hot stew. It smelled wonderful, and I dived in as soon as was polite. As we ate, I asked, "When you talked to Evelyn did she say anything that would help, like who she was meeting, where she was staying, why she had come to the desert?"

He put down his spoon, rubbed his chin thoughtfully, and finally answered, "Well, no, not really. She told me she was on an archeological dig." Then he smiled and got in his own dig by adding, "Sort of like your rock hunting, I suspect, because I don't know of any significant site around there. When I asked how she got out there, she basically told me to mind my own business. She said that unless she was breaking some law, I was to go away and leave her alone. I was in a hurry to get to my office and didn't need some crazy woman to make a bad week worse, so I took her at her word and left."

He looked into my face and shrugged. "It's one of those things you wish you had done differently, but . . ."

He quit talking and ate a few bites, then added, "You're lucky Camas just thinks you're incompetent. Think he's got me figured for his prime suspect. After all, she was killed practically at my house. In fact, that may be the tangent he took off on instead of contacting you. I hear he has been asking a lot of very personal questions regarding my love life."

"Well, that's typical cop mentality for–" I blushed. "Sorry."

He laughed. "No offense taken. Some policemen don't look further than the nearest relative or first person connected to the scene. Maybe now that he knows who she was, he'll back off on me."

I studied him for a moment, then confessed, "There are a few details I sort of forgot to tell Agent Camas. I don't normally hold out on law enforcement, but I had no real information and, ah, . . ."

He smiled. "There may be a few things that escaped my memory too." He looked nervously at the stack of mail piled on one side of the table, then looked at my face for a long moment. After an uncomfortably long silence he pulled out a pencil, tore a scrap of paper from a piece of junk mail, and began writing. When he finished he turned the paper around and there, in the neat box-letter style many policemen use in their written reports, were the words: HIGH POCKETS.

I was stunned.

Seeing my expression, he said, "You know what this means, don't you?"

In answer, I took the scrap of paper, folded it, and stuffed it in my bra. "It's from an old World War II movie. The heroine was a spy who slipped notes in her bra. High Pockets was her code name. You said Evelyn didn't talk to you. How did you know?"

"When I come home at night I dump the day's mail here in a pile. About once a week or so I sort through it, pay bills, answer letters, and so forth. A few days after her death I was going through my mail and I found this buried in the pile." He dug down to the bottom of the pile and pulled out a white envelope with no address on it. Inside were two pieces of paper. He read me the first one.

"If something happens to me, I think a woman may come here and inquire after me. If she does, please give her this note. Please show it to no one else. You will know the right person because she will know the meaning of the words High Pockets."

I took the note. "That is Evelyn's hand-writing. At least it looks like her hand-written speech."

"By the time I found this, it was clear that Camas was trying hard to make me his suspect. So I was not inclined to take him a note written by a dead woman and try to explain how it had been in my house for several days. Now I'm glad I saved it. Maybe it will make sense to you. It's a puzzle that has been driving me nuts." He handed me the second note and I was startled to see the familiar words.

"It is my private joke that the safe drop is in the old astrological

gardens at the Nautical University. In the burrocity, scientific knowledge has been withheld from the people, so my pursuers will not understand the significance of the great granite spheres which chart the stars and planets. But someone among the Hidden Ones may know enough to get my joke. I leave my last information buried beneath the sphere that represents Atland, thus I am the first to get to the new planet."

FOURTEEN

On the drive back to Flagstaff, I checked my cell phone for messages and found a short but disturbing message from Sam. It said simply, "Diana Hunter needs an extended vacation in Arizona. Leave her there, and don't go to her apartment."

At the airport I bought new tickets for cash using a phony driver's license under my current alias. My laptop could be carried aboard, but since I had the Walther, the suitcase had to be checked. The itinerary I was able to put together meant long waits to catch available flights in both Flagstaff and Phoenix. The trip took longer than driving home, but it was necessary to brush out my tracks. It also meant a second night in a motel in Flagstaff, but after the day I'd had, I needed the rest. As my dear ol' daddy used to say, "If you have time to spare, go by air." On the long trip home I tried to sort out all the pieces of the puzzle. First I placed a set of imaginary parentheses around all the mumbo jumbo about Mars and Red 19, not eliminating it from my equation, just setting it off as an independent variable. I would solve for verifiable fact first.

Borson had set me up to seek Red 19. By following that lead I'd found Evelyn. Could his real goal have been to have me locate Evelyn? Unknown.

Were those hour-long talks really part of the selection process or were they just intended to gain my trust? Unknown. Why was I chosen? I hoped it wasn't because I was the most gullible. Evelyn was attacked, frightened, and decided to run away rather than follow her itinerary. Within a week of our meeting she was murdered in the same way as Antia in the *Martian Diary*. Who besides Borson, Evelyn, and I would know that detail? Unknown.

No ID was left on the body, and her fingerprints were removed to prevent or delay identification. Was my card left in her bra because the killer didn't find it, or so the FBI would call me? Why would Borson want to delay ID? Did he? Did he kill her?

What had Evelyn done in that week? Who had she gone to see in Arizona? What was the motive for murdering her? All unknown.

Why did the FBI wait so long to call me, and who was watching my place?

Enough! Those were all useless questions. What real leads did I have that I could pursue? When Evelyn had run off without filing a complaint, there seemed little use in following up on the boat used in the kidnap attempt. Now, checking the CF number was high on my list. Sam was working on information on Borson. Maybe he would have a good lead or two. Evelyn said three of her colleagues in Costa Rica had been killed. I would have to get online and see what I could learn about the murder of environmental activists in Costa Rica. There were also the three people I met at the environmental conference in Long Beach: Guillermo Jesus Montegro y Monteblan, and Ken and Judith Hoffman. Why did they disappear so quickly?

At John Wayne Airport, I waited bleary-eyed for my one piece of luggage. Renting a car under my pseudonym, I left my easily identifiable 57 T-Bird sitting in the expensive airport parking lot. Oh well, if Borson was going to shower me with cash, I might as well put it to good use. Sam could have someone pick it up later. I headed for the Yellow Umbrella Hotel in Bluff Beach.

This old hotel had been quite a Hollywood retreat in the 1920s and 1930s. All the elegant suites, complete with kitchens and wet bars, were terraced down the bluff so each room had its own patio overlooking the ocean. Of course, a lot of things have changed since those days. The rooms are no longer elegant; in fact, they stink of dirty carpet, stained upholstery, and musty, moldy walls. However, the old place still offers two things that made it a desirable retreat in the old days. Each room still has its own ocean-view patio, and the privacy of its clients is still guaranteed. No eyebrow is raised if Mr. and Mrs. Smith register, and no ID is required. No one gets past the security gates to visit any guest until the guest approves the visit. If a hasty escape is needed, the path from the apartments leads to a private beach and waiting boat. It was the perfect place to set up operations and go after answers and Evelyn's killer.

FIFTEEN

I registered under my alias, Champs O'Shaughnessy and deposited my limited luggage in the penthouse suite on the top floor of the Yellow Umbrella. From there I walked two blocks to a mom and pop store and carried home sandwich makings and a bottle of Grants. Fifteen minutes later, with a sandwich in one hand and a glass nearby, I called Sam. I had no idea how Borson was getting to me, and I had decided that my first step would be to make sure I wasn't walking around with an electronic bug.

J. Edgar answered Sam's phone. Putting on my best East Texas drawl I said, "Well, hello there, darlin'. This is Champs O'Shaughnessy just in from the great state of Texas. Is your boss there? I have a hurry up need to have a word with him."

Sam picked up. "Hello, Champs. I been wondering when you would blow into town. Where are you?"

"Oh, I'm havin' myself a little holiday here at the beach. Staying in that hideaway where we met the sheik and his bride. You remember?"

"Sure."

"You also remember that they had a little electrical problem you helped them with. S'pose you could help me with it too?"

"I'll be right over."

It would take Sam about fifteen minutes to drive from his classic old California bungalow in San Pedro to my temporary quarters in Bluff Beach. While I waited, I turned on the laptop, pulled up the Borson report, checked the boat CF number, and put in my second call.

"DMV. Good afternoon, this is Tamara. How may I help you?"

"Hi, Tamara, this is Diana Hunter. I would like to run registration on one CF number, please." As she typed, I supplied the CF number, my account ID, and my password.

"The registered owner is Offshore Deep Driller, Inc. The legal owner is Blue Morpho Global Investments. There is a Department of Justice report as of 29

October. Do you receive address information on this account, Ms. Hunter?"

"Not this time. No process service needed. You said a DOJ report? So you are saying that this boat was reported stolen on the 29th of October, right?"

"Yes."

"Does the DOJ do an investigation on that, or do they just maintain a state index as reported by local enforcement?"

"I'm sorry, I really don't know. You would have to talk with the DOJ on that."

"Okay, thanks."

I dialed the 800 number I had for the Department of Justice and got one of those interminable message machine menus. Waiting none-too-patiently, I finally was allowed to press zero to talk to a staff member. The phone rang and I got another recording telling me that their staff was available from nine a.m. to noon and one p.m. to four. I looked at my watch, 12:40. Shit! Twenty minutes was too long to wait so I called the Sheriff's Department, Harbor Patrol, to see if they knew how boat theft reports were handled. I got an operator message that said the area code had changed. Damn! With mounting frustration I tried the new area code and got hold of a deputy who hadn't a clue what I was talking about. He didn't even know the DOJ got stolen vehicle reports. I apologized for bothering him and said I would call the DOJ. Damn, damn! I slammed down the receiver and sat staring at my watch and steaming.

I reread the registration information, looking for another angle. Blue Morpho Global Investments had to be connected to Blue Morpho Petroleum, Inc. I was staring at the phone, debating my next move, when it rang.

"Hello."

"This is the front desk, Mrs. O'Shaughnessy. Are you expecting a gentleman named Sam?"

"Yes, please, send him right up."

Sam came in carrying a large satchel with his debugging equipment and went to work without a word, not only checking all my possessions, but the entire room. "You're clean, ma' dear. Now we can relax and chat."

"Thanks, Sam. Why did you warn me off going to my apartment? Did you find a bug there?"

"Yes, I did. Probably found it before your plane took off for Arizona on Friday. But that's not why I told you to stay away. There's somebody watching your building. I've been trying to ID the two guys who trade off watch but don't have anything on them yet. They're definitely not pros. On Friday afternoon I brought your stuff out right under their noses and they never knew it. I've got Yeabot, your PC, and filing cabinet at my place. You're all set up for operation, complete with a secure phone line. You can move in tomorrow."

He paused and I could tell from his expression that more bad news was coming.

"Before I got back over there Saturday, they managed to break in and pretty well trash the place. It was strictly amateur night. They hacked around the locks with a fire axe, for Pete's sake."

There was another ominous pause, and I braced myself for the real news.

"At least we can be fairly certain it wasn't your friend Borson. He would have known everything he could want to know from his video-tape."

"What! What video-tape?"

He gave me a self-satisfied grin. "Borson must have some connections in the business because he had a piece of top-secret, state-of-the-art hardware installed in your television. I had trouble even finding someone who knew me well enough to tell me what it was. My past associates call it a Big Brother chip. You remember in the book *1984* how the televisions watched the people like a security camera?"

"Yes, don't tell me . . . "

"Uh huh. The set didn't even need to be on. Borson got a twenty-four-hour-a-day video, with sound. Of course he'll know that I found it. Would have seen me debugging the place; so we lost the advantage there, and he'll know about me and any other people you have had in your apartment, and about Yeabot."

I closed my eyes and shook my head as I thought about the damage control that would be necessary on this one.

"But, it's not all bad news. I did figure out how he was tapping into your computer. Clever damn program. In your first emails with him he installed a small program that allowed him to dial up your modem, send future messages and plant them in your C-drive. I am still analyzing the program to see what else it does, but I cleaned that all out of your computer and added a program that will recognize any similar attempts as a virus."

"Thanks, Sam. You really are good."

His face lit in an almost mischievous smile. He was actually enjoying all this. "I haven't gotten to the good part yet. The good part is I was able to get a trace on the outgoing signal from that Big Brother chip. You will never guess where that signal went." He didn't wait for me to guess. "The executive floor of Heartland and

Home Insurance Corporation, biggest damn insurance conglomerate in the country."

He waited as I processed this incongruity. Bewildered I asked, "What was he doing there?"

"The correct question is: What does he do there?"

"Okay, what does he do there?"

"His real name is Nathan Niedlemyer, a.k.a. Nate. He is the youngest vice president in the company, came up through the accounting end of things, does master programming and planning in things like actuarial tables, loss projections, long-term planning for the health and wealth of his company."

"Son of a gun! He *is* a bean counter. I pegged him for that when I first met him. But how the hell does that . . . it makes no sense. What was his connection to Evelyn, to Mars and the red stuff . . . and to murder?"

"I don't know, but tomorrow morning at eight a.m. he will be conducting a training seminar for his regional managers. I tapped into his computer and inserted an extra attendee, Clara Shimmerhorn of Story City, Iowa. Here is your badge, Ms. Shimmerhorn. I used my computer to fudge up your picture a little bit. Richard is expecting you at Coiffeurs Americain tomorrow at six a.m., so he can make you up to go with the picture. See what you can find out at the training session."

I smiled at him. "You are a real magician, Sam. Great work as always. Thanks."

"Yeah, well, I have a rather personal interest in this son of a bitch. He's the first person to get a jump on me since I retired. I gotta know what cards he holds and how he intends to play them. By the way, I won't be any further away than your lapel. That badge is wired."

SIXTEEN

Monday morning I was up by five a.m. and within minutes was on the way to Rick's Coiffeurs Americain in Beverly Hills. Owner Richard Barton is a diminutive Englishman who has charmed his way into Hollywood and Beverly Hills society. He is also the world's greatest fan of the movie *Casablanca*. His salon decor is a careful imitation of the set of Rick's Café Americain, and he often livens the place up by hiring impersonators to appear as Humphrey Bogart and Ingrid Bergman or Sidney Greenstreet and Peter Lorry. I don't even know if Barton is his real name. In casual conversations in the salon he often drops hints that he has a mysterious past, but that could be just his Richard Blaine act.

Four years ago a con artist ripped off Richard's entire retirement savings in a real estate swindle in Palmdale. Like most victims, Richard soon learned that the police simply referred him to a private attorney, and the attorney charged him another small fortune to get a judgment. Nine times out of ten a judgment in a fraud case like Richard's is worthless. The con has either spent the money or hidden it beyond the reach of the court or legal investigation. I had seen it happen dozens of times, but I liked Richard so well that I did something I had never done before. I conned a con. Of course the operation called for unorthodox, if not felonious, activities, so I try to refrain from such solutions these days. But it did work slick. Not only did I recover all of Richard's retirement, but I gained myself a friend and disguise master.

Working from Sam's computer-doctored photo, Richard gave me dark brown hair, brown contacts under horn-rimmed glasses, and padding to round out my body to a size eighteen. Not a complete disguise, but there would probably be hundreds attending, and I didn't expect to get too close to Borson, or, rather, Niedlemyer.

On the way to the downtown Los Angeles hotel where the seminar was being held, I bought an appropriately frumpy suit for my Clara Shimmerhorn character. It wasn't hard to find one. If you want truly ugly colors, cheap fabrics, and styles that would be unflattering to anyone, just go to the large-size section of any store. The industry bias is so obvious it's a wonder large women haven't started lynching the designers.

It was 10:45 by the time I got to the hotel, but with an insurance seminar, I didn't expect to miss much. I displayed my Shimmerhorn ID, picked up my seminar packet, and headed for the morning session in the River Room. Before I even got the door open, I could hear a loud, angry voice echoing around the cavernous hall.

". . . half the folks are already out of work because of those God damn tree huggers, and I haven't seen any of that bullshit proven. I'll be damned if I'll go back to Oregon and raise insurance rates on my people because of some fairy tale about global warming."

Unlike most of the suited attendees, the speaker wore a plaid shirt, jeans with suspenders, and a billed cap. The woolen shirt was open, exposing a T-shirt that read, "TRY WIPING YOUR BUTT WITH A SPOTTED OWL." He was a huge man, six foot five, over three hundred pounds, and very little of that bulk was fat. His eyebrows and eyelashes were so blond that they were almost white. I would have bet money that this guy should have been at a logging tattoo, rather than an insurance seminar, and I wouldn't have been surprised if he'd had a large blue ox waiting patiently in the parking lot.

"So you can take this shit," he shook the conference packet menacingly at Borson/Niedlemyer, "and shove it up your ass, because I'll quit and go on God damn welfare before I'll help this company screw over my people."

Well, so much for my not missing anything by arriving late.

SEVENTEEN

The Oregon Paul Bunyan looked around the conference hall, seeing shock and disapproval on many faces. Some folks seated nearby were actually leaning away to distance themselves from him. I liked him immediately. He reminded me of my dad, rough, tough, independent, and incorruptibly principled. I selected a chair just two away from him.

As he looked into the disapproving faces around him, his tone changed from angry to resigned. "Hell," he said, "I've been there before."

As he sat down, he caught the smile on my face and did a double take. The look he gave me said he was ready to take me on if I was laughing at him. I gave him a thumb's up. His expression changed, and he gave me a conspiratorial wink.

The audience reaction was mixed. At first there were some audible criticisms of Paul Bunyan's language and opinions, then some loud and strongly expressed approval.

As Niedlemyer waited out the audience, he was smiling affably and nodding his head in understanding. Only the dark red flush of his neck and ears revealed that he wasn't as cool as he was pretending to be. His eyes moved from Bunyan to me, first a glance, then he looked back and held me in his gaze for several seconds. While being subjected to his close examination, I noticed that the audience seated in a semicircle around his podium was not as large as I had anticipated. Perhaps plopping myself down at the center of attention was not the cleverest thing I could have done.

When the audience quieted, he spoke in a calm, reasonable, non-confrontational voice, dripping with empathy. "I know you have been there before, Sven. I know that when ecological concerns shut down your logging business in Oregon, you had to go on welfare for a while to feed your family. I also know how hard it was for a man like you to do that. The important thing is that you did it so you could survive. Then you adapted. You learned a new business, and you adapted and survived." He paused, and there was quiet throughout the hall.

"I sincerely hope you do not quit, Sven, because you have the qualities your people and all of us will need. Our neighbors, our states, our country, and, yes, our insurance company, will need to adapt in order to survive. Will you hear me out, Sven?"

Sven clenched his jaws as he considered his answer. "I'll listen, Nate, but I won't promise anything."

"Nate." That was a more fitting handle for this tidy little man than Borson. He had won a momentary truce with Sven and had quieted the fractious audience, but I doubted he could really win hearts and minds in this crowd. Though they might have disapproved of Sven's earthy language, most of the audience seemed to agree with him in principal. They didn't appear to be toting Sierra Club cards.

"That's fair enough. You're right, Sven. There is still debate about global warming, and I'm not here today to tell you I have all the answers. I'm here to tell you what we know for sure, what we think is possible, and how we propose to prepare ourselves, our company, and our insured. First, let's examine what we actually know. What can we designate as fact?

"Fact one: We know the global mean temperature is going up at an alarming rate, more than one degree Fahrenheit over the Twentieth century. The thirteen hottest years occurred since 1980.

"Fact two: We know there is a natural greenhouse effect. That is, the gasses of our atmosphere, such as water vapor, CO_2, methane, and nitrous oxide, trap heat and radiate it back to the Earth, keeping the Earth warmer than it would be from just the sun's rays.

"Fact three: We know that man's activities have greatly increased the greenhouse gasses. With the burning of fossil fuels, CO_2 has increased thirty percent. Right now we are dumping seven billion metric tons a year into the atmosphere, and it stays up there for a hundred years. Methane has increased five times as fast. Those extra gasses add extra heat to the planet. The hotter it gets, the more water evaporates. The more water vapor in the air, the more it heats up. In short, the hotter it gets, the hotter it gets. Every year more emerging nations–"

"Wait a minute! Whose fact is this?"

The interruption came from a gentleman to my left who sported a thousand-dollar suit, a beautifully coiffed head of gray hair, and an East Texas twang to his speech.

"Every time one of those flower sniffers comes on TV like Chicken Little to claim the sky is falling, some more sensible scientist comes on and gives a very different interpretation of the 'facts.' We don't know that it's humans doing this.

This old world has warmed and cooled lots of times before. You start shutting down oil wells and cattle ranches, you'll see what real disaster is."

There was a general hubbub as the audience mumbled their agreement or disagreement. Before Nate regained control, Sven rose again and chimed in.

"That's right. All those damn hippies have to do is claim some rat or bird is endangered, and the next thing you know the whole damn town is outta work. It's not enough they wrecked the loggin' business, now they hafta start in on oil. Guess next they'll want us to go back to horses." He paused and added with a grin, "Now that could cause some real pollution that you city folks might not be familiar with."

An uneasy laugh tittered through the crowd. Nate let it play out, then, ignoring Sven, he turned to the Texan and asked, "David, why are you so sure that this scientist is more sensible?"

"Well, because he's not just some nut out there burning for a cause. He's not a politician or a government mooch just trying to save his own job. He doesn't have an axe to grind."

"I see. Are you sure he has no axe to grind? Please turn to page seven in your conference packets. This is a list of 'scientists, organizations, and think tanks who are supported directly by the oil and coal industry, and the amounts of cash they receive annually. Their job is to make sure that any information contrary to industry interest is countered by an opposing view. If the scientists you are listening to are like these, they do have an axe to grind."

The expression on David's face made verbal response unnecessary. Nate smiled and said quite affably, "David, you look like you don't believe me."

"Well, if you want to be frank about it, no, I don't. You're trying to tell me that the oil industry can buy off every newspaper and TV station in our country, and I'm sorry, but I don't believe that. We still have a free country here."

This drew enthusiastic applause.

"Exactly, David. We do have a free country and a free press, and that is precisely how it's done." He paused to allow his audience to chew on that one.

"One of the best traits of our free press is that its members usually try to present both sides of an issue. But in this case, that very quality of fairness in reporting allows oil interests to use a few key spokesmen to present their side of the issue against the opinion of more than two thousand international scientists. The newspapers and television news give equal time to both sides, making it look like an even argument, but it is not."

David folded his arms across his chest and closed his eyes. He might as well have stuck his fingers in his ears.

"David, don't take my word for it. Research it for yourself. Of course, you will have to read something besides Lyle Gorman's editorial in the *East Texas Times*. Get on the Internet and read world opinion. You will learn that there is virtually unanimous agreement by every other industrial country in the world that we are facing a crisis in global warming. Europe is even considering trade embargos to make the United States join in reducing greenhouse gas emissions."

That was definitely the wrong tack. The East Texan shouted back, "That's exactly why we should quit dumping money into that damned UN to support those commie bastards. We are the most powerful and richest nation on Earth, and nobody has the right to tell us how to run our country. We been doing just fine by ourselves. How the hell do you think we got to be numero uno, huh?"

A man in the first row stood up and didn't wait for Nate to call on him. "You're telling me the whole rest of the world knows we're headed for disaster, and the oil guys are keeping it secret. Give me a break."

The noise level in the room rose several decibels, and Nate had to lean into the mike and speak loudly. "Please sit down, Harry. David, Sven, all of you, I'll pay you each one hundred dollars to do your own research. I'll give a thousand dollars to anyone who can prove that global warming is not a real threat to our country, our company bottom line, and, our jobs, yours and mine."

Their jobs! Maybe I was wrong about Nate's persuasive abilities. One of Nixon's aides was supposed to have a cartoon on his wall that said something on the order of, "If you have them by the balls, their hearts and minds will follow."

Nate continued to talk over the audience clamor. "No, I'll make that five thousand to anyone who can prove global warming is not a threat."

Carrot and stick, now he at least had their attention. They quieted. "Many of your offices have already suffered tremendous losses due to extreme weather events. In the last twenty years we have witnessed the worst floods, fires, hurricanes, and tornados ever recorded by man." He paused, then with a very charming, little boy grin, added, "Well, unless you count the flood reported by Noah."

That won him a laugh and lessened the tensions in the room. "In the last twenty years of the twentieth century, our industry paid for damages in forty-two weather-related disasters that cost over one billion dollars each. Thirty-six of these events occurred between 1988 and 1999, costing us one hundred and seventy billion dollars. In May of 1999 we had a single tornado event that spawned more than seventy-five tornadoes. One of them was more than a half a mile across and stayed on the ground for four hours. And it didn't just blow Dorothy over the rainbow. Fifty-four people died. Over ten thousand homes and businesses were damaged or destroyed. You beginning to see a pattern here?

You could hear a pin drop. No one even coughed.

Now look at the tables in your conference packets and follow that pattern into the twenty-first century and notice our company losses. I am sorry to tell you the evidence suggests this is only the beginning. As global warming increases, so will extreme weather disasters. How much can our company, or any insurance company, take before we go bankrupt? What good can we do for our employees or our insured if we're broke?"

A neatly dressed woman in the first row raised her hand. Nate said, "Yes, Kay?"

I was beginning to see a pattern here, and it wasn't just a weather pattern. So far everyone Nate spoke to he knew by sight and name. Did he know all his regional managers that well? If so, Clara Shimmerhorn was in deep trouble.

Kay rose and said, "Okay, so say we accept global warming, but you said it was warming at an alarming rate, and you also said it had only gone up one degree in the last hundred years. In Tucson our temperature can change forty degrees from noon to midnight. I can't see why one degree would make that much difference."

That gave the audience a small laugh, and Nate smiled. "I can understand why that is confusing, but the thing is, we aren't talking about just a local temperature, we're talking about a world average or mean temperature. To put it in perspective, you know about the ice ages when much of Europe and the U.S. were covered by glaciers?"

Kay nodded.

"Do you know how much the world mean temperature had to drop to start an ice age? Four degrees centigrade. Just four degrees. Some scientists are now predicting an increase of three degrees. Some are predicting even more. If the mean temperature rises by even the most conservative estimate of three degrees, the effects will be disastrous worldwide."

He turned and looked directly at me. "For instance, Mrs. Shimmerhorn, our Midwest will become too arid to produce crops. What would the folks in your area of Story City, Iowa, do if there was no rain for crops, and no crops to feed people and livestock? Across the world in Mali the people already face that plight. Since the 1970s an entire region of lakes has dried up, and people who were once self-reliant farmers and fishermen now face famine. Desertification is happening in dozens of places all over the globe, right now."

I gave him no answer but sat in stunned silence. How did he do that? I was too far away for him to read my name tag. Had he memorized all the photos in the computer roster, or did he simply know exactly who I was? He held me in his gaze for a few seconds as a slight smile played on his lips. It might have been simple geniality, or it might have been a Cheshire cat, "gotcha."

"Situations like the one in Mali are part of what your UN money goes for, David, part of where our excess grain goes. If our Midwest turns to dust and desert, the famine will become worldwide because our Midwest plains are the world's bread basket.

"On the other hand, it could mean good news for Canada and Russia. As our latitudes are overheated and turn to dust, Canadian and Russian prairies may warm just enough to become the new producers of the world's grain. That would certainly make a change in the world trade balance, wouldn't it? It could even affect our position as numero uno."

Consternation registered on David's face as Nate scored a bull's-eye. "David, the goal here is not to shut down oil wells or cattle ranches, but to devise plans for our nation's continued prosperity. That means finding better answers than turning up the air conditioner.

"Kay, if the world mean temperature goes up three degrees Fahrenheit by 2100, your mean summer temperature in Tucson will be one hundred degrees. That is not your high, but your average. Your highs would fall between a hundred and thirty to a hundred and forty. How many of your seniors would survive that kind of heat? How far would your water and power stretch under those conditions?" Kay sat down heavily with no more comment.

"Sven, ever since 1999 heat and drought have contributed to horrific annual forest fires that have destroyed hundreds of thousands of acres of trees throughout the west. If the world continues to warm there will be great loss of temperate forests. That is not only tragic to loggers, nature lovers, and animal life, but it makes fewer trees to absorb less of the CO_2 we dump into the air, which makes it hotter yet. The hotter it gets, the hotter it gets.

"Kyle, Mary Beth, both of you cover areas that have serious coastal erosion problems. There is now very frightening evidence that the great ice sheets of Antarctica and the arctic may be melting rapidly. The European Space agency is now warning of the collapse of the Wilkins ices shelf. As they melt and the ocean water warms and expands, the world's mean ocean levels are rising. The optimists have been predicting six feet, the pessimists thirty feet. Now international climate scientists are beginning to think sea levels could rise three times that of the official worst-case estimates. That could completely wipe out some small island nations. With the invading seas you can expect damage to our fresh water supplies, sewage facilities, and loss of our most expensive real estate. Even at that, we could be getting off light. At the end of the last ice age, world oceans rose three hundred feet. One can only guess at how many ancient coastal habitats are buried three hundred feet beneath the sea."

He had more than caught their attention. He had touched each individual where he lived.

"How bad will it get? We don't know. Could it all start cooling off again? Possibly, but not likely. David, you said this world has warmed and cooled many times. That's true, but according to the Milankovitch solar radiations cycles, which you will learn more about this afternoon, we should be in the middle of a cooling trend right now. Instead, it's getting hotter. Since Milankovitch's formula has proven accurate throughout Earth's history, this warming trend can only be explained by human impact on the world's atmosphere. Our burning of fossil fuels has changed the world.

"So, how do we make plans? What do we do to protect our company and our insured against the possible hazards of global warming? Will your region of the country face more rain and flood, more hurricanes and tornados, or more drought, fire, and crop loss? That's what we'll discuss this afternoon in our regional sessions. Have a good lunch. See you at one o'clock."

I gathered my belongings, joined the crowd heading for the dining room, and was about to catch up with Sven when someone grabbed my arm. The grasp was firm enough to halt and hard enough to hurt. I turned, both startled and angered, and found myself looking into Nate's face. There was a smile on his lips; however, his eyes were anything but friendly. "Diana, I believe we have a matter to discuss."

EIGHTEEN

"Why don't you join me for lunch in my private office?"

"Nate, you have an office? I thought you just conducted business in the park."

He was still clutching my arm, and my anger made my voice loud enough to turn a few heads. Nate's eyes shifted around to take in the curious looks, then he laughed as if I had made a joke. Then he said, "Only when we're doing the ecology survey, my dear. Today I think my office will be much more comfortable."

Looking down at his hand on my arm, I replied through a clenched-teeth smile, "I think I'd rather take my chances in MacArthur Park at midnight."

He dropped my arm like it was hot and looked lamely at his offending hand as if it had acted upon its own volition. "It's great to see you again, my dear," he said warmly, then gave me a hug and a peck on the cheek as if we were long-lost buddies. As he did, he whispered in my ear, "Diana, please, there are watchers."

As he pulled back, I could see the fear in his eyes. Either this guy was genuinely frightened or he was a wonderful actor. Knowing Sam was listening to my lapel mike I asked, "Okay Nate, but I have something to take care of first. Where is your office? I'll meet you there in about five minutes."

"Good! I'm in the Jason building, right across the street, suite 1200. Thanks."

He turned and walked away, and I watched him wend his way through the crowd, dispensing hugs and kisses as if this were a family reunion instead of an insurance conference. My cell phone rang. "Yeah Sam?"

"I thought we agreed you would steer clear of any close encounters."

"The situation is a little different than anticipated, and I do have a lot of questions for him to answer. You get that location?"

"Yeah, I'm on the way. Be careful."

While Nate was still schmoozing his way through the crowd, I walked across the street and took the Jason building elevator to the 11th floor. Quietly I entered the fire staircase and started for the 12th floor. As I rounded the landing, I caught a very surprised-looking Sam sitting on the top step near the door. Always prepared, Sam wore the coverall uniform of a ubiquitous electrical service company and had a toolbox of legitimate-looking equipment.

Covering his surprise, he said, "Good girl! You learned something on your last case, didn't you?"

"Yeah, I guess so." In my last case I had been trapped on an upper floor by some unpleasant people and had learned the benefit of fire stairs and caution.

"Well, I checked the hall for you," he said. "His office is locked and no time to check it out. I don't see any muscle, but the place is lousy with both surveillance and counter-surveillance equipment. He will probably know you're wearing a wire, but that's okay. Put him on notice not to pull anything. Here, take a look."

He reached under the top tool tray and handed me a video screen about the size of a pocket TV. It was hooked to a tiny wire that slipped under the door, and on the screen I could see a fish bowl view of the entire hall. As I watched, the elevator opened. A waiter stepped out and pushed a food cart down the hall to suite 1200. He unlocked the door and entered, leaving the door standing open. I handed the screen back to Sam, quietly opened the fire door, and waved Sam a goodbye.

As I walked quietly past the office door, I could see the waiter's back as he set out lunch on a small round table. I hit the elevator button to open and close the door, then clomped loudly back up the hall, humming to myself. When I reached the open door, I gave two friendly raps on the wood and said, "Hi, Nate."

The waiter whipped around, and I feigned surprise and laughed. "Whoops, guess I beat him back here. Oh, coffee, wonderful! Could I get you to pour me a cup of that? I missed mine and was yawning all through the morning session."

His occupational desire to present excellent service vied with his suspicion that there might be something not quite kosher about my entering Nate's office. As he served me, however, the routine won out over the troubling prospect of questioning my presence. I pulled a twenty from my purse and slipped it in his hand as I ushered him out the door saying, "Let's leave the rest covered to stay warm until he gets here."

With the door shut, I looked around Nate's office. I was sure I would be the star of Nate's office surveillance video, but I didn't even care. He had certainly gotten a good view of my apartment. At least my bedroom and bathroom were walled off from his surveillance.

His large, prestigious corner office had windows on two sides, giving him a spectacular view of the city. It was sparsely furnished, no hard wood, only easily replaceable pine and man-made materials, not the ostentatious display one normally expects from VP quarters. It was neat as a pin. That was predictable.

The first file cabinet held only insurance papers; the second was dedicated to weather and global warming. Nate had been doing his research for years. A wooden cabinet held what I was looking for, video tapes. I was determined to retrieve the ones of my apartment and searched through his neatly organized cabinet with careless abandon, dumping the tapes on the floor.

I did not hear the door open, but despite the surprise, I managed not to jump when Nate said, "Good afternoon, Diana."

Without taking my hands from the file cabinet I replied, "Hi ya, Nate."

He shut the door and punched in a code on the security control panel, then hung his jacket in the closet. Moving to his desk, he pushed a button that closed the drapes on all the windows. Then he opened a gadget on the top of his desk revealing a flat video screen and a number of controls. When the screen lighted it showed one small blinking red light. He compressed his lips slightly as he considered the light. Looking at me and at the mess I had made on the floor, he said, "I think you'll find what you're looking for in the out-basket on the front of my desk. I had them out to give to you this morning."

As I walked around the desk, he watched the little blinking dot on his screen. I could see that when I moved, it moved. Leaning over the top of his desk to get a better view, I could see that the screen contained a floor plan of the office and all of its furnishings. My red dot and I were now directly in front of his desk. As I leaned forward, so did Nate. Speaking in the general direction of my lapel, he said, "And good afternoon, Sam."

"Neat gadget," I said.

"Yes, it's a helpful tool, and those drapes are of a special, very expensive material that prevents anyone from picking up the vibrations of our conversation on the window pane. So now that we know that Sam is the only one listening, we can talk."

From his out-basket I picked up four video tapes with my initials and a date. Well, that eliminated any question in my mind as to whether or not he knew I was coming today.

"Over in the hall you said there were watchers. Now I see you're serious about that. Who's spying on you, Nate?"

"Let's eat, shall we? We don't have much time. Sorry I can't invite you to join us, Sam, but I only ordered for two."

We settled in at the small round table, and Nate played mother and served us. It looked and smelled delicious, and like the picnic lunches he had served me, was completely vegetarian. As he filled our plates he said, "I don't have time for chit chat, Diana. I need to know if you found the diary."

"I'll have answers before I give any. Who is spying on you, Nate?"

He shrugged. "Just standard corporate security."

"Right, and I suppose you're going to tell me that your corporate security has access to the Big Brother chip you put in my TV."

To my amazement, Nate lost it. He slammed his fork down and his face went red. His eyes were red and watery. Fatigue? Or had he actually been having a good cry? Whatever cool he had managed this morning was gone. In a loud voice he said, "No, the guy I had sweep my office for bugs found that chip in that video surveillance camera over the door, just like Sam found it in your TV."

He leaned forward and touched both of my arms with his hands. His voice changed to a plea as he asked, "Diana, please don't ask any more questions. I can't answer them, and believe it or not I am trying to protect you as well as myself. The only way to do that is to pass that damned diary on to its next Caretaker and forget we ever saw it. If we don't do that, and do it fast, we are in as much danger as Evelyn was."

Stunned, I sat a moment evaluating him and deciding on my response. "That's a very convincing performance, but then you have played all of your roles well, *Mr. Borson*, and played me for a sucker. I don't care if the very hounds of Hell are chasing us. I don't intend to play blindman's bluff anymore. I want the facts. First fact: Did you kill Evelyn or have her killed?"

He was silent, examining me. "Would you believe me if I told you no?"

"Who did?"

"I don't know."

I slammed my closed fist down on the pine table, rattling the dishes. "Whoever killed her had to have read the diary. You must have at least a short list of suspects. Who else knew about that diary?"

"Diana, I don't know which group did it, and knowing anything about them will just put you in danger. I won't have another death on my hands if I can help it. I'm so sorry I involved you in this, but I didn't know . . . so you might as well stop with the questions. I won't answer them."

I had imagined several possible scenarios for this interview, including ones that had made me bring both my stun gun and my Walther. This, however, wasn't one of them. His fear seemed genuine, but I was determined to have some answers. It was time to play my trump card. From my wallet I pulled out the business card for Special Agent Neal Camas. Handing it to him, I said, "In Arizona I had a very interesting talk with Agent Camas."

His eyes moved slowly from the card to my face. "Did you tell him about the diary?"

"No. I told him about my disappearing clients, the ones I met in city parks and on bicycle trails, and failed to get their address or phone number. He got a good chuckle out of that. Somehow, he seemed to think it reflected rather poorly on my professionalism. And you know what? I had to agree with him. I did promise him that if I ever heard from *Mr. Borson* again, I would get back to him with the address and phone number. I believe he is quite eager to talk with you about Evelyn's death. Now, as much as I disliked this little prick, either you answer my questions or I call him up and answer his questions, all of them: diary, red stuff and all."

Nate put both elbows on the table, folded one hand over the other, and rested his chin in the cup formed by his thumbs. His eyes strayed in the general direction of the drapes, and he sat silent for a full minute. Finally, looking back at me, he said, "Okay, Diana, you give me no choice. I'll tell you the whole story and hope to hell it keeps you from doing something that would sign both our death warrants."

NINETEEN

He opened his office safe, took out a large manila file, and placed it on the table. As he pulled out his first exhibit, I was astonished to see that it was an eight-by-ten-picture frame with three pictures of himself and Evelyn, looking like happy lovers. One picture was in front of Niagara Falls, one in front of an enormous glacier, and one on a tropical beach somewhere.

"We met two and a half years ago at a global warming seminar in Costa Rica." His voice cracked with emotion and he paused. I sat absolutely spellbound. Nothing he could have told me would have surprised me more. What was wrong with my people reader? I hadn't had a clue.

Regaining control, he continued in a matter-of-fact tone. "We had a lot of common interests and spent as much time together as possible. She always worked it so we met outside the United States, except for that one time that we took a quick trip to Niagara during a holiday in Canada. Eventually she told me about the warrant for her arrest after her protest at Blue Morpho Petroleum, but not until her lawyer had succeeded in getting all of the charges dropped. She still didn't tell me about Mars and Red 19---not then, anyway.

"We were on our last trip, the one to Tahiti, when the house in San Jose, Costa Rica, burned. Evelyn and her colleagues had used the place as a headquarters for their environmental movement. Everyone inside was killed, and Evelyn later told me that they were all dead before the fire started.

"She was totally changed after that: haunted, paranoid, distant, distracted. Half the time she wouldn't even hear what I was saying to her. Finally she began to tell me about this secret society she belonged to, the Caretakers of the *Martian Diary*. It was upsetting to see that she believed this tale about Martian pollution destroying that planet's atmosphere and Martians migrating here. I told myself that the deaths of her friends, and her accidental escape, had just temporarily unhinged her mind. I was trying to be supportive and protective and humor her until she got over the shock. I didn't know then that she had started with the Martian stuff years before."

He had been staring at the drapes but now hesitated and looked into my face. "By that time I was hopelessly in love with her and would have done anything she asked. So, when she told me that she had been ordered to pass the diary on and wanted me to be the new Caretaker, I agreed without asking too many questions. My mistake.

"Before she could give me the disc, we had to meet with one of her society members, who put me through weeks of indoctrination. Sometimes I could hardly keep a straight face. Other times I thought about cults like Jonestown or that group that believed they were going up to join the mother ship when the comet came by. I often worried about what I was getting into. Perhaps the most frightening moments were when part of this tale actually began to sound plausible. Then I questioned my own mental stability. The bottom line to the indoctrination was that I was to guard the disc, find a safe hiding place for it, and never reveal its existence to anyone unless told to by the society. The society teaches that for eons this information has been handed down in some form: parchment, verbal memory, and now, CD ROM." He laughed self-consciously at the ludicrous statement he had just made.

There was another pause "Soon after I was confirmed as Caretaker, Evelyn began working on me, relentlessly. She was absolutely convinced that Blue Morpho was very close to developing the type of fuel that produced Red 19 as a byproduct, some chemical combination that I think was supposed to include helium and lead. She was determined that I should publish the diary and her Blue Morpho information electronically– transmit it all at once to every insurance company, every scientist, every environmentalist in the world. If I didn't do it like that, zap it instantly over the Internet, 'they' would stop me."

I was trying not to interrupt but had to ask, "They who? Blue Morpho or the Martian cult?"

"At the time I thought she was talking about her Caretaker friends. Lately, I haven't been so sure. My Caretaker contact tells me that the persons who killed her friends and burned the house were thugs associated with Blue Morpho.

"Anyway, when she told me that part about the helium and lead, I made some quip about it going up like a lead balloon. We had the biggest fight we ever had. Her reaction was so crazy, I had to promise her I would help before I could calm her down. I never made light of the subject again, never questioned her at all. The one thing I insisted on was that we could not email such an accusation unless we had more information about Blue Morpho's fuel experiments. It seemed like a good compromise, but I know now that my plan was not good enough for her.

"The day after I agreed to help her, I started getting very angry admonishments from Caretakers warning me not to reveal the diary. There were mysterious messages on the phone, the computer, right on my desk, even after the office had been locked. The security video showed no intrusion. They seemed to know everything I did. Scared the hell out of me."

I couldn't resist the sarcasm. "Gee, I seem to know exactly what you mean."

He paused long enough to acknowledge the rebuke. "I know, it's not much of an excuse, but I'm trying to explain why I . . . I hired a man from Sam's line of work to find out how they were spying on me and to set up counter measures to protect myself. Victor, my spy versus spy guy, debugged my office, took the chip he found in my surveillance video camera, and planted it in your TV. He also helped me set up the computer program.

"I told myself at the time that I was protecting both of us by making sure you didn't reveal the information. It was a vile thing for me to do. I am sorry, Diana." He looked into my face, expecting forgiveness.

His expectation made me furious and triggered my outrage. "Oh, right! There's always a good reason to invade another's privacy, and the James Bond glamour of the Cold War removed any worry about illegality, immorality, or principle. From Nixon's Watergate crew to the database the local supermarket keeps on all its customers, to the illegal wire taps now going on in the name of national security, we all think our need overrides the law. But in the final analysis, that's just the quickest way to loose our freedom."

For a moment he seemed taken aback by my rant, then conceded, "You're right. Once you allow the end to justify the means . . . but it started so innocently. All I wanted was a thorough and careful investigation so I could show Evelyn there were no Martian conspiracies. I wanted to convince her to drop out of the society and continue the wonderful relationship we had started. I was hoping your report would do that for me. I was dumbfounded when you found Evelyn. It never dawned on me that you could do that. When I read the first paragraph of your report and saw that Evelyn had been attacked, the whole world changed. All of a sudden it was real and dangerous and I–"

"Wait a minute. How did you know about the attack? The report I sent you on email came back as a bad address."

"Actually, I sent that error message. Those emails were never really on any Net server. Too public. The program I installed on your computer captured your mail to me. The minute you typed in my address. Every letter of the message was captured and encrypted and sent directly to my computer by direct phone line."

With my lack of technical expertise, I was trying to work through that, but my expression evidently looked accusatory rather than simply confused. His voice became defensive.

"By then all hell was breaking loose. The day before Evelyn had gone ballistic. She was calling me, wanting to know why some woman named Diana Hunter was talking to everyone on the expo staff about her. I had a Caretaker come up to me at lunch and tell me in person that I could never reveal the *Martian Diary*. The day after your email was terrible. Even though Victor cleaned all the bugs from my office and set me up with state-of-the-art counter-surveillance equipment, the society still knew, before I did, that Evelyn had let herself in and stolen the disc and new access code from my safe."

"Evelyn broke in here?"

"She didn't exactly have to break in. I'm afraid I trusted her with everything, including my office key. She knew where I kept the combination to the safe."

"I don't understand. Why did she give it to you and then steal it back? Why didn't she publish it herself in the first place?"

"She had tried, but I wasn't told that until after she had taken it back. She made two hard copies of the diary and sent one off to a regular print publisher along with accusations against Blue Morpho. The publisher sent it to his legal department, and somehow a copy was leaked to Morpho Petroleum. A week later, three people in Costa Rica were dead. Both copies of the manuscript, one in the Costa Rica house and the one with the publisher, disappeared. At least that's what I am told by The Caretakers.

"My contact even showed me 'evidence' that Morpho had ordered the 'novel' destroyed and any witnesses silenced, but I never knew whether to believe that. I did verify that an editor at Martino Press read the diary, but all she would say was that their company had decided not to publish it. Under the circumstances, I figured the most prudent thing was cut off all communications with you, and hope that neither the Caretakers nor Morpho knew you had seen it. I had planned to never contact you again."

"So why did you?"

"As far as I knew, Evelyn had simply stolen the disc and gone underground. After that day on the river, she never contacted me or anyone I knew.

I figured that the next thing I would hear of her would be when the diary hit the Internet. Strangely, perhaps just selfishly, I never really thought of the possibility that she was in danger. I was too angry with her for choosing the diary over me and leaving me." He pulled a stack of paper from the file, hesitated a few moments, then handed me the papers.

I leafed through them and realized that it was the entire FBI file on Evelyn's "Jane Doe" murder. The top memo noted that a business card and been found on Jane Doe's body and suggested that a private investigator named Diana Hunter be contacted to identify the body. Across the memo in red ink was a hand-written note saying, "No mention of the disc by FBI. Find the disc. New Caretaker has been chosen."

"That was just sitting on my desk one morning when I came in. The description of Evelyn's murder was so . . . I knew you needed to read the diary about Antia and . . . That's when I sent you the next excerpt from the diary. I thought that any day you would get the call from the FBI. A hellish week went by before they called. My last message had to wait until you heard from them or . . . I knew you would wonder how in the hell I knew.

My old suspicions about my pal Borson/Nate came flooding back. I had him in a lie. "Yes, and there is something else I wonder. I wonder just how you sent me excerpts from the diary if Evelyn had stolen the disc?"

From his file he pulled a compact disc. "This is my program that I used to interface with your computer. The original disc was protected, so I had been hand-typing the files on this CD. I programmed your disk to self-destruct when you reached the end of the file, so you couldn't do the same thing. I swear to God, Diana, I had no idea I would be using it to tell you about Evelyn's death. I . . . loved her."

I looked from the disc to his face. His moist eyes and his expression full of genuine pain made me give up the last of my suspicions. "I'm sorry, Nate. I wish I had been better able to help her. I'm sorry I–"

"Don't. She was so driven by this vision, this damn diary, she might as well have been possessed. Neither of us could have done anything to stop her. I just don't want anyone else hurt. I just want to give the disc back and forget I ever heard of it. Please, Diana, tell me. Did you find the disc?"

TWENTY

"Nate, who killed Evelyn?"

His voice changed from pleading to yelling. "I already told you, I don't know! It doesn't matter now. Weren't you listening to anything I said? Whether Blue Morpho or the Caretakers did it, they just want that diary kept secret. Let's just give it to them and get the hell out of it."

"Fine. You ready to give up your identity, your looks, your job, your friends and family and disappear permanently?"

"Of course not. Why should I?"

"Suppose your first suspicions were correct. Suppose the Caretakers killed Evelyn and her three coworkers because they had seen the diary. You and I have both seen it too. Maybe all they are waiting for is to get it back before they kill us. Even though you debugged your office, they knew before you did that Evelyn had stolen the disc. How did they do that? Someone managed to get a complete FBI file and place it on your desk. Who did that, and how was it done? They defied both your security and the FBI.

"Suppose the information the Caretakers gave you is the truth, that Blue Morpho killed Evelyn's friends in Costa Rica. It's quite possible. That boat that tried to grab Evelyn was registered to one of Morpho's corporations. What if they also found and killed Evelyn after she stole the disc from you. What else do they know? How did they find out? What would keep them from killing you and me?"

"Damn it, Diana! I thought you were going to help me, not scare me senseless."

"I'm trying to help you, but you have to deal with reality here!"

He looked totally defeated. "How? As you have already pointed out, they can get to me no matter what security I have."

"That's why we have to know which group was willing to commit murder in order to possess the diary. If it's the Caretakers, and they are some sort of weird cult, they could be very dangerous to deal with because they will believe that anything they do is justified by their cause. But the one thing they want is to keep the diary safe and silent unless they choose to reveal it in their own time and their own way. That is our bargaining chip. Our safety is in keeping the disc from them with the threat that it will be exposed if anything happens to us."

He thought that through, his own mind now beginning to work in analytical mode. "What if Morpho murdered Evelyn? What if they really are experimenting with a product that would destroy our atmosphere and make this world as barren as Mars?"

"Is that what Red 19 is supposed to do?"

He nodded, then shrugged. "Something like that. I don't really understand it or know if it's even possible. Evelyn said it was like the ozone hole, only it would eventually deplete all gases in our atmosphere, even water vapor, and dissipate them into space."

I was silent for a moment while I tried to digest that one. "Well, that's two problems. Let's deal with the immediate one first, murder. If Morpho thugs committed murder, it wasn't the executive floor that ordered the hit. That would be done by a black operations group buried somewhere within the security or PR branches, like those who supply silent muscle or bribery to coerce countries that refuse to supply them with the oil leases or –"

Diana saw Nate's jaw drop, and new concern registered on his face.
"What?"

"No wonder he's been so helpful!"

"Who?"

"Harriman Woods, Morpho's vice president for public relations. For the last two weeks he has been all over me offering every sort of assistance in preparation for this global warming conference. He was in the audience today. I just figured Morpho was covering its bases so it could counter anything we said here with the usual disinformation. It never . . . I just wouldn't think . . . I mean, he's PR, I would expect disinformation, but murder? He's a member of the Brentwood Country Club, for Christ's sake."

There was a knock at the door that made us both jump. I followed Nate to his desk and watched as he pushed a button on the surveillance monitor. A video of the hallway appeared, showing a man in electrician coveralls standing at the door. I smiled. "I guess Sam is hungry."

Nate went to the door, opened it, and Sam strode in with a wide grin on his face. "Hello, boys and girls. Someone call for an electronic sweep of this place?" Without waiting for an answer, he started unloading equipment. He checked everything in the room, including us, and came to the same conclusion Nate's desktop unit had. The only bug in the room was on my lapel.

"Okay," said Sam as he walked to the desk. "Mind if I take a look at your system here?"

"Help yourself," replied Nate, but Sam already was.

His fingers danced over the computer keys as he ran the specs on the security system. "Okay, can be only one thing. Nate, when you come in you check in on that alarm pad by the door and assume surveillance control, right?"

"Yes."

"And when you leave you check out again, right?"

"Yes."

"And when you're not in the office, who monitors the security?"

"Our corporate security monitors the whole building."

"Right, and central security takes manpower, usually people who are paid just slightly above minimum wage. No mystery here. No matter how fancy the gadgets, security eventually depends on people. Someone in your central security either belongs to the Caretakers or has a lucrative sideline supplying them with information. When Evelyn broke in, your security videos were feeding into central security rather than your own desktop monitor. Someone saw Evelyn on the monitor and reported it to the Caretakers. Maybe not just the Caretakers. Someone who's dirty might not have any qualms about collecting for information twice."

I mentally tallied a few of the disasters that complication could cause. "Nate, who sent the FBI file, Morpho or Caretakers?"

"Oh, that was definitely the Caretakers."

"Why so certain?"

"Because I was contacted by the same Caretaker I have dealt with all along. He showed up at lunch the next day and asked if I got the file and gave me instructions to contact them if I heard anything about the missing disc."

Sam looked over his half eye-glasses and in his fatherly tone said, "So you have this Morpho guy hanging off your flank at the conference and the Caretakers entering your office at will and joining you for lunch." Sam turned to me. "I think it is a very good thing you left Diana Hunter out there in Arizona, and I believe Mr. Niedlemyer should leave immediately, for a quiet, secluded vacation."

TWENTY-ONE

It took a bit of doing, but we managed to convince Nate to report in sick, send his assistant to complete the afternoon conference, and leave unseen in Sam's car. Then Sam and I helped him with a disappearing act. I called Richard and borrowed his cabin at Big Bear, while Sam rented a car for Nate under an alias. Promising it would be only a few days, we bundled a worried, depressed Nate into the rental car and pointed him toward Big Bear.

Next I picked up my few belongings at the Yellow Umbrella, moved to Sam's house in San Pedro, and settled in to work the case. The only solid lead I had was the boat, and I decided to trace it and see where it led. To help with the task, I used the scanner, computer, and printer to create a bit of helpful paperwork. I decided to maintain the Shimmerhorn persona, but peeled off the padding and costume and put on the more comfortable pant suit I had taken to Arizona. It still had a few suitcase wrinkles but was serviceable. Armed with the paper tools I had created for the Shimmerhorn Insurance Agency, I headed out to Terminal Island.

Like a divided fiefdom, Terminal Island is partitioned down the middle, providing domain to the two great ports of Los Angeles and Long Beach. Side by side they sit, in constant cutthroat competition to wear the title of the busiest port in the country. It was late, but I had a couple hours before businesses closed for the day.

As I drove down several small streets, the rather shabby-looking buildings belied the fact that much of the world's wealth passed through here. A few oil wells still dotted the island, but now it was mostly occupied by huge stacks of cargo containers. A forest of giant gantry cranes and smaller mobile cranes moved inbound containers from freighters to railroad cars and truck trailers and loaded the outbound ones onto the freighters. A friend of mine who works for the U.S. Customs office says they get a chance to inspect less than five percent of those big boxes. Pretty good odds for smugglers.

Winding my way past older-looking office buildings and warehouses, I spotted the names of several oil companies, freight-forwarding companies, chemical companies, and other business that make high use of the harbor. None of them seemed to feel that their port buildings were the place to put forth a highly polished corporate image. It was therefore somewhat of a shock when I pulled up in front of the address for Blue Morpho Global Investments. I double-checked the address. Here in the midst of this dingy port sat a palace of smoky gray glass surrounded by a Japanese garden that was manicured and sculpted like cut green jade. There were oddly shaped gray glass towers jutting out at unexpected angles, creating a surprising, pleasing, and unique building. It must surely have won an architectural prize or two, but what was it doing here?

There was no name on the building, and the place was surrounded by a security wall with a buzzer at the gate. I pressed the button, and a woman's husky voice said, "May I help you?" This phrase is one of the most fallacious utterances in the English language. The speaker almost never means to offer assistance of any kind. In this case, I translated the words and the tone as, "Who the hell are you and what do you want?"

When my Maker deprived me of visual memory, She tried to make up for the deficit by providing me with superior auditory and olfactory memory. My ear for accents was honed by a nomadic childhood, as my dad moved us from mine to mine around the world. It developed into a pretty fair talent. I conjured up an audio memory of my college friend Carolyn Larson, and appropriated her light Norwegian accent.

"Good afternoon. I am sorry to trouble you, but I am Clara Shimmerhorn of the Shimmerhorn Insurance Agency and I would be grateful if you could assist me with some small information on a claim."

"What kind of claim?"

"Only a little one, a slight boat bumping. Please could I come in and talk to you? I will only take two minutes of your time."

There was no further answer, but the gate lock buzzed and opened. I followed the walkway to the building and heard another click as I reached for the door handle. Behind a large wooden desk in the atrium entry sat the gatekeeper. She was at least fifty-five, had dry, badly bleached hair, and a face so hard I would expect her to be tending bar in one of San Pedro's tough little taverns, not running the front desk of a corporate office. I checked her name plate.

"How do you do, Mrs. Fagan. I am Mrs. Shimmerhorn." I presented my business card and an accident claim form I had created at Sam's. Fagan picked them up, glanced briefly at the form, then looked at me impatiently.

"I just need to get one small piece of information from you, please, Mrs. Fagan. My clients were boating in the inner harbor over by Seal Beach and had a slight run-in with another boat. It caused some damage to the hull and the electronics. Nothing major, no injuries, just . . ."

"Mrs. Shimmerhorn, get to the point. What do you want?"

"Oh, well, as I was explaining we are trying to settle this claim, but we can not seem to find the other boat or the boat owners. We have learned that at the time of the accident the boat had been stolen but . . ."

"Was this a boat owned by our company or what?"

"Oh, no, Mrs. Fagan, but you see, you hold the lien on the boat and I am hoping you might be able to give me the current address of the company that owns it or the marina and boat slip where it is kept."

"Then I am sorry you wasted your time. You should have called. It is against company policy to give any information regarding our accounts. Good day."

"Oh. Then I am so sorry to have to waste your time. I hoped we might do this the easy way. I apologize, but I must then present you with these subpoenas. Here is one for you, one for your company president, one for your accounts manager, and a subpoena *duces tecum* for the specific records of the boat and–"

"Hold on, hold on. Let me see what I can do." She grabbed back the claim form, pressed the intercom and searched the form for details.

"Charlene," she bellowed in her rusty, cigarette-alto.

"Yes, Mrs. Fagan?"

"Look up Offshore Deep Driller, Inc., and give me their address."

"Just a moment." Voices, laughter, and paper shuffling played over the open intercom while we waited.

"Here it is. I only have a U.S. address for them. They're based out of Venezuela, I think. It's just Box 1902, 1792 East Martinez Street, San Pedro, California."

Fagan and I both scribbled down the address. Before she could hang up I asked, "Does she have the boat slip?"

"Do you see a loan for a boat?"

"Four of them."

Fagan grimaced. I pointed to the CF number on the claim form, and she read it to the clerk who then gave us the name of a marina and a slip number. Success in less than five minutes. I gathered up my fake subpoenas and gave Fagan a smile. "Your company is lucky to have someone as efficient as you to cut through the red tape for them. Thank you so much."

With a smile as phony as mine she laced her whiskey voice with heavy sarcasm. "Oh, you're just so welcome."

The marina Charlene had come up with was right on Terminal Island. It was not one of the glamorous marinas you find in Long Beach or Newport Beach where the yuppies keep their pleasure yachts. The boats here are nestled into a little niche of the working harbor; most of them looked just as grubby as the surrounding buildings. Many were live-aboards, and were so covered with plants, bicycles, BBQs, boxes, and other paraphernalia of daily life that they could not have been out of their boat slips in years.

I stood on the bank watching a pair of giant cranes load a freighter that was docked just across the channel. The smaller crane wheeled back to a pile of containers, picked one up, and carried it to the gantry crane. The gantry lifted the container up and out over the ship, then lowered it carefully into place on deck. Amazing machines. I thought about the thousands of men who used to do the loading with simpler devices and with the strength of their backs. A lot of time and back injuries were saved by going to containers and cranes, but thousands of jobs lost. I wondered which way served mankind best.

As I watched the cranes, an old man watched me. He sat on the deck of his old trawler in a rocking chair that had just barely enough room to rock without hitting any of the piles of stuff stacked around the deck.

I followed the marina to the ocean end, noting the slip numbers as I went. His eyes followed me. How many others peeked out of portholes to check out the stranger who so obviously didn't belong to this small boat community? On the way back, I saw that the space for the speedboat was just two slips up from the old man. It was empty. Continuing up the walkway, I checked each boat slip in case the boat I was looking for had moved. It was nowhere in this marina. I returned to the old man in his rocking chair.

"Good afternoon."

He rocked the chair a couple of times to launch himself, then stood on wobbly legs and hobbled over to the bow of the boat. "I'll bet you're a social worker."

I smiled. Sticking with my Norwegian accent, I asked, "Oh? What makes you think that?"

He looked surprised, then delighted, then set me for a loss by answering me in Norwegian. Not having the vaguest idea what he said, I smiled, "Oh, how wonderful! You speak Norwegian."

He was so pleased with himself. "Ha, I knew it the minute you opened your mouth. I'm a regular Henry Higgins, just like Rex Harrison. I can pick out a man's accent every time. But, no, I don't speak it, 'cept that little bit and a few words not so polite. Picked that much up in the Merchant Marine. Knew a lot of you *Scandawhovians* in those days."

"That's very good. Not many people would know exactly what country I am from. But you lose the other bet. I'm not a social worker, I'm an insurance investigator."

"Insurance, huh. You sure you're not here to hunt down ol' Brad Commins for his child support payments?" His milky gray eyes were probably covered with cataracts, but it didn't seem to have slowed his observation of life around him. In addition, he had that eagerness to talk that so often afflicts the old and lonely. He was an investigator's delight.

"No," I answered, "but if I were, I'll bet you would be the one who could help me. Actually, I'm just here to settle a small insurance claim. I'm trying to find the speedboat that is supposed to be in slip twelve. Is it out for the day or moved for good?"

"Actually, it's probably more like out for good." He laughed at his own play on words. "Damn thing woulda sunk right there if I hadn't called the Coast Guard."

"Really? What happened?"

"Well, she was docked here, oh, seven, eight months ago, and almost never went out. Two or three times somebody took some suit-wearing fellas out for some sort of pleasure ride or something. Out just a few hours, and then back to just sit there, growin' barnacles. Kinda a shame for such an expensive boat.

"Then these two thugs shows up one day, maybe a month ago. They was dropped off by a motorboat. No name or marking I could see, but it looked like a lighter off one a them foreign freighters. These guys was worthless. They didn't know an anchor from an ostrich. Damn near hit three boats before they got the thing out of the marina. I knew it when I saw the way they handled that boat. I knew they would never get it back in one piece. They didn't. Come back later that morning with cracks in the hull, leaking like a sieve, and just docked her and left her to sink. They left on the same lighter that brung um. Nobody knew who owned her, so I just called the Coast Guard and they hauled her off to White's."

"What is White's?"

"Old boatyard over in San Pedro. Real busy when we had a fishing fleet. Now it's more of a wreckin yard than a boatyard."

"These two men, can you describe them for me?"

"Well, my eyes aren't so good that I could give you much of the fine detail, like eye color and such. I can tell you they weren't too tall, maybe five foot eight or nine. They was all dressed up to be sailors, only they must a gotten their ideas about sailors from old movies: bell-bottom trousers, watch caps, and such. Looked pretty damn silly. I can tell you one thing, though. They was Venezuelans."

"Why are you so certain they were Venezolanos?"

"Why, their accent, of course. Those Venezuelans have a distinctive accent, completely different from them other Spanish speakers. But then I can tell what country most Spanish speakers are from. They most of them have their own little differences, ya know. Strikes me like you know something about their lingo too. That's how they call themselves, they say *Venezolanos*, like that."

Whoops. Maybe I underestimated this old man. "You really are good with those accents. Did you notice anything else about them? Did they take any cargo or anything on board?"

The old man started to laugh. "Yes, they did take something aboard, and they probably managed to wreck that too. Least ways they never brung it back."

I knew the answer before I asked but had to have him confirm it. "What was it they took and didn't bring back?"

"A bicycle."

TWENTY-TWO

I had spent two years in Ciudad Piar, Venezuela, while my dad consulted on a few problems at the iron mine there, so I didn't question the old man's identification of a Venezolano accent. Even though there were regional and social variations, there were enough distinctive characteristics to make it identifiable to someone with a good ear.

Putting the other pieces together with the old man's information, the picture seemed quite clear, but then clear pictures are often drawn from potentially dangerous assumptions. It looked like the boat owner, Deep Driller, Inc., was based in Venezuela. A couple thugs from there were probably brought onshore illegally and given the speedboat and orders to kidnap or kill Evelyn. After their crime, they were taken right back to the ship and returned to Venezuela. Police here wouldn't have a prayer of finding them. They never existed in this country. I decided there was no point in even trying to find them, but I could still check out the boat and the mailbox. The company had to have some contact to handle things here in the States.

It was almost dark by the time I left the marina and worked my way around San Pedro to White's Boatyard. A cold, wet onshore breeze greeted me as I stepped out of the car. I grabbed my windbreaker, slipped my stun gun in the pocket, and zipped up the jacket.

There was a two-story blue-and-white building in the center of the yard, a blue wooden gate in front, and a wire fence trimmed in barbed wire around the perimeter. Starting at water's edge on one side, I followed the perimeter fence around the small peninsula to where it touched the water on the other side. I decided the old man was right. "Wreckin' yard" was a better description, or maybe junkyard. Inside the fence was a tangled collection of boats, boat parts, and machinery. Many of the pieces of metal and wood defied my attempts to guess what they were. One object, however, was easy to identify. Stacked among the rubble was the speedboat that had been used in the attack on Evelyn.

The sign on the gate said "closed". I wasn't sure if it meant for today or forever, but I could see a light in an upstairs room of the building. Thinking someone might be working late or perhaps living here as a night watchman, I looked for a bell or buzzer. At the gate was an old ship's bell with a mallet dangling by a rope. I picked up the mallet and gave the bell a tentative tap. When that brought no response, I really let go and pounded on the thing.

As the sound reverberated around the silent peninsula, I looked to see if I had disturbed anyone else and realized there was no one else to disturb. The only neighbors were other junkyards filled with remnants of old conveyer belts that had once been used to fill the freighters with bulk cargo in the days before cargo containers. My ears still ringing, I felt like I had triggered the alarm at the gate to Hades. With a growing sense of apprehension, I had to control an urge to run to my car and get the hell out of there. It was one of those eerie premonitions that hindsight tells us we should have listened to.

Before I could consciously evaluate my instincts, however, a light came on in one of the first-floor rooms and the door opened. A huge bull mastiff lunged from the door and took only five or six bounds before he hit the gate with such power I was afraid the gate would break loose from its rickety supports and topple right over.

Terrified of dogs, I backed up several steps, slipped my hand into my windbreaker pocket, and wrapped it snugly around my stun gun. It was the only weapon I had with me. The Walther was in the trunk of my rental car. The LAPD and the LA County Sheriff refuse to give anyone a permit to carry a concealed weapon; so, law-abiding citizen that I am, I tend not to carry a gun unless I feel I may be in a life-threatening situation. The funny thing about life-threatening situations is they can happen when you don't expect them.

A short man in a dark-colored turtleneck sweater followed the dog to the gate and asked in a heavy Spanish accent, "What do you want?"

"Good evening. I am sorry to disturb you so late, but I am Clara Shimmerhorn, and I am trying to settle an insurance claim on that speedboat over there."

He looked briefly toward the boat and replied, "But we made no insurance claim."

"Ah, no, you see the claim was made by my client, the people who were in the other boat."

"What other boat?"

"The one that was hit by that boat."

In his anxiety, he slipped into Spanish. His first sentence made my jaw drop, and I sucked in a gulp of air as realization hit me. He'd said, "I did not hit no boat." He definitely used the verb form for first person-singular, and he said the word "I." Instead of pronouncing it as *yo,* he pronounced it *jo.* As he continued in Spanish, telling me he hit only a submerged grocery cart in the river, his accent left no doubt. He was *Venezolano!*

I saw his face change from annoyed and defensive to suspicious, and felt myself tense as I realized my own stupidity. With my poor visual memory, I might not have been able to describe this guy to a police artist, but now, as he stared at me over the gate, there was no doubt in my mind. The last time I saw this man he was hunched over the wheel of that speed-boat. I had assumed that as soon as these fellows had finished their task, they'd been shipped out. Perhaps they hadn't finished the task. They had missed Evelyn. Questions raced through my mind. Why had they been kept with the boat? Were they living here as night watchmen? Had someone anticipated my searching for the boat? Were they just waiting here to see who showed up? They? Where was the other one?

At the same moment I asked myself that question, I heard a sound behind me. I turned just in time to see his arm descend toward my head. My motion redirected his aim, and the blow fell on the top front of my head instead of the back. The zap connected with my skull, my teeth jarred together, instant pain filled my head, and blood ran down my face. As I fell to the ground, I could hear the two of them yelling at each other, but my brain was too scrambled to even try to understand what they were saying. I was struggling to regain my feet and defend myself when I was hit on both shoulders and knocked backward. The next thing I knew, the bull mastiff had his jaws around my throat. I lay there as this growling terror tightened his hold. The Venezolano who had piloted the boat was at my ear, yelling commands to the dog and to me. To the dog he spoke in Spanish. To me he said, "Hold still or he will rip out your throat."

I knew and understood what he said, but fear and panic filled me, and my arm was already moving. I pulled the stun gun from my pocket and jammed it into the dog's gut and squeezed the trigger. He whimpered and growled at the same time, making an unearthly sound, but he didn't let go. He would carry out his charge if it killed him. I felt his jaws tighten, teeth puncturing my neck, and I brought my other arm up and grabbed his lower jaw. My hand was inside his mouth when he finally got enough juice from the stun gun that his whole body jerked convulsively and went limp. I shoved him off me and tried to get up, but a number nine boot connected with my stomach. I vomited a watery bile that ran down the pavement and under my head. As evidence of my mental condition, the last thing I remember thinking was a totally discrepant concern: Would that vomit running in my ear give me an ear infection?

TWENTY-THREE

I must have been awake earlier, because I knew before I touched my head that there would be a bandage on it. I also knew I was lying on a canvas cot and was covered with a rough woolen blanket. Running my hand around the cold metal pipe legs of the cot, I felt laces attached to canvas and confirmed memory there too. To learn anything else would require opening my eyes. My head throbbed and I had a vague memory of pain and nausea when I had tried to sit up before. It was tempting to just go back to sleep.

Despite my desire to escape into dreamland, somebody on my internal board of directors was figuratively shaking me awake. It was the Intrepid Investigator part of me asking questions like, "Why did they zap me on the head and then bandage and care for me?" The Coward in me said, "I don't want to know, I just want to sleep and forget it. Maybe when I wake up again it will be all gone."

Then someone on my committee threw in the clincher. "If you don't wake up now, they might see to it you never get another opportunity." On that thought I opened my eyes.

Lying on my left side, I could see light from an adjoining room shining through all the cracks around the door. In the corner to the right of the door was a washbasin. To see what was to the left, I would have to move my head, and I wasn't quite ready to do that. A vague murmur came from the next room, but not loud enough for me to make out what was said.

The voices triggered another memory. They had been arguing over me. The one who had zapped me wanted to kill me. The other one wouldn't let him and kept repeating in Spanish, *"We have instructions."*

Suddenly I heard a new voice, louder, definitely English speaking, and I could even make out some of his words. Someone or something would arrive about noon. Who? What? I had to hear more. Slowly and carefully I raised myself to a sitting position and waited for the dizziness and nausea to subside. The throbbing headache increased.

Ambient light from outside entered through the window on the wall opposite from the door, lighting that side of the room. Carefully, I stood and walked to the window. Suspicions confirmed. I was in an upstairs room of the building that was inside the boatyard. I tried the window and couldn't budge it, but in my condition I didn't feel up to much effort. Even if I got it open, I didn't see any way to get down from the second floor. At the moment the pain in my head took precedence over everything, even conversation from the next room.

At the end of the room I could see a door partly open. If memory served, the dark interior beyond would be the bathroom. I started for it, but partway there I had to pause and hold onto the wall while the room spun. When the spinning slowed, I walked carefully to the bathroom, felt for the light switch, silently shut the door and flipped on the light. Shouldn't have done that. The small wattage bulb over the sink seemed like a sunburst in my eyes. I flipped it off and waited a moment. Then with my eyes shut, I turned it on again. Opening my eyes a tiny slit, I pulled the cabinet door open, found the bottle of Excedrin, and poured three pills into my hand. As I reached for the glass on the sink, another of those isolated memories flashed in my aching brain. The old pipes in this bathroom had made a terrible noise before. I didn't want my captors to know I was awake, so I tossed the pills into my mouth and began chewing. The noise of my teeth cracking and crunching the pills rumbled through my head and sounded loud enough to be heard in the next room.

I turned off the light, opened the door, and stood there a moment waiting for my eyes to readjust to the semi-darkness. Then, as quietly as possible, I made my way to the door that led to the next room. Lying on the floor, I peeked through the half-inch gap under the door. I could see the legs of wooden chairs and the scarred and scratched bottom of an old pedestal table. Two men were seated and one standing. The English-speaking man was giving instructions to the two Venezolanos, and I caught a few words here and there. ". . . water will . . . to be laced. The food and refuge . . . the other one are fine. Better get two of batteries . . ." Then he raised his voice and I heard all of the next sentence. "Don't look at me like that, Morro. We want her to arrive healthy and in one piece."

I liked the sound of part of that. It seemed to be at least a temporary reprieve. But where was I to "arrive" and what would happen then? I just wished I could have caught more of the first part.

"But it's only about a hundred miles to the plant, why . . . "

"She's not going to the plant. . . . her . . . south."

"Why?"

"That's not for you to worry about. Do your job and . . . with pay. I've got to go. Call me if you have any problems."

He was leaving, and I had to try to get a look at him. I stood up and tried the door handle. It wasn't locked. I opened the door just a crack, but the damn thing screeched like the opening of *The Inner Sanctum*. All speech stopped. Then the guy who spoke English started cursing. Too late now to try to be secretive. I opened the door and got a good look at him. Using my own little observation technique, I put the picture I saw into words: about six foot, sandy brown hair, jowly face, brown eyes, heavy body with a slight paunch, grey slacks, white shirt, no tie, collar open, brown shoes, and expensive-looking gold watch. Most interesting of all was the bright yellow cap with an iridescent blue butterfly logo and the corporate name, Blue Morpho Petroleum. It also helped that I had seen him before. This guy sat next to the Texan who had spoken up at Nate's conference. I would bet my Danny Kaye video collection that this guy was Harriman Woods, the Morpho PR guy that had been hanging around Nate.

Seeing me looking at him, he whirled and headed for the door. "Put her out and keep her that way until you get her loaded. Don't fuck this one up."

The two Venezulanos were already moving in my direction, and I was in no shape to offer much resistance. In short order I found myself on the cot being forced to swallow some vile-tasting liquid. The taste triggered another memory flash. Oh, yeah, I remembered this stuff. They had given me some after they bandaged my head. I turned on my side and felt very smug because I had managed to keep some of their knockout juice in my cheek. I remember letting it run out onto the canvas beneath my head, but that was the last thing I remembered.

TWENTY-FOUR

The headache was much better, and I didn't want to do anything to disturb that, so instead of trying to sit up, I had been quietly noting changes in my surroundings. My conclusion was that I must be in a different room. There was no longer light from under the door. The bed I was on had a wood frame with a foam mattress. On the wall where there should be a window, I could see only some tiny holes. I knew it was daytime because sunlight streamed in though the holes in shafts filled with dancing dust motes. Even so, it was much darker than the other room.

There was a loud noise. Sounded like a diesel truck but was too close for that. Sounded like it was right inside the house. Smelled like a diesel too. What the hell were they running?

Sitting up on the edge of the bed, I could make out the outline of a night stand and lamp. I felt all around the lamp base until I found a switch. As I turned the round rheostat switch, the light grew, and I could see that my lamp was actually a battery-powered camping lantern.

I was in some sort of small rectangular storeroom. There was a bed, a box that served as a night stand, and a porta-potty. All the walls were lined with boxes. On one end the boxes went to the ceiling, looked like they were stacked several rows deep, and had some sort of cargo net over them. All the rest of the walls had boxes stacked about five feet high. Where was the door? A momentary panic gripped me, but I pushed the claustrophobic thoughts aside.

I focused on the bottle of water and the Excedrin sitting beside the lamp, hard evidence that someone cared about my comfort. It wouldn't be the guy who wanted to kill me. I remembered the words of the fellow giving orders. "*They want her to arrive healthy and in one piece.*" But arrive where and how?

A chill went down my spine as I had a terrible suspicion of *how*. Picking up the lantern, I walked to the end of the room for a closer inspection of the line running vertically down the center. "Oh God, please no." That line was where the doors met, doors at the end of a cargo container. "Shit!"

I set the lamp down and began moving the two rows of boxes stacked in front of the doors. Noticing that they were filled with bottled water and canned food, I hoped they hadn't put all this here for my use. There was enough for a journey to Mars. Boxes out of the way, I examined the doors. With mounting panic I found there was no handle, no catch, no release of any kind. Whatever opening mechanism the damn thing had was on the outside. Resorting to frantic and irrational force, I threw myself at the doors, jarring my whole body and starting my head hurting all over again. No amount of shoving and pushing budged them.

Retrieving the lantern, I sat back down on the bed, then almost at once stood up again. Trying not to panic, I began checking the boxes, making a mental inventory. The box that served as a night stand was filled with extra batteries for the lantern. The boxes along the wall held sanitary bags for the porta-potty, toilet paper, plastic silverware, a can opener, paper plates, and dozens of boxes of water and food. Quite a picnic basket. Did they use this container for smuggling people in and out on a regular basis, or was this all for me? How long did they intend to keep me in here?

I took slow, relaxing breaths, trying to keep my mind clear of the fear that had started me trembling and threatened to overpower my thought process. I chanted my own personal litany: "*Emotion floods the intellect, emotion floods the intellect.*"

I had to focus on something that would keep my mind working. Mentally, I began writing a report, trying to think of all the details, addresses and numbers, names and descriptions, but my mind kept drifting back to the fear of being in tiny closed places. Then my breath would come short and shallow and I would start to tremble again.

A door slammed and the engine noise altered. That was a diesel I was hearing, and my little home was attached to it. I leaped up and pulled down a couple boxes from the wall with the tiny holes. Now I realized what they were. My friend Barbara, who is a U.S. Custom's inspector, told me that sometimes they drill holes through the metal walls of the containers or "cans" as she calls them, in order to check for false walls. Sometimes the drill comes out with white powder on the bit.

Climbing the boxes like steps, I made my way up to where I could see out through the holes. The truck and trailer were parked in the boatyard. No point yelling for help here. They would learn I was awake and knock me out again. Judging by the shadows around the junk in the yard, it was just after noon. Well, now I knew what it was that was to arrive at noon. This was one time I found little joy in satisfying my curiosity.

I was hyperventilating. Had to focus. The boxes behind the cargo net.

What's in them? I unhooked the net and began lifting the lids on the file boxes and searching through the papers. At first I was hopeful because they were all Morpho files, but as I rifled through box after box it became apparent that there was no smoking gun here. These were all ordinary personnel files: hires, fires, medical claims, et cetera. It seemed totally weird to find them here, but at the time I couldn't concentrate well enough to even hazard a guess as to why these papers were here.

Gears shifted. As the truck began to move, I left the files and returned to my window seat on the boxes. Peering out the tiny portholes, I watched for recognizable landmarks and tried to keep some sense of direction. When I recognized the route, the fear seemed to start in the pit of my stomach and seep like a drug through my body, paralyzing both physical movement and mental reason. By the time we reached the shipping dock, I was in full panic, unable to think of anything but the scene I had watched the day before. The cranes had loaded the containers aboard, not only filling the hold, but stacking them row upon row on deck. All I could think about was the fact that I would be entombed, buried with containers on top, bottom, and all sides.

Would there be air? How long would the ship be at sea? How sick would I get? Since earliest memory I have been claustrophobic. Hell, I almost panic pulling a turtleneck sweater over my head. How could I stand being buried alive? All the supplies that my captors had so thoughtfully left for my journey would mean nothing. When the crane slammed down container after container on top of me, I would simply go mad.

As the truck came to a stop, I curled into a fetal position on the top row of boxes and lay so still I barely breathed. Part of my brain was numb and the part that worked drifted in strange directions, making no attempt to deal with my current situation. The word "nimwat" took shape in my thoughts, and I tried to remember what it meant. Oh yes, it was the creature in the *Martian Diary* that got frightened and curled up in a ball, just as Antia had done. I giggled insanely as I considered the irony: Antia terrified of open space, me terrified of closed space. Antia survived because they blindfolded her so she couldn't see the vastness. Some member of my internal board who hadn't totally lost her wits reached out and switched off the lantern.

At the same moment there was a loud metal on metal sound. The container I was in rose and lurched, tossing me and several boxes to the floor. Sitting on the floor among the fallen boxes, I saw a large patch of light coming from the wall where the boxes had been. Hope revived my paralyzed brain and I began tearing madly at the rest of the boxes.

There was a long gash in the metal wall of the container, crescent shaped, running more than a foot down the side of the wall. At the bottom was a hole about the size of my fist. I kicked at the opening but found that despite the gash, the wall was quite substantial. Peering out of the hole, I could see the metal legs of the crane, a huge stack of containers, and people walking around the dock.

Turning on the lantern again, I grabbed a couple cans of beans and began pounding on the wall and yelling out the hole. I screamed until I was hoarse but no one seemed to hear me. One guy walked right past the crane, and though I pounded and yelled as loudly as I could, he kept right on going without ever looking up. The noise from the ships, the cranes, and other machinery on the dock drowned out my yells.

Despite the setback, I was now determined to keep my wits. If they couldn't hear me, I would have to make them see me, and I would have to do it fast. The crane, which had been stationary for several moments, was now turning. I could see the dark hull of the ship and the waiting gantry crane at the other end of the dock. This mobile crane would carry the container to the gantry crane and the gantry would lift it up and move it out over the ship, then settle it down into place. If they got me that far, I would be signed on for the whole cruise.

I tore boxes open, looking for something to signal with. I shoved a small can of fruit juice through the hole and watched it hit the asphalt unnoticed. Two more, same results. I took one of the porta-potty bags and poked it partway through the hole, attached a second, then a third and fourth. A longshoreman with a clipboard was checking containers, but she wasn't seeing my signal. Color! After pulling off my windbreaker with its sea-green and bright yellow colors, I attached it by a sleeve to my signal and shoved it through the hole. The woman with the clipboard finished her scribbling and looked away. In desperation I tied three more bags to my signal so it dangled down from the container like a great kite tail.

As the crane rolled slowly past the longshoreman's position, I was watching out the gash in the wall, pounding with my bean cans and yelling. The kite tail floated past, almost touching her head. Her mouth fell open and she did a classic double-take. She signaled the operator to bring the crane to a stop, and then walked over to take a closer look. From directly beneath the container she could hear my yells for help, and I could hear her welcome words.

"Hold on, I'll have the door open in a minute."

TWENTY-FIVE

The crane set my container down gently on the dock, and the longshoreman broke the seal and opened the doors. I must have looked a sight because her facial expression changed from concerned to shocked, and her first words were, "I'll call Customs, and they can get you to a doctor."

"Please, wait. I don't need a doctor right now. When you call Customs, please, ask for Barbara Donald. Tell her that Diana Hunter needs to talk with her."

She looked doubtful.

"I'm an investigator, but I have no ID on me, and she knows me personally. It will save a lot of time if you can get hold of her."

"I'll try, but I can't guarantee she'll be available. It might take a while. You sure you don't need a doctor?"

"No, I'm okay." I would have liked to continue browsing through the file boxes, but the longshoreman locked up the container doors and escorted me to the office, where one of her coworkers kept an eye on me. While I waited for Barbara to be located and dispatched, I tried to make sense of what I had seen in the container and what had happened to me. Despite the brevity of my search, I had made one interesting discovery. All those personnel records were from the office in Paso Nuevo. That was the plant where Evelyn Lilac had staged her protest against Blue Morpho and their experimental fuel. Why were they in a cargo container that was used to smuggle people out of the country? Given time I might be able to find some answer, maybe a mysterious illness caused by the experimental process, or maybe the silencing of insider whistle blowers. Now I wouldn't have the opportunity to find out.

In less than an hour a uniformed customs inspector entered the office, but it was not Barbara Donald. Instead it was a grim-faced young man determined to maintain that attitude of control that law enforcement professionals like to call *presence*. He whipped out a notepad and began asking questions.

"Look, I'm sorry, but please call Barbara Donald and tell her Diana Hunter is here. She is the only one I will talk to."

Another blue uniform came through the door, and a familiar voice said, "Hello, Diana."

I looked up to see Barbara with a confused look on her face. I smiled at the young man and said, "Boy, you guys really work fast, thanks." He almost smiled before he caught himself.

Barbara smiled. "Scott, I'd like you to meet Diana Hunter, private investigator. Diana, this is Scott Johns." She examined my various wounds and bruises and shook her head. "We better have a doctor look at you. What the heck got hold of your neck?"

"A bull mastiff, but how about I tell you on the way to White's Boatyard? The guys who tried to send me on this all-expense paid cruise are living there. Not only can you charge them with trying to Shanghai me, but you can get one up on an arrogant, chauvinist FBI agent in Arizona who has a murder case he can't solve."

She managed to maintain what might have been interpreted as a thin smile while she eyeballed me and considered my request. "Sounds like you need to talk with the police."

"By the time we finish talking, these guys could be on their way back to Venezuela. I think I was their last task here. They are probably also here illegally, so you could get them on that charge too. FBI and INS points."

A knowing look passed between Barbara and Scott, and Barbara asked, "These guys were Venezuelans?"

"Yes, why?"

"Describe them."

"Both about five foot eight, maybe a hundred and forty pounds, swarthy, dark haired, one had hair down past his ears and a beard, the other one had short hair and was clean shaven. Why?"

"You better come with us, Diana." With no further explanation, she loaded Scott and me into a car and drove around the harbor to the LAPD building on B Street. Having known and worked with Barbara for several years, I just kept my mouth shut and waited to see what official little surprise she had for me. In the quiet of the car I put my head back and closed my eyes. As current reality displaced the fear and adrenaline of the last twenty hours, I began to tremble and realized I should not have been so macho about seeing a doctor.

Inside the LAPD station Barbara spoke briefly to a sergeant. Then we waited. Her only explanation was that they were setting up a lineup. In a few minutes I was ushered into a darkened room. Through the one-way glass I saw five guys standing in a row. To my amazement there stood my two Venezolano captors. For the second time in an hour, I looked at Barbara and Scott and said, "Boy, you guys really do work fast."

Barbara gave me a self-satisfied smile and said, "That's what Sergeant Lewis said too."

After making the ID I waited outside with Barbara. "How did you do that? You must have had those guys before I got to the dock."

"When your call came in, we were here turning them over to the LAPD for temporary detainment until a number of things could be checked out. They had driven into the dock area at high speed, just ahead of a CHP car and tried to get aboard that ship before the chippie could grab them. He was faster than they were. Customs got called in to go aboard and check with the captain to verify their claims that they were members of his crew. He said they were, but couldn't produce the paperwork to prove it. In the meantime the CHP had determined that the car they were driving was an Avis rental registered to a woman."

"Was the woman who rented it named Clara Shimmerhorn?"

She first looked surprised, then as she processed it, suspicious. "Yes, Diana. Someone you know, perhaps?"

"We're, ah, acquainted, but I really wouldn't like to try to explain that to the LAPD right now, if we can avoid it."

She looked at me for several seconds, evaluation ending in disapproval. "If you were legitimately working undercover, the alias shouldn't be hard to explain, should it?"

"Okay, message understood."

My headache was coming back and I was exhausted. "Barbara, do you have anything for a headache?"

She took a close look at me and her "officer in charge" expression dissolved into one of friendship. "Will you give us a formal statement on these guys?"

"Of course."

"Wait here a minute and I'll see if I can set it up for later in the day. You do look like hell."

"Thanks! The bull mastiff doesn't look too hot either.

TWENTY-SIX

I didn't want to talk until I'd had time to organize my thoughts, so on the way to Barbara's I put my head back and pretended to go to sleep. It didn't take a lot of pretending.

It had always been my policy to turn over criminal information to the proper authorities so they could do their jobs of arrest and prosecution. That left me to do the type of work I do best, and earned me the respect and cooperation of the authorities I dealt with. In this case, however, I had done everything wrong from the get-go. Top of the list was the fact that I hadn't reported the bike trail incident to Special Agent Camas. He was going to want my license for that one. Now, how was I going to give the police information to charge the Venezolanos and connect them to Evelyn's murder without getting myself in more trouble? Which truth to admit to, and which lie to stick to? Ah, what a tangled web we weave . . .

Showered, medicated, and bandaged, I returned to the PD station with Barbara and was given a brief introduction to a detective named Walsom. He was medium height, heavy set, with a considerable paunch. His gray hair and lined face made him look ready for retirement. Either he had been around long enough that he had lost his need to maintain a stony-faced image, or he was more at ease because I came with Barbara on a case that was of little interest to him. In a friendly and casual manner he invited Barbara to sit in on the interview and offered us coffee. After a few preliminary identification questions, he asked me to tell him how I was acquainted with the two men in custody.

"About two months ago a man named Borson asked me to help an environmental activist named Evelyn Lilac with research material for a science fiction book. It was all about Martians polluting Mars, then coming to Earth. It all sounded like such nonsense that I am afraid I didn't treat it as professionally as I should have. In fact, I don't even have a contact number or address on Borson."

Walsom nodded. I knew that he would understand this because police must deal with vast numbers of people who are half a bubble off. When Governor Ronny Reagan closed the mental hospitals, the effective result was that the mentally ill were dumped out on the streets. The police were left to deal with them, but were given no resources to do so. Doing a sort of criminal triage to sort serious cases from frivolous is now a large part of their job. Within the police culture there is an almost proverbial story that most young recruits hear at some point in their training. It usually tells of a crazy who comes to the station complaining that the Martians are sending rays into his brain. It ends with the older cop telling his recruit, "So I told him to wear a hat lined with tinfoil so the rays couldn't hurt him, and he want off happy as a lamb." It's not the police who must be blamed for the callous lack of concern taught by this proverb. A helpless shrug and a tinfoil hat are the only tools society gives them.

Having danced gingerly around the fact that I had not obtained proper ID on my subjects, I moved on to my next mistake, failure to report the incident on the bike trail.

"Evelyn was in town very briefly to speak at an environmental expo in Long Beach. Since her time was so limited, I agreed to meet with her and talk about her book during her bike ride. That's where I first saw the two guys you have in custody. When I caught up to Evelyn on the bike trail, the long-haired guy had pulled her off her bike and was trying to load her into a waiting speedboat. The guy with the shorter haircut was at the steering wheel of the boat. I ran my bike into the one on shore, knocked him down the embankment, and the two of them took off in the speedboat."

Here, of course, I failed to mention that I'd had a concealed weapon in my bike bag and that I had drawn and brandished it.

"Evelyn and I had a talk back at her motel and she concluded, quite rightly, that I knew little about the environmental movement. She decided she didn't need my help and rode off in a yellow cab."

Walsom asked the obvious question. "Did you report this attempted kidnap?"

"I'm sorry, no. Evelyn wouldn't even talk about it, much less file a complaint with police."

"Did anyone else witness the incident on the river?"

"No."

Despite his years of straight-faced practice, I could read the "no case here" look in his expression.

"However, the whole case took on new significance this week when the FBI asked me to come to Arizona to identify a body. It was Professor Lilac, and she had been murdered by someone chopping off the top of her skull like they were opening a coconut."

Now I had his attention. "If you happen to find a machete in the Venezolanos' belongings or at White's Boatyard, you might want to check it for a murder weapon. If you find anything to tie them to that murder, the guy in charge of the case is Special Agent Camas in Flagstaff." I paused and smiled for effect. "I'm sure the FBI would love to have the LAPD clean up its case for them."

He returned my smile and said, "Well, if we do, you can be sure that won't be the way it will hit the papers."

Good. That little aside placed Walsom and me in the same camp and gave me an opening to explain my little problem with Camas. "I'm afraid I was quite shaken by seeing Evelyn's body, and I never thought at the time to mention the incident on the river."

His poker face was betrayed by a slight lifting of the eyebrows.

"After I got back home I started thinking about it. I dug out the case file, looked up my notes and saw that I had the CF number of the boat. I was trying to check that out to see if I could find anything for the FBI when I ran into the Venezolanos again."

Now the old pro locked down his face in a perfect expressionless mask. I had just admitted to having a piece of information that could have been useful in preventing or solving a murder and had not reported it. That is the sort of thing that makes cops have little respect for private investigators.

In my defense I said, "Evelyn flatly rejected any and all assistance and disappeared. If I had brought in that tale, with no victim, you guys would have processed and filed it. How could I explain that I had this potential client who didn't hire me, who disappeared, and had been trying to hire me to chase down Martians?"

That defense might have had some validity if I had told Camas the truth once I learned of the murder. There was no way to explain that I held out on Camas because I thought he would ridicule me or because he was an asshole. His insular, macho, superior attitude may be the sort of thing that makes private investigators have little respect for many police officers, but that wasn't going to wash here. Walsom nodded but now maintained his professional distance.

I continued my tale of how I ended up in the container, but knew that any consideration or cooperation I might have gotten from this guy had just gone out the window. With the amount of the story I was admitting to, there was no reasonable explanation for my use of an undercover identity, so I left that out and also failed to mention the bit about the phony subpoenas. As I fluffed over this part, I stole one surreptitious look at Barbara, but her face gave away nothing. Walsom asked no questions about my methods. He probably had guessed and didn't really want to know.

When I finished, Walsom sat back and considered my statement. "Too bad you had to go through what you did the last twenty-four hours, when a call to Agent Camas could have put it all in his court."

"Yes sir," I answered contritely.

"Well, with your testimony we can probably get the DA to go for charges related to your kidnaping, but if their attorneys come up with any illegal actions on your part, the perps will probably walk."

He began picking up the paperwork on the table and then with a dismissive air added, "Better have our photographer get some pictures of your wounds and bruises."

In the moment of silence that followed, I realized he wasn't going to chase any phantom case regarding the FBI and a dead body in Arizona. Reason told me I was just going to dig myself in deeper, but I couldn't let it alone.

"What about the murder of Evelyn Lilac?"

"What about it?"

"I think these two Venezolano thugs you have in custody killed her, and I think they are tied to Blue Morpho Petroleum."

I could not read his face. The stakes were now higher and his professional demeanor more rigid. "Do you have further evidence that you *forgot* to tell us to support that allegation?"

"No, but there are three things in the information I just gave you. First, the speedboat used to snatch Evelyn was registered to Offshore Deep Driller, Inc., and the lien holder is Blue Morpho Global Investments.BMGI is the financial arm of Blue Morpho, and Deep Driller is probably some drilling subsidiary. Second, the guy who was in the room at White's boatyard giving orders after they grabbed me was wearing a Morpho company cap. Get these guys to ID him and you have a direct connection to the corporation. If you can find him, I could ID him too. And third, that container I was in was filled with supplies for my journey and with personnel papers from Morpho's Paso Nuevo plant. You could check on how these Venezuelans got into the country and who set them up to live in the old house at the boatyard. You could search for a murder weapon and try to get these guys to cop to the murder or implicate their boss at Morpho."

In the silence that followed, I realized that as my frustration boiled out, my voice volume had risen. Walsom made no response.

I was making the mistake of telling him how to do his business, a fatal error, yet I couldn't stop. It was like picking at an itchy scab until you scratch it off and bleed all over yourself.

"If nothing else, you could start with asking Morpho why their container was used to Shanghai someone and why all their personnel records were being shipped out."

Barbara had been sitting quietly in the corner listening, her presence an unofficial courtesy. She spoke for the first time. "I can answer part of that question. The whole Paso Nuevo plant was shipped out. Most of the cans left over two months ago. That ship was taking the last few cans to the new Morpho research facility in Costa Rica."

That surprised me. "Costa Rica, not Venezuela?"

She nodded. "Yes. The ship will dock in Venezuela eventually, but that can you were in stops in Limon, Costa Rica."

The casual, friendly tone that Walsom had used at the beginning of this session was replaced with cold, professional reproach. "Thank you for your statement, Ms. Hunter. In regard to that Arizona murder case, I would advise that you contact the proper jurisdiction and report *all* the information you have."

TWENTY-SEVEN

As Barbara drove me back to the dock I slumped down in the passenger seat in a silent blue funk. She was enough of a friend not to chastise me, but her silence spoke volumes.

Fortunately for me, the rental car had been ignored in the convergence of jurisdictions. Neither the CHP, Customs, nor LAPD had thought to tow the thing or even take the keys out of the ignition. I thanked Barbara, reclaimed the car, and retrieved the Walther I had left in the trunk.

Unfortunately, the oversight of my rental car was extended to the container and the ship. The ship's captain had the container loaded and the ship under power and out through Angeles Gate to the open sea. Whatever information was in that container, it was on its way to the new plant in Costa Rica.

Like a mauled kitten, I slunk away. I drove my damaged reputation and wounded pride toward Sam's house in San Pedro.

In Sam's guest room I enjoyed the best night's sleep I'd had in a week, then gave myself the next morning off. I slept in late and had a leisurely breakfast with Sam. Always clear-sighted and pragmatic, Sam guided me through a post mortem of both my errors and the flaws inherent in the police and FBI systems. His suggestion was that I write a well-worded report to Camas and send it by email to minimize my exposure and maximize the information I could provide.

I spent two hours composing the report, aided by Sam's expertise on cover-your-ass writing. Once done and polished, I made a copy for my files and hit send.

For the afternoon, I drove into Bluff Beach, picked up my cleaning and a deli picnic, and returned to Sam's. We loaded the picnic and some wine onto his boat, motored slowly to one of the oil islands in the harbor and put down an anchor. While I fished and sunned, he played with his underwater robot, taking digital pictures of the pollution on the harbor floor. The pictures he got guaranteed the fish I caught would be gently released. No way would I want to eat anything that swam in that water.

For dinner we motored over to the Bluff Beach dock and tied up, then treated ourselves to a wonderful fish dinner at the Ocean Way Grill. I reassured myself that their fish had all been caught somewhere that was safe from pollution, and shut my mind to the nagging suspicion that there was no such place on the planet.

After dinner we returned to Sam's house and sat up until the wee hours of the morning. We sipped brandy while Sam told stories of the Cold War and the Drug War, some wonderful, some horrifying. If we had known what was going on at the LAPD station across town, we could not have had such a pleasant and relaxing evening.

I was awakened the next morning at 10:37 by the angry, no, furious voice of Agent Camas, leaving a message on Sam's answering machine.

"Hunter, God-damn you, pick up the fucking phone!"

I stared at the machine a moment like it was part of a bad dream. How did he find me at Sam's? Then the fog lifted and I remembered that Sam had rigged my phone to forward calls to his house.

Sam was standing in the doorway holding a cup of coffee. He smiled and said, "Sounds a wee tad upset, doesn't he?"

"Yes, he does."

He stood staring at the wall a moment, and I knew his computer-like brain was going through all the variables. "Shit, I thought that was a damn good report. Wonder what bee got in his skivvies. Don't think you want to talk with him while he's this hot. He'd probably toss you in a federal cell on so many charges it would take you a year just to sort out a defense. Think I'll pay a quick trip to your apartment and remove the call-forwarding program. The way it's rigged, I don't think he would even detect it, but just to be sure–"

He turned to leave and looked back. "When he sees the condition of your apartment, he'll probably give up on chasing you down, but just in case, you better clear the decks for action. Get showered and dressed and ready to roll. I'll call you after I check your pad."

My shower took just two and a half minutes, but Sam was gone and the house quiet by the time I got to the kitchen for that first cup of coffee. I jumped at the sound of a phone ringing, but this time it was Sam's phone and his J. Edgar answered it.

The little robot took a message and then turned to me. "Sam says I should turn on the radio for Diana to KWSP, right now." The news announcer's voice began immediately from one of J. Edgar's speakers.

". . . his statement later. At this time all we have is a brief announcement from Lieutenant Patrick Marshal, saying that two prisoners were shot by a sniper late yesterday evening. The unidentified men, who were taken into custody yesterday, were being transported from the San Pedro police station to the jail at Parker Center. The officers loading the prisoners into the car were not harmed."

"Fascinating report, Dick. Any information on who these men were or why they were being held?"

"None, Mark. An earlier report that they were in custody on smuggling charges has now been denied. We have also heard that the FBI is involved in this case, but we have no verification of that at this time."

"Great report, Dick. We will be back to you for any updates."

As the announcer cut to commercial, I sank down into a chair. The dead men had to be the two Venezolanos, and I'd bet my last dollar that Special Agent Camas made that call to me from San Pedro. He must have gotten my report and flown straight to LA. No wonder he was breathing flame when he called me. Murder suspects he could have had if I had given him that boat CF number, murdered. He was going to want a lot more than my license, and I don't look good in striped suits.

"J. Edgar, please keep that station on, but mute the volume. I want to hear more on that same story. Also, check both radio and television for other reports. Turn up the volume if you find something, and make audio and video records of all reports."

Without a clue as to where I would be going, I began packing. Fortunately there was little to pack: a few clothes and toiletries, stun gun, fanny pack, Walther and bullets. I saved the entire Evelyn Lilac file to a CD and packed it in the laptop case.

The volume came up on the TV as J. Edgar played an ongoing report. Detective Walsom stood just outside the station door, looking worn and haggard. A semicircle of reporters clamored around him with mikes, cameras and video cams as he read from a prepared speech.

"Two men being held on kidnaping charges at LAPD's San Pedro Division were shot and killed by sniper fire while officers were attempting to move them to Parker Center last night at 9:45. Their names are being held until their identities can be confirmed and their next of kin notified. The investigation into this matter will be handled jointly between local authorities and the FBI with help from INS. Further information will be released as it becomes available."

He folded the notepaper and, ignoring shouted questions, returned to the station house.

Wonderful. Camas undoubtedly would have treated the PD to a royal flaying for letting his suspects get killed right under their noses. I hoped Walsom would remember that he'd told me to report any information I had to the FBI. Whether he blamed me for Camas or not, he would want my hide. Since the station was letting Walsom play "Meet the Press" he was probably tagged to take the fall for this mess. Poor guy looked ready for retirement, but nobody wants to go out under a cloud. Now I would have a second law enforcement officer who would be happy to toss my ass in jail forever.

I was about to have J. Edgar mute the TV when something caught my attention. In the back of the crowd was a baseball cap with an iridescent blue butterfly on it. "J. Edgar, play back the last thirty seconds of that report. Freeze frame right there."

I walked over to the screen. "Can you blow up this section here?" The screen filled with a closeup of the man in the cap. "Can you give me better resolution?" The picture cleared and became slightly smaller. "Oh, my God! Print that, J. Edgar."

I could clearly read the name Blue Morpho and identify this man as the same person who ordered me canned for shipment to Costa Rica. The possibility of coincidence was out of the question. "The arrogance of it. He doesn't even worry about wearing his company logo to the scene of the crime. Is he that stupid, or is he so untouchable he doesn't have to be careful?"

I was talking to myself again, but J. Edgar thought I was talking to him and answered.

"Context of questions not specified. Answer unknown. Would you like his identification file?"

I looked at the little robot. I have never known what all Sam had this guy programmed to do and would never impose upon our friendship by asking such an indelicate question. "Can you give me his identity, J. Edgar?"

"His image matches one of my data records to eighty-nine percent. Would you like to view the record?"

"Yes, please."

Sam walked in the door just as I finished reading the six-page bio on Harry Winczewski. He was a nineteen-year career officer in military intelligence and the commander of an elite black ops force with a budget carefully hidden as military child welfare and education. He had been forced out of the service when his continued presence might have exposed secrets regarding Ollie North, Ronny Reagan, and Irangate. I knew him as Harriman Woods of Blue Morpho.

I handed Sam the bio and the picture of Woods/Winczewski printed from the news report. "Saw one of my kidnappers on television, and J. Edgar offered to ID him for me. I hope it was okay to accept."

Sam didn't answer. He stared at the image. "Silly son of a bitch. He still likes to show off his colors and rank. Never was able to teach him subtlety."

"You know this guy?"

He sat on the couch beside me. "Was this the guy at White's Boatyard?"

With that question, his face took on an expression I had never seen. His voice was low, controlled, in a tone I had never heard. This was the old Sam, the one who ran black operations for U.S. military intelligence. My gentle companion had suddenly morphed into someone I didn't know, someone cold, hard, and dangerous.

I nodded.

"You read the bio?"

Another nod.

"You understand what this means? You can't fuck with this guy, Diana."

"And how do I keep him from fu . . . messing with me?"

Sam didn't answer. I knew he was processing an answer, and I waited. He hit the picture with the back of his free hand.

"There were a lot of guys like him in the service. They're the reason I got out. They have no real understanding of freedom, of the true brilliance of our constitution. They are totally immoral and unprincipled, with no true sense of patriotism. For them it was just a game in which the end justified any means."

I had never heard Sam speak so passionately. He looked back down at the picture and shook his head.

"The worst thing about it was, the end didn't even have to make good sense. In most cases the real purpose was just to make good dollars. Most of what we did wasn't for freedom or democracy, it was to prop up some fucking zillionaire corporation."

I nodded. "Well, I guess now he's gone to work for the end client. I think this is the guy who has been sniffing around Nate for the last two weeks. I saw him at the insurance seminar as well as at White's. My guess is he didn't find whatever it was that Evelyn had on Morpho, and he's nosing around Nate for a lead."

"That Martian crap? He's a crazy son of a bitch, but I don't think he'd bite on science fiction bait."

"I have been thinking about that, too, and about the articles I read on Evelyn's first attempt to expose the problem with Morpho's fuel. I think she had more than the *Martian Diary*. I think she had some sort of scientific proof, maybe some of Morpho's own secret studies or something. She had something that scared the shit out of them."

"Diana, do you have any idea the kind of power you're up against here? You think those clowns and puppets we elect to Washington really run this country? No. The world is no longer run by nations, it's run by international, interlocking corporations. What you are after isn't just Morpho. You're going after the most powerful industry in the world. They'll swat you like a fly."

I believed him. "Sam, I'm basically a coward, and I have no delusions about my ability to deal with this kind of organization. I would gladly drop it and hope to hell Evelyn's story of ecological destruction was just an environmental nightmare. But do you believe Harriman Woods is going to drop it? He is already onto Nate. He already saw me. I may have been disguised, and he may not know my name yet, but how long do you think it will take him to ferret it out? Do I have any real choice?"

Sam studied his hands for a moment, then scratched his head, then interlaced his fingers on the top of his curly gray locks, and sat staring out the window. I waited quietly for several minutes.

"Costa Rica," he said, then looked back at me. "That week between the day you saw Evelyn on the bike trail and the date she was found dead in the wash, she spent four days in Costa Rica. She flew from Orange County to San Jose, then back to New York. Then she flew to Phoenix two days before she was murdered."

"How do you know that?"

He smiled. "You think I've just been sitting on my butt while you've been gone?" Thoughtfully, he continued, "I just didn't know what to make of it until now. If they had found what they wanted on Evelyn, Harry wouldn't still be looking. My guess is she stashed it in Costa Rica. I guess finding it first is the best life insurance."

"Well, I've always wanted to see the rain forests of Costa Rica before they disappear."

"Yeah, well, we just have to make sure *you* don't disappear." He pulled me to him and hugged me.

"You remember the story I told you last night? The one code-named "Pied

Piper" that you made me stop telling in the middle?"

I remembered the story all right. It was the one that was so horrific that I couldn't bear to hear it. I pulled back and looked in Sam's face, waiting for what I knew he was going to say.

"It was Harry Winczewski who dreamed up the idea of sending those village kids back to their parents a piece at a time."

My stomach turned over in revulsion. I know my face showed my horror.

"Diana, you're going to have to be like the prairie dog with plenty of back doors to dive for cover, a half a dozen backup identities, lots of money, and some trustworthy help. I still have some contacts. I'll make a call or two."

"OK, and I'll get started on those backup identities."

TWENTY-EIGHT

The next morning I was scheduled for special treatment at Rick's Coiffeurs Americain. After I took a long soak in the hot tub and received an hour-long massage, Richard began my "beauty" treatments. I'd requested a disguise that would age me but not require face mask or body padding because that might be detected and cause questions and grief. He complied with uncanny artistry: fingernails short and broken, hair salt-and-pepper gray with that look of just growing out of a bad permanent, leg hair unshaven, varicose veins on the legs, liver spots on the hands, sunspots on the face, a light sprinkling of chin and mustache whiskers, eye bags and shadows, eyebrows thinned to wispy stubs, and every line on my face delicately deepened, all with makeup that would not wash off with ordinary soap and water. I was appalled as I watched myself age.

Someone said, "Rick, what have you done? She was beautiful when she came in."

I knew the voice instantly but didn't identify the speaker at first. In that split second before I looked up to see who it was, I felt a joyous response as if someone I knew and loved had just walked into the room. With my pupils narrowed in the bright makeup light and the rest of the room fairly dark, the woman behind me was only a shadowed silhouette, but that was enough. The hat brim pulled down slightly over one eye, the famous profile, and most of all, the voice and accent. Ingrid Bergman had just walked into the room. Perhaps it would be more accurate to say Ilsa Lund, for the actress was costumed in the suit and hat from that wonderful parting scene in Casablanca.

I turned around to get a better look. "Please, say something else."

"What would you like me to say?"

"That is amazing. You have the voice and accent down perfectly. That is the best Bergman I have ever heard."

She laughed, still in character it seemed, because it was Ilsa's quiet, controlled little laugh. "That," she said, "is the only thing about me that is real. All the rest I owe to Rick."

"Yeah," said Rick in his very poor Bogart, "Of all the beauty shops and all the spas in Beverly Hills, she had to walk into mine."

"It's a good thing you hire your Bogart, Rick."

He gave me a look but returned to his normal voice, which was closer to Tom Conte.

"The minute I heard this lady speak, I knew I had to have her as my permanent Ilsa. Now I not only have an impersonator, but she also serves as my full-time receptionist, that is, when she's not off digging up old bones."

"Yes, that's what he says, but the truth is he knew my husband had died and I needed work. He is a soft touch, this one."

"Don't say such things. Every out-of-work actor in Hollywood will be in here looking for a gig."

I was still spellbound. "No, you are wonderful. Face, body, voice, accent, you're perfect."

"You certainly are," said Richard wistfully. There was something so obvious in his voice that I realized he was hopelessly in love with this creation of his. Shades of Pygmalion. But of course, he would be. Rick of Rick's Coiffeurs Americain finally finds his Ilsa. There was an awkward silence because all three of us had heard that telltale note in Richard's voice.

"OK, girls, I suppose you expect lunch too. Demanding, demanding, all the time. I never get a moment to myself. I just happen to have a quiet table for three reserved. Come along."

I looked at the old woman in the mirror. "You're not really going to take me out in public looking like this are you?" In fact, what I was really wondering was if there was any chance that either Camas or Walsom might happen into the restaurant and yell, "Seize that woman!"

"Well, of course I am. It will be a good chance for you to practice your Aunt Tillie walk and your Midwestern drawl. And Diana, if you're going to fit that polyester jacket properly for the role, lose the bra."

The staff at Musso and Frank's is just about immune to the dizzying luster of stardom. They have seen them all, the stars, directors, writers, and musicians; but none the less, the appearance of a young and beautiful Ingrid Bergman turned every head in the place. It was almost like stop-motion photography. All conversation and all eating stopped as gawking diners and waiters followed our procession to a secluded wooden booth at the back. I really didn't need to worry about my appearance. Next to Ilsa, I might as well have been invisible.

As we ate, I got to know the real woman, Sophia Hamerstat, and found her every bit as fascinating as the character she was hired to impersonate. Sophia's husband had been a famous, if somewhat unorthodox, archeologist, and she had traveled with him to the ends of the Earth. Though she avoided discussing personal information, it was obvious that their marriage had been more than a romance and more than a professional partnership. She and her late husband had been soul mates who shared their passion for archeology and for each other. My heart went out to Richard. I could understand why he would fall in love with this woman who possessed such a strange combination of strength, joy, and sadness, but how could he possibly hope to take the place of the idealized ghost she still loved?

The real surprise, however, came when her comments added a new mystery to my current case and made the hair stand up on my arms.

On hearing that I was going to Costa Rica, she said. "Ah, you go to the land where the night frog sings. Paul and I went there." Then she studied me like she was reading my mind and said, "You must go to the Diquis to see the mystery spheres. They are granite balls cut so perfectly spherical that even with today's technology it would be hard to replicate. There is not one culture in the known history of the area that would have been capable of making them, yet thousands of them have been found. The indigenous population conquered by the Spaniards in the fifteen hundreds said the Old Ones had made them and that their purpose had something to do with the sky. My husband believed they were once arranged to chart the heavens and teach astronomy, navigation, and mathematics to a great seafaring culture, now forgotten in time."

Her description of the spheres and their purpose sounded so much like those in Antia's last diary entry that astonishment registered on my face. Sophia misinterpreted my expression as disbelief and a controlled anger seeped into her voice. "But then he believed a lot of things that brought ridicule from his colleagues."

"No, Sophia, I have read somewhere of such a university, a place with granite spheres where they taught astronomy and navigation. Did your husband write a book on this idea? Is his theory something someone else could have read and picked up on?"

When she realized I was not ridiculing her husband's work, the defensive tone relaxed and was replaced with one of sadness and regret. "No, no book. He wrote a paper, but no scholarly journal in his field would publish it. With a choice of publishing in a magazine of doubtful scholarship or not publishing, he chose not to publish. To read it, one would have to check out the single copy of his graduate thesis from the University of Costa Rica library. Others, however, are now giving some credence to the idea, so I am not surprised you have read of it."

For the rest of our lunch I allowed Richard and Sophia to carry the conversation while I considered what the chances were that Evelyn had found Paul Hamerstat's thesis. She had lived four years in Costa Rica and had taught at the university in San Jose. It was possible. Did that prove the *Martian Diary* was her creation? If so, who were the Caretakers watching Nate? Were they also Evelyn's creation? More unanswerable questions. Perhaps I would find the answers in Costa Rica.

TWENTY-NINE

I walked through the echoing concrete building, appraising the dirty walls and following the signs to what appeared to be the Customs desk and the lone Customs inspector. After eight hours on the plane, it wasn't hard to move with the stiff-jointed old lady walk I had been practicing. I actually appreciated leaning on the cane. It wasn't necessary to worry about my disguise for Customs, however, for the man at the desk never even looked directly at me. When I hesitated at his post, he impatiently waved me and my bags toward the open doorway.

Once outside, I stood blinking in the bright sunlight. My first steps onto Costa Rican soil were not what my travel handbook had led me to expect. Though I knew that coffee and banana fincas and great parks of protected tropical forests were out there somewhere, my first view of CR was a small alley, surrounded by concrete walls, filled with yellow taxis and terrible tailpipe exhaust.

I walked toward the line of cabs, my breathing becoming shallow as I tried not to inhale the noxious fumes. I paused involuntarily at a shiny new yellow cab that was like the rest with one exception. Emblazoned on the side in letters of forest green was the name *The Green Machine*. The moment I hesitated, the driver was out of his car, smiling and reaching for my bags.

"Buenas, Senora. You go to San Jose?"

I held tight to the bags, and he stopped and met my eyes. He looked to be in his early thirties, brown hair, blue eyes, and a serious demeanor hidden beneath a charming smile. "Los Yoses," I responded. "Why do you call this bright yellow taxi the Green Machine?"

"The taxi is yellow but the machine is green. Catalytic converter, unleaded gas, low emissions, and great gas mileage." He smiled and patted the fender. "It is all new and all mine."

He reached for the bags again. I held on and asked, "How much to Los Yoses?"

"Twenty U.S."

"I thought is was a ten-dollar ride into town."

"To San Jose in a pollutions machine, yes. To Los Yoses is more far. And with me, you get a driver who speak English and give you a clean, green ride."

I liked this guy. I handed him my bags and climbed in. As he shoved his Green Machine in gear, he looked at me in the rear-view mirror. "Where you want to go in Los Yoses?"

"Just a second," I said as I dug into my bag for my note with the directions. Sam and I had decided that renting an apartment from a private party in a suburb would be safer than staying in a hotel in the city, and would help preserve my cover. On the Internet, I had contacted a woman named Maria Campos who had advertised an apartment in the *Tico Times* newspaper. We made a deal and I asked her for a street address, only to receive a cyber laugh as she typed "LOL". She wrote back, "No one in Costa Rica uses a street address. In fact most people don't even know the name of the street they live on. Locations are given in terms of how many meters they are from known landmarks. She had then typed me very specific instructions to give the cab driver. Hesitantly I asked, "Do you know the *Mas X Menos* market?"

"Sure. But you say, '*Mas por Menos*.' It mean more for less."

"English, Green Machine, and Spanish lessons. Such a deal."

He checked the mirror to see if I was joking or complaining. Reassured by my smile, he beamed me his boyish grin. "My name is Roberto. Hire my taxi by the day and I also give you a very good price."

"Thanks, Roberto." I handed him Maria's directions to her home. "My name is Matilda, but most people call me Aunt Tillie."

"*Tia Tillie, muy bien.*"

The ride from the airport took us by freeway to downtown San Jose, then by narrow, crowded streets through the city to the suburb of Los Yoses. The car exhaust was near asphyxiation levels, and I hadn't had a ride quite like it since age nine when an aunt took me on Mr. Toad's Wild Ride at Disneyland. Stopping at red lights and stop signs seemed to be optional, and the right of way went to the guy who was pushiest and fastest. Roberto squeezed his little Green Machine through tight knots of traffic where I was sure we had no more than two inches of clearance. He also placed a great deal more faith in his fellow drivers than my defensive driving methods allowed for. By the time we arrived at our destination, I realized that everyone here drove the same way and that Roberto was quite skilled at the local sport. With this realization, I decided against renting a car.

Maria was waiting outside her home and waved us down to make sure we didn't miss the house. As Roberto got my bags, Maria and I traded introductions.

Like every place I had seen on the drive here, Maria's property was surrounded by a high wall, which was crowned with three rows of barbed wire. This was another first impression that belied the guidebook assurances that Costa Rica has a very low crime rate. If crime was so low, why was every home and business fortified?

She led us through the wooden gate to her inner courtyard. Stepping into her yard was like leaving a black and white Kansas and entering the Technicolor land of Oz. The walls were covered in three colors of bougainvillea, red, magenta, and light orange. The patio was effusively planted in various types of hibiscus, small palms, banana plants as well as other shrubs and trees I was at a loss to identify. Two trees were festooned with dozens of bromeliads and tilanzias clinging to the trunks and limbs like brightly colored sconces. Scattered about the yard was an assortment of pots filled with multicolored orchids ranging in size from a half an inch long to five inches across. As the profusion of color and sweet fragrance delighted my senses and nurtured my soul, the eight sleepless hours on the plane and the exhaust-filled fright-ride from the airport slipped into the almost forgotten past. A huge blue and gold macaw sat on a perch in the middle of the garden and let out a mighty screech as we walked by.

"Oh, you have a guacamaya."

Maria looked embarrassed. "I'm sorry. Quiet, Sammy."

"Sammy pretty bird," replied the macaw.

I laughed at him and he preened. "Oh, not a problem. We had guacs in Venezuela when I was a kid. I'm delighted with him."

We climbed the flagstone stairs to the apartment on the second floor of Maria's house and Roberto deposited my bags. As I paid him, I asked if he was available the next day and made a deal with him on an all-day rate.

Maria showed me around the apartment, checking me out on all the appliances and making sure I had everything I would need to be comfortable. She had even stocked the refrigerator with a pitcher of lemonade and a casserole dinner in case I got in too late to shop.

Once they were both gone, I poured a glass of lemonade, went out on the balcony and sat down on the rattan couch. The view was lovely and the weather was glorious, about 72 degrees, a few scattered clouds, and a cool, gentle breeze. I was asleep in sixty seconds.

CHAPTER THIRTY

I sat back in the patio chair at Café Ruisenior and drained the last sweet drop of my second coffee. I had Roberto pick me up early so we could start our day with breakfast and had asked him to recommend a place where I could get a good cup of espresso coffee. Surprisingly, espresso in not popular in this coffee producing country, and a latte is hard to find. During breakfast we had chatted and I had learned that he had a wife and a fourteen year old son who was both an outstanding soccer player and a straight-A student. This small family was obviously his joy and the thing that grounded him.

Roberto beamed me his charming and slightly flirtatious smile. "Well, Tia Tillie, how was your latte?"

"Perfect, and the bakery goodies are wonderful. I will spend many of my mornings here."

"I'm glad you like it, but I don't know how you can drink that stuff. It's too strong. You should try a nice cup of Costa Rican coffee, not so dark and strong."

"Maybe next time," I answered, but I was thinking of the cup of Costa Rican coffee that Evelyn had served me. The memory of her sad, pail face as she rode off in the taxi caused a wave of sadness and distracted me momentarily.

Roberto stood and handed me my cane, his action pulling me back to the present. I pushed back from the table and gathered up my computer and purse and he led the way to his cab. Putting my equipment in the back, I climbed in front with Roberto. We made a stop at the Mas por Menos grocery store so I could get a bottle of scotch and a few vitals for the apartment, then a stop for me to buy a local cell phone. After that we headed toward downtown.

"Roberto, this is such a delightful place but the exhaust from the cars on the boulevard is almost enough to ruin it. It's like sucking on a bus tail pipe almost everywhere we go."

"Yes, the air is very bad, too many diesels, no emissions control."

"How come? I thought Costa Rica was ahead of the entire world in environmental protection, but you had the only green machine at the airport."

"Until now it was no good to have catalytic converters because the leaded gas just ruined them and still polluted."

"But leaded gas has been illegal for years."

"In the U.S., not here, not in most of the Third World countries. And besides, government taxes make it easy to import used cars and very expensive to import new, unleaded gas ones. I must be away from my family for two years in the U.S. to make that much."

My admiration for this industrious young entrepreneur rose several notches. "I'll bet that was hard. Seems like a strange government policy. I wonder why."

In about ten minutes he had me to my first destination, a home in downtown San Jose that had been converted into the offices of the *Tico Times*, an English-language newspaper.

"I'll be a couple hours here, Roberto, so feel free to take some other fares. Just pick me up about eleven, OK?"

He shrugged. "OK."

I explained to the young woman at the door that I wanted to do a bit or research. She issued me a visitor's badge and called a reporter to help me. Fifteen minutes later a woman arrived, introducing herself as Helen. From her frazzled and slightly resentful demeanor, I suspected that I had arrived in the middle of a big story or at press deadline. However, it was her reaction to my request for information on the fire at Evelyn's house that was the shocker.

She blanched, becoming so pale I was afraid she was going to pass out on me. As she reached for the wall to support herself, I took her hand. "Let's sit down over here on the couch. Are you all right?"

She nodded but sank onto the couch. "Why are you asking about that story?"

I had a cover story about being Evelyn's aunt from Iowa, but she was so visibly shaken that I just said, "I wanted to see if there had been any follow-up on the investigation, any response to Evelyn's claims that all three victims were already dead when the fire started."

"Who are you?"

"I'm an investigator from the States." Seeing her doubtful look, I hoped she would not ask for my license as it was not made out to Tia Tillie.

She considered me a moment, then shrugged. "It will be in the paper tomorrow, anyway. There was a reporter from another paper, *Costa Rica Hoy*, who was following that story. He disappeared three weeks ago and was just found this morning in the morgue."

"How did he die?"

"The police say he overdosed in Sabania Park the night he disappeared, but they can't explain where his body was for the last three weeks. His friends had already checked the morgue."

The color returning to her face, she stood up. "If you want to research our newspaper, all the volumes are up there on those shelves. Help yourself, but it might not be a very safe time to be too curious about that story."

She turned and walked away leaving me staring at the shelf of both loose leaf and bound volumes. The young woman at the front desk confirmed my suspicion that there was no index, so I picked up the volume that covered the right period of time and searched it page by page.

By the time Roberto picked me up I had made copies of all the stories I could find on Evelyn, her work, and Lilac Environmental Institute. I had also copied the only story I found regarding the disappearance of reporter Mark Rojas. Sitting in the front passenger seat, I stared blankly at the material and considered where to go next. In the States I would run every name and address through an assortment of computer databases, develop a number of leads, then follow them. None of my databases had data in Costa Rica, however. Well, back to BC: Before Computer.

"Roberto, I need a phone book and I need to visit the newspaper *Costa Rica Hoy.*"

He reached under the front seat and magically produced a region-wide phone book. I smiled and said, "Could you be faster next time?"

He chuckled, put the car in gear, and pulled out into traffic.

Costa Rica Hoy was like an armed camp. Plain-clothes security barred our entrance and we were carefully screened outside the door. I was required to show my passport, tell them where I was staying, and state my business. When I said I was at the Selva Verde hotel and wanted to look through their old papers for a story they had printed on my niece, Roberto's eyes widened slightly and he studied me thoughtfully.

After a brief conference with someone inside, the guard declined to admit me, saying he was sorry but the office was closed due to the death of an employee. He invited me to come back next week if I was still in town.

Back in the car, I studied the phone book and Roberto studied me. "You speak pretty good Spanish. Funny accent. Not like most from the U.S."

"I learned my Spanish in Mexico and Venezuela. It's been a lot of years, though, and I've forgotten much."

"What were you doing in those places?"

"I was being a kid. My dad was opening an iron mine in Venezuela and an opal mine in Mexico."

The phone book had a long list of Rojas, but none with the first name of Mark. Most listings had no address or had only a postal box. "Roberto, is there an office supply someplace close?"

"Si, you want to go there next?"

I nodded, noticing that he was dying to ask more but too polite to do so. While he waited in the car, I got a medium-sized box, brown wrapping paper, some mailing labels, an ink pen with washable blue ink, and some scotch tape.

On the way back to the car, I passed a small working man's sidewalk café. I had seen them everywhere we drove that morning, and Roberto had told me that here such lunch spots are called "sodas." The delicious aromas emitting from it reminded me it was past lunchtime. I flashed Roberto a hand signaled-question, pointing to my mouth and then to the Gallo Pinto Soda. He nodded, turned off the engine, and joined me. As we lunched on rice, beans, and fried banana, I asked for a third order to go. Roberto was explaining the tradition of the term *Gallo Pinto*.

"It means 'spotted rooster' because its colors looks like one with the white rice, and black beans, green cilantro, and red chile. It's sort of a . . . ."

As I put the Styrofoam container with the third helping into the box, he paused to stare at what I was doing.

". . . It's sort of a joke, the man who has no chicken eats spotted rooster, but it is a dish we . . . "

I then wrapped the box of *Gallo Pinto* in the brown paper and applied the address label.

" . . . it's a dish we take great pride in. But not so much that we make presents of it."

On the return address I wrote "TIA TILLIE'S KITCHEN, Avenida 6, Calles 5/7." For the mailing address, I wrote MARK ROJAS on the first line, then made up another address in San Jose. I dipped the corner of my paper napkin in my water and smudged the address until it was totally illegible.

"What are you doing?"

I met his eyes but avoided his question. "Finished with lunch, Roberto?"

He gave me what I was now recognizing as a characteristic shrug. "Sure."

Back in the car, I pointed to the first Rojas in the phone book and handed Roberto the local cell phone I had bought. "I need someone with a local accent to call these people and ask if this is the home of Mark Rojas. Could you do that for me? If they ask why, you can tell them we have a delivery for him."

He looked at the cell phone and looked up at me. "Tia Tillie, are you a cop?"

"No"

"Mark Rojas was a good reporter, but dangerous. I must know what you are doing. I think it could be dangerous too."

I had been studying Roberto for two days and made my decision quickly. "Do you know who Professor Evelyn Lilac was?"

Again the shrug. "I do not know her but I have of course heard of the Lilac Foundation. Everybody has and they . . . Was?"

I nodded. "She was found murdered in Arizona. I am trying to find out a little about her life here, her friends and her enemies, to try to help find her murderer."

"You are a cop."

"No, a private investigator. My little investigation is not official, and I need it to be very quiet."

He smiled, almost laughed. "San Jose is not so big a city, and Mark Rojas has disappeared. You go to deliver *Gallo Pinto* to Mark Rojas all over town and your investigation won't be very quiet. Gossip here is faster than email."

"Maybe, but I don't have the resources to find people here that I do in the States."

He shrugged. "But you have me."

"You know where Mark Rojas lived?"

"No, but I know where his girlfriend work . . .wait . . .You did it again. You said lived. Is he . . .?"

I nodded. "It will be in tomorrow's papers."

Roberto shook his head, shoved the car in gear, and drove a short way across the inner city, navigating expertly along the narrow, congested, mostly one-way streets.

As we passed an attractive older hotel, he pointed and said, "That is the Selva Verde hotel you give to the paper. You pick a nice one. It have big rooms, restaurant, casino. Many fisherman stay there. Some fish for marlin, some fish for pretty young Ticas in the Golden Macaw Bar." He gave me a self-satisfied grin, then socked it to me with a final pointed observation. "But, not so many older aunts stay there."

We drove past an attractive city park, and as Roberto paused in traffic, I noticed an older mansion with the delightfully romantic name of Key Largo. In his constant tour guide mode, Roberto pointed it out and said it was a very lively night spot. Then with a mischievous grin, he added, "So if Tia Tillie doesn't find what she want at the Golden Macaw, she could check out the action at the Key Largo." It occurred to me that this kid could turn into a real smart ass.

Circling the park, he rounded the corner and stopped in front of a huge two-story building that from the outside resembled a concrete bunker. It was surrounded by a tall chain-link fence that was topped by the ubiquitous strands of barbed wire. The windows on the upper floor were all covered with dark drapes. The entrance, a huge set of heavy wooded doors, was blocked by two armed guards. Even before I noticed the name over the entrance, I was speculating as to its probable uses, and most of the ones I considered were salacious. As we pulled around to the entrance and I saw the name, I had to laugh. It was aptly named The Shady Lady. Where was Roberto leading me?

THIRTY-ONE

Hollywood could not create a better den of iniquity than this real-life one, but in the shuttered, under-lit gloom of the afternoon, it was just a big, empty, decrepit, bar that stank of stale beer and aged floors and walls. I suspected that the dark lighting was in lieu of cleaning and painting. Not even the life-sized posters of can-can dancers that hung in the shadows at the back of the stage could add any glamour to this dive.

The bar lined three of the walls so that one need never be too far from a drink, but only one small section was lighted and in use in the afternoon. The only two people in the place were the bartender, a hard-looking woman who was probably in her forties, and a pretty young woman seated on a bar stool. They sat gossiping quietly while a muted television flickered silently on the wall behind them. I had no doubt that there would be women in the upstairs rooms, but at this hour they would be resting up for their night's work. At night, when the place was gyrating with human bodies and afloat with booze, it was probably exciting enough to satisfy at least the prurient interests, but at this hour it was just distasteful. I wondered what Mark Rojas's girlfriend did here.

Either Roberto was very good at people reading, or I was becoming entirely too transparent for this business. He turned to me and said, "At the day Patricia is the assistant bookkeeper here and at night she sell flowers and earrings to the customers. Don't worry, Tia Tillie, I wouldn't bring you to such a place at night."

Roberto greeted the woman behind the bar as Elina and gave a polite nod to the one seated. Elina returned his greeting and looked suspiciously at me as I limped in, leaning heavily on my cane. She asked what we would have, and Roberto ordered us each a beer. As she drew the beers, he introduced me as a visitor from the United States and said I was interested in some of the hand-carved wooden earrings that Patricia made. He asked when she would be in or if we might go to her home to see the earrings.

When Elina set the beers in front of us, her face was a mask, and she mumbled a quiet, "*Un momento.*" She picked up the phone, dialed just two digits, turned her back to us and spoke softly. She hung up and walked over to Roberto. Speaking in a very quiet voice she told him that Patricia was staying at the Shady Lady for a day or two and would be down in a few moments with her earring box. She would meet us in the outside garden. Roberto thanked her, picked up our beers, and led me to the garden.

The "garden" was a rather bleak cement patio which nested in the center of the U shaped building and was not visible from the front entrance. It's only redeeming virtue was that it had a nice view of the city park beyond. Once seated on a concrete bench, Roberto leaned over and reported confidentially, "The employees here think the owner has the whole place bugged with tape recorders and video. I don't know if it is so, but they won't talk much inside."

I nodded and sipped my beer. Across the street the small park offered gardens configured around a domed, circular structure that was built in the style of a neo-Roman temple. My ever-observant companion followed my gaze and said, "That is the Parque Morazan with the Temple of Music in the center. It is like one in Paris. Very pretty park, no?"

"Yes, very pretty," I answered, but I was actually more interested in the man in the baseball cap who was leaning against one of the Ionic-style columns. I could not see him clearly. He was too far away and in the shadow of the temple, but his hat and body shape were familiar enough to be disturbing.

Patricia stepped out of a side door and joined us, giving Roberto a friendly salutation and me a polite one in English. She and Roberto made small talk for a few moments while she waited for me to ask to see the earrings.

When she opened the box I found myself totally distracted from everything else by exquisite, original pieces of art. As she displayed earrings carved in unique shapes from many natural woods, she told me the Costa Rican names and origins of each wood. She took great pains to explain how she came by the raw materials and wanted me to know that she was careful not to buy from those who poached from protected forest. I had planned on buying a pair or two to break the ice with her, but found myself so genuinely enchanted by her art that I had selected six pairs before I got around to the real purpose of my visit.

It was Roberto who brought us back to the subject. "I'm very sorry to hear about Mark, Patricia."

She nodded but was unable to summon any words.

He continued tenderly. "Patricia, I'm afraid there's more bad news. Evelyn

Lilac was murdered in the United States. This lady is here to learn something that might help find Evelyn's murderer. Can you talk with her?"

She considered me for a long time. "If Evelyn was killed in the United States, why look for her murderer here?"

I put my wallet and the earrings in my purse as I answered. "Because I believe she was killed by someone who didn't want her to complete the environmental work she was doing here. I am trying to learn as much as I can about her work and the other deaths associated with her work."

She turned to Roberto and spoke in very rapid Spanish. I didn't catch it all but got enough to know that she was telling him this was too dangerous, that five people had already died, and that he must stop working for me or I would get him killed.

As she was speaking, I caught a slight movement out of the corner of my eye. I leaned back against the concrete bench so I might see more without turning my head. The man in the baseball cap had left his post by the column and was leaning against a tree that was just across the street. The iridescent blue butterfly on his cap reflected the sunlight.

As he raised his camera, I stood between him and the two young people, turned my derriere his direction and bent over. That should give him a great shot of Aunt Tillie's cotton slip and knee-high roll-up hose.

I picked up the box of earrings and said, "You know, I've thought of a few other people back home who would love these." Then in a low voice I instructed them. "In the park behind me is a man in a baseball cap with a butterfly on it. Don't let him see you look, but try to get a peek at him as you look at me. Tell me if you've ever seen him before."

I had spoken low enough and fast enough that Patricia had missed it and Roberto had to repeat it in Spanish. By the time he had finished and they were able to steal a look in the direction of the park, Roberto reported, "There is no one there."

Patricia took back her box of earrings and glowered at me. "I don't need to see him. I already see him twice. I don't know if he follows me and now sees you, or if he follows you and now knows where I am. Either way we are all dead." She said this mechanically, woodenly, without the emotion she had shown when she'd tried to warn Roberto. She was not only expecting death, but with the loss of Mark, almost seemed to welcome it.

"Don't count us out yet, Patricia. Maybe we can help each other and get this guy before he gets us."

She shook her head. "That is what Mark thought, but this guy owns everybody, even the police." She started to turn and walk away, but I held her arm.

"Please, tell me, where did you see him before?"

She looked at my hand on her arm and I let go. She thought for a moment, then shrugged and said, "The first time was in a restaurant. It was me, Mark, and a computer friend, a German name Carl. Carl sell Mark a computer program. He did not tell me what it was but he pay a lot of money for it. He joke that he was going to be a big Internet publisher. I see that guy with the cap sitting at a table near to us and think he is listening to us. After that meeting, Mark took me home. I never see him alive again."

"The next time?"

"Yesterday. I came home to find someone break up my house looking for something. While I was waiting for my uncle to come and help me, I see that man. He sits a few houses down the street in the shadows and just watch me. I think he was the one in my house. That is why I stay here."

"What about the computer guy, Carl? Has this guy been looking around Carl's too?"

She shrugged. "Two days after Mark disappear, Carl disappear. A reporter at *Hoy* find out Carl fly to Germany. He leave all his belongings, even his computer, and tell no friends where he go."

I was processing what she had told us when she added, "Roberto, we get the autopsy report today." She paused, trying to control the tears that were welling up in her eyes. Her voice broke as she continued. "Mark was tortured many times in many horrible ways. He died of this torture. Get out of this. Go hide and forget it."

Again I took her arm to keep her from fleeing into the club. "Patricia, you need to hide also. I can help. I can send you to a friend in California who will keep you safe."

She wrenched away from me and turned toward the door. Then she paused, turned back, and gave me a look I could not interpret. Standing so that I was between her and Roberto's line of sight, she reached inside the earring box, lifted the felt-lined bottom, and pulled out a CD in a paper envelope. She leaned in close and slipped the disc in my purse. "Here is a special pair of earrings as a present if you promise to leave Roberto out of this." With that she turned and went inside.

THIRTY-TWO

When she refused my help and turned to go into the house, Patricia had the same look of fear and resignation that Evelyn had the last time I saw her alive. It was unbearable to think that it might happen again and that I was helpless to stop it. How can you force someone to accept help? As Roberto drove me home, I was terribly afraid for both these young people. Patricia obviously didn't trust the police, and considering the suspicious circumstances relating to Mark's murder, her suspicions might have some substance.

As Roberto drove us back to Los Yoses, I was quite sure we were now being followed. On the way to my apartment I made my plans. "Roberto, Patricia is right. This is getting too dangerous, and Tia Tillie is going home. I want you to drop me and never come back here. If anyone should ask you about me, remember, they may have been watching us, so tell them the absolute truth about where you took me and when. You don't know me, or anything about why I stopped where I did. I was just another fare you picked up at the airport. You took me to Patricia because I had heard she made nice earrings and had asked you to, not because you recommended her. I bought six pairs of earrings and you took me home. That's it. Get it?"

He was silent a moment and then said, "I will pick you up for your plane in the morning. I will be your bodyguard and see you get away safely."

"Roberto, cabs here are plentiful. All I have to do is step out the door of Maria's house and flag one down. I'll get to the airport just fine. You and your family will have to live here. Think about your son and what happened to Mark and stay away from me. Is that clear?"

He took a while to answer, then shrugged. "Yes."

As soon as I got up to my apartment, I grabbed a plate of leftover casserole, poured a scotch on ice, then sat down and put the disc into my laptop. I opened it with no problem, but it was written in a computer language that was Greek to me. I turned on the voice system, activated the scrambler and the encryption programs, plugged the modem into the phone, and dialed up Sam's number. He answered on the first ring.

"Hello."

"Hi, Sam. The programs you gave me are on. If I were to send you a copy of a disc written in a programming language, would it come through OK?"

"Should, yes."

"Stand by." I copied the disc and zapped it to him as an attachment. He sent a return message: "Received yours, will examine and report."

I left the laptop plugged in with the call alert on and began my packing.

In about an hour Sam called back. "It's basically an Internet mailing program designed somewhat like a virus, but not designed to do any harm. First, it's addressed to a large number of specific people, mostly news, media, scientific, environmental, and political types. Then, after it's sent to that list, it will access the mailing list of each person and send its message to everyone they have on their list. There is no message yet, but there is a place to insert one. Here's the tricky part. It transmits as an email with no attachment showing. The minute you click 'read,' the hidden programming quietly begins mailing copies. Scary damn program. Where the hell did you get it?"

"Long story. I suspect it is something Evelyn ordered through a friend, but the programmer didn't deliver until after she was dead. The middleman, a local reporter, was tortured to death, and your friend in the Blue Morpho hat looks like the chief suspect. Right now he's nosing around the reporter's girlfriend, who is scared to death but won't let me help her."

"Has Woods seen you?"

"He got a glimpse of Aunt Tillie." I looked out the window to where the surveillance car had stopped two blocks down the street. "So far he hasn't followed up, and tomorrow Aunt Tillie's out of here." It was only technically a lie. Someone had followed us to the house, watched as I paid Roberto, then set up surveillance a couple blocks away. I was just thankful he hadn't turned right around and followed Roberto's taxi. There was no point in telling Sam. He could do nothing but worry.

"No, Diana, don't give him the chance. Get out of there tonight."

"Can't, Sam, no plane. But I am all set for tomorrow morning. After Tillie boards the plane I will need everything up and running for Dolores Gomez. Got to get busy. More later." I hung up and unplugged before he could ask any questions.

I loaded my Walther, set portable noise alarms on both doors, and went to bed.

THIRTY-THREE

I slept lightly and was up early. I went downstairs and apologized to my landlady, explaining that there was an emergency and I had to return home but that she was, of course, entitled to the entire month's rent. She made faint protest, then agreed that she would have the expense of advertising and might not find a renter quickly.

No sooner was I back in my apartment than the phone rang.

"Hello."

"Tia Tillie, are you all right?" His voice was frantic.

"Yes, Roberto, I told you not to contact me again. What's wrong?"

"Patricia was strangled last night, right up there in the upstairs room of the Shady Lady, even with the guards downstairs. Police are all over the place this morning, but not last night. I had to know if they . . . if you are all right."

"What phone are you using?"

"A pay phone on the street."

"Good man. I'm fine and I'm getting out of here this afternoon so don't worry about me, just distance yourself from all of this. Promise me!"

"Yes, I will. Goodbye. Be careful, Tia Tillie."

"Goodbye, Roberto."

"Patricia! Damn!" One more sad, frightened face to haunt my conscience and make me wonder if I could have done something differently, something to have protected her. Everywhere I turned in this case someone was killed or endangered. I was beginning to feel like Typhoid Mary.

I had already planned to get rid of Tia Tillie, but now I would have to polish up the plan a bit. From my second-story window, I could see two cars parked about two blocks down the street. It looked like there might be a driver sitting in one of them, but I couldn't be sure. From my back balcony, I saw no cars but did see Maria working in the garden. I was thankful for all the high walls and barbed wire.

I unwrapped the cardboard box, discarded the day-old *Gallo Pinto*, unloaded my pistol, then wrapped it and my ammo in paper towels and packed them in the box. It might be chancy without it today, but I couldn't risk any type of drop off that might be seen by my shadow, and I couldn't have it on me for today's business.

Slapping a new label on the brown paper, I addressed the package to Dolores Gomez, care of the Hotel Aurola Holiday Inn in San Jose. Then I called Federal Express and asked specifically for an afternoon pickup. Walking down the back stairs, I joined Maria in the garden. "Maria, I wonder if I might ask you a small favor?"

"Anything I can do."

"I've called for a Federal Express pickup, but they couldn't get here until this afternoon. Could you please give them this package?"

"Of course. Oh, it's heavy, isn't it?"

"Yes, it is. Thank you." I eyed the old orange and pink knitted cardigan that Maria had hanging on the line. "Maria, the plane sometimes gets so cold, and I forgot a sweater. If I promise to mail it back, could I borrow that sweater?"

She seemed nonplused by the request, but like most of the Ticos I had met so far, she was too polite to refuse. "It is very old, but if you want it, keep it."

"Thank you, but I will mail it back to you."

I went back upstairs and made myself a cup of coffee and sat out on my balcony for the last time. While part of my mind tried to work out all the variables and all the things that could go wrong with my improvised plan, another part was thinking what a pleasant place this would be to come back to. Coffee finished, I reluctantly turned to the next task.

Change of plans meant change of packing. Years of business trips taught me to travel light: one small suitcase on wheels, like the ones the flight attendants use, and a large tote-bag purse with an 'across the body strap' for security, and a few secrets of its own. Both can go onboard with me, and I never have to check baggage unless I am carrying a firearm.

From my suitcase I took my plastic makeup bag, a dark brown wig, and my laptop, and loaded them into the purse. I checked out the rest of the stuff, making sure there was nothing but the thrift shop clothing I had bought for Aunt Tillie. There could be nothing that could be traced. As a backup plan, I took a pair of wrinkle-proof polyester pants and a blouse, rolled them into small tight little balls, and stuffed them in the purse. I zipped up the case, headed out the front door, and flagged down a cab.

As my taxi carried me downhill, we drove right past the surveillance car.

The man in it chose that moment to turn and reach into the back seat, so I could not be sure it was Woods. All the way to the airport, however, that car shadowed us. He was very good, his tail loose and unobtrusive, but a single car surveillance can never be invisible.

At the Juan Santamaria Airport, my driver set my suitcase up on its wheels and pulled up the handle so I could wheel it in. I draped the distinctive orange and pink sweater over the case and settled the security strap of the purse strap over my head , across my chest and under one arm. Using the cane and pulling the case, I entered the airport in my now practiced old lady walk. My shadow left his car in the loading zone and followed me as I waddled through the airport, past the metal detectors, and into the area where my airline had six gates.

I could now see that it was someone other than Harriman Woods. Dressed in blue jeans and a navy colored T-shirt, this guy was younger, blond, very muscular, and not so stupid or arrogant as to wear a company cap. So there were at least two of them in Costa Rica. Which one had made his way into the Key Largo and killed Patricia last night? Where was Woods and what was he up to while Muscles was following me? What would Muscles' instructions be? They were still searching for something, and since Aunt Tillie was probably the last person to see Patricia alive, Aunt Tillie would be the next logical target to be searched.

My flight didn't take off for hours and that was just fine for my plans. I didn't go near the check-in counter but settled into a chair and opened a magazine.

My shadow went out to the ticket counter and checked the outbound flights. Finding no easy answer there, he wandered back to watch me for a clue as to which flight I might get on.

Two hours went by before I finally saw what I had been waiting for. Three flight attendants came off a plane and headed for the ladies' room each pulling a small flight bag identical to mine. I rose stiffly, picked up my purse and cane, grabbed hold of my suitcase and pulled it along, entering the restroom right on the heels of the flight attendants. I picked the one closest to my size and watched as she and the other two parked their bags beside the vanity mirror in the front corner of the room. Two of them entered the little booths, but, unfortunately for me, one stayed out combing her hair, washing her hands, and watching the bags. Plan B.

I walked in until my bag was right beside the others. Then I stumbled, catching myself against the booth with my left hand and dropping the cane so it clattered to the tile floor just the other side of the stewardess at the washbasin. When she turned away from me toward the noise, I reached down with my left hand, picked up the sweater from my case, draped it over the stewardess's case and then rested my hand on the handle of her case. The one at the mirror bent over, picked up my cane and carried it to me, asking, "Are you all right?"

"Yes, just clumsy I guess. Thank you."

I entered the first booth, pulling the suitcase with me. When the helpful stewardess at the wash-basin took her turn in one of the booths, I walked back out to the waiting area.

Watching me sitting there reading my magazine was driving Muscles nuts. Patience was not his virtue. When my plane was at the gate and almost ready for the first boarding, I finally stood and collected my gear. Muscles followed me as I limped over to check-in. He stood near, trying to be nonchalant, until he was sure this was my flight. Then he raced for the ticket counter, leaving a cloud of Aramis cologne in his wake.

I asked to board early because my hip was hurting me, and was obliged by a very nice young man. Once out of sight of the waiting passengers, I shoved the cane into the pocket of the case and walked rapidly down the jetway to the plane. Timing on this maneuver was going to be tricky.

Flight attendants were fully occupied front and rear of the plane, and I made my way to the restroom in the middle of the aircraft. Opening the bathroom door, I shoved the case through and wedged it into a spot on top of the toilet. As I stepped in and shut the door I tried not to think about how small this little room seemed.

Now the question was, had my long wait at the airport been worthwhile? I unzipped the case and was relieved to find one dirty flight attendant's uniform. The polyester pants and blouse that I had in my purse would do in a pinch, but the uniform was much better. As long as people in uniforms are in places they are expected to be, they might as well be invisible.

I took all the stuff out of my purse and balanced it on the laptop on the floor. Turning my purse inside out changed its color from worn-out tan to shiny navy blue and changed its design from open tote-bag type to one with a pocket flap and lock. I checked the secret compartment, putting Aunt Tillie's passport in and taking Dolores Gomez's out.

First I applied the cleansing cream Richard had given me to remove my wash-proof makeup. The problem was I didn't have the necessary fifteen to twenty minutes that Richard recommended to soak loose the makeup. I stripped off the Tia Tillie dress and slip and put on the flight attendant's uniform. The skirt and blouse were snug but workable and the jacket, worn unbuttoned, disguised the tightness. The shoes, however, were torture.

The cabin speakers crackled with brief status checks between the flight attendants and the pilot and indicated that boarding was almost finished. Using a damp paper towel, I wiped off the years along with the cream. Amazingly, it worked fairly well. At least it would get me out of here, and I could do a second application later. Too bad we can't do this with real age lines.

Someone knocked on the restroom door and said, "You need to take your seat now."

"OK," I replied. I dabbed on a little lipstick, crammed my salt-and-pepper gray hair into a skull cap, and pulled the brown wig down snugly. I put the laptop, makeup bag, and other belongings in my purse, crammed the sweater and Aunt Tillie's clothes into the flight bag, and opened the door.

While the real flight attendants were occupied with getting their passengers belted and upright, I made my way to the front station and looked for anything that looked like a passenger manifest. With Tia Tillie no longer on the plane, those flight attendants were going to come up short on their nose count. I saw nothing and wondered if the manifest was on computer. Then I heard the captain order the doors to be closed and the jetway withdrawn. Shit, if I didn't get off now, I would be on my way back to LA for real.

A stewardess entered the station and did a double take. "Are you on our crew?"

"No, I, ah, I just came aboard to let you know one of your passengers escaped."

"Escaped?"

I laughed. "Just joking." She didn't crack a smile. "An old lady, she was feeling ill and got back off, almost passed out in the waiting area. She's with the paramedics."

"One off, and one unauthorized. It's going to be one of those flights. OK, did you by any chance get this sick passenger's name?"

"Yes, Matilda Ferguson."

"Okay, thanks, you better get off unless you want to try for a deadhead to LAX."

"Right, have a good flight." I smiled, she glared, and I backed out of the work station and headed down the jetway.

As I passed the ticket counter I could see Muscles pounding on the counter, and the entire airport could hear him demanding a ticket. The poor ticket agent, wilting back from him, was backed up by two supervisors, all trying to explain why he was too late to purchase a ticket for an international flight. When one of them told him that the plane was already pulling away from the gate, he gave them a royal cursing in an accent that was British, probably London's south side.

Tia Tillie was safely on her way home, and Dolores Gomez of El Paso was on her way to a lovely large suite at the Aurola Holiday Inn.

THIRTY-FOUR

The wide windows of my luxurious tenth-floor suite provided a panoramic view of San Jose. I wrote Maria's address on the label of a new box and started to pack her sweater, but the view and my own thoughts stopped me. Looking down across Parque Morazan, I could see the dark mansion that was the Shady Lady, and I sat for several moments just staring at it. Maybe this case was just making me nuts, but all of a sudden I had a vision of Maria, wearing this sweater and dying because she was mistaken for Aunt Tillie.

I pulled a small pair of scissors from my purse and began cutting the sweater into bits of knotted yarn. The tiny scissors had to gnaw their way through the thick hunks of knitted flowers and soon my cutting became an attack. Tears flooded my eyes, almost blinding me, as I tore into the sweater as if it were responsible for the deaths of these two young women who had briefly touched my life. I quit cutting and gave in to a cry that had been building since I first saw Evelyn in the morgue in Flagstaff.

When I could no longer breathe, I was forced to get myself under control. Then calmly and methodically, I continued the destruction of the sweater. No one would ever take the chance of wearing that sweater and being killed because of my investigation. Dropping the pieces in the garbage, I vowed that no one else was going to get killed, period. I would go after Woods and his black operations team and maybe even the entire Blue Morpho Petroleum corporation. I even had a glimmer of how I was going to do it.

I set up my computer, plugged into the electricity and phone, turned on the encoder, and sent Sam a short message. "Dolores in place. Is her CV ready?"

Within an hour I had received and decoded a file attached to a note from Sam.

The note said, "The new plant manager down there has container loads of Paso Nuevo records and has no staff in place to deal with them, so Dolores is now a records management specialist. This is a new field growing out of the 'paperless' world of computers, which is manufacturing paper records at an alarming rate.

Corporations all over the country are running out of warehouse storage room and are employing specialists to figure out what to store, what to scan, and what to toss.

"I gave Dolores a librarian's background so that part would be something you already know. Planting a curriculum vitae that could be traced and verified was easy compared to finding enough information for you to bone up on this field. It's too new for anyone to have written much on it, but since many of the people doing it seem to be flying by the seat of their pants, that shouldn't be a problem. Some material will be delivered to you along with your credentials. The attached file has some websites you can check. Read fast. An old pal of mine has arranged for you to attend a dinner party at the U.S. ambassador's home tomorrow night. Get acquainted with James Nolan, the new plant manager for the Blue Morpho research facility, and see if Dolores can get hired to help him with his paper mess."

The phone rang as I was finishing the note. It could be only one person. "Hi, Sam."

"Hi, beautiful. You get the stuff?

"Yeah, looks great. Thanks.

"Got one more little piece of equipment coming. Tonight a special messenger will arrive with a new laptop, loaded with a records specialist's working file. Stash your old laptop in the hotel safe. Someone at the new location might try to take a peek at your hard drive. Understand?"

"Yes, thanks. By the way, in case I need a backup, who is your old pal? Is it someone down here?" There was a long silence and I realized I had asked a stupid question and wasn't going to get an answer. Working with Sam meant that I stepped over that line, out of the world of private, legal investigation, and into the shadow world of 'spy guys' rules. Sam would never expose his contact. "Sorry, Sam. Dumb question."

"You won't be completely alone, but Harriman Woods is chief of security at the plant. Watch your back, beautiful."

While my tiny printer was busy spitting out pages of Sam's attachment, I began a day of rest and luxury. First I turned my gray hair dark brown, added brown contact lenses, and did a more thorough job of removing the old lady makeup. Next I sank into a hot bubble bath in a Jacuzzi tub, shaved my legs and underarms, and read the printout. Clean, refreshed, and grateful to feel and look young again, I took out the bottle of body makeup that Richard had given me and applied a wash-proof golden brown tan, all over my body.

In the hotel gift shop, I bought a lightweight sweatsuit, a basic brown street dress, tennis shoes, and a pair of brown flats. Dressed in the sweats and tennies, I headed for the women's fitness center for a workout and massage, followed by two hours in the beauty shop and another shower. Hair and makeup done, I put on the dress and headed for the San Pedro Mall. Dolores was a high-rolling consultant and needed an appropriate wardrobe. It was a tough assignment, but somebody had to do it.

When they closed the stores and I could shop no more, I had the packages delivered to my hotel and grabbed a taxi for Le Chandelier, a classic French restaurant that my hotel concierge had recommended. It turned out to be in a spectacular Mediterranean-style mansion with beamed ceiling, fireplace, sculpture garden, and wonderful paintings, many painted by the chef.

I placed myself in the hands of my waiter and asked him to make all my food choices for the evening. He started me out with a salad of marinated salmon and hearts of palm in a melon and mint vinaigrette dressing that was delicious, proceeded to shrimp and champagne mousse that melted in my mouth, then a cream of pejibaye soup I could get addicted to. I asked what pejibaye was, and he showed me a small persimmon-colored fruit that came from a native peach palm.

Each course was accompanied by an appropriate wine, and he served a lemon sorbet to cleanse the palate before bringing my main course of châteaubriand. By the time he followed up with pastries and coffee, I had mentally raised his tip and the tip to the concierge twice. It was a spectacular dinner, completing a wonderful day of escape, but as I headed back to the hotel and to reality, I felt like the condemned after a hearty last meal.

THIRTY-FIVE

To my delight the ambassador's chief was also familiar with the peach palm fruit. As I tried to sip my cream of pejibaye soup daintily without dripping on my lovely new silk blouse, James Nolan slurped his rapidly, with much clanging and banging of the spoon as he tried to scrape up the last few drops. Though the noise was muted by the general din of conversation in the ambassador's large dining room, it was sufficient to summon the attentive server, who offered Nolan seconds. Nolan looked surprised, then looked at me as if asking my opinion or permission. Surprised and curious, I obliged him.

Leaning in close I said, "There are probably four more courses. Wouldn't want to dull your appetite."

He responded like an obedient child. Mildly disappointed, he hesitated a moment, looking at the empty bowl, then dropped his soup spoon into the bowl and handed it to the surprised server. "Guess I better not, but thanks anyway."

The server was too well trained to show his disapproval to Nolan, but with a sharp look and a barely perceptible movement of his head, he summoned a busboy to collect the offending dirty bowl from his hands.

"What the hell was that made of, anyway? I've never tasted anything like it."

"It's made with pejibayes, or palm peach, a small round fruit that grows on a type of palm tree they cultivate here."

"You must have been here a while to know all this stuff. You work down here?"

One of my favorite things about PI work is the way the oddest pieces of general knowledge can find their way into working a case. "I've been here about six weeks consulting for a chip maker who has a plant in San Jose."

"Oh, so you're one of those high tech types, huh?"

"Not really. I do set up some scanning programs but my job is to help companies establish and maintain a records retention system."

Our next course was served. Nolan waited to see which utensil I would

select, then dived into the tomato aspic with the same gusto he had the soup. I'm
sure the food was every bit as good as my meal last night, but in the disciplined
tension of this evening, I might as well have been eating sawdust.

Sam's friend had made excellent arrangements for my cover. He'd sent a
car to bring me to the ambassador's house in San Rafael de Escazú, a country club
suburb west of downtown, and arranged for me to sit next to James Nolan at dinner.
I was tense, expecting the same sort of man as Harriman Woods, but James turned
out to be somewhat of a surprise. He looked to be in his forties, was about six foot
two, and had curly, light brown hair and blue eyes. Though he had no detectable
regional accent, he had the tan, verbal expressions, and general demeanor of a
California-raised surfer. His brightly colored surfer shirt gave the impression that his
dark, conservative suit and tie must be borrowed for the occasion. As I watched him
inhale his aspic in three bites, I wondered if he could really be working for the same
company as Harriman Woods.

"Records retention. Is that like filing systems?"

The question was asked casually, head down, looking at the empty bowl
instead of me, but his voice carried a sharp undertone of interest.

"It's an entire system for all forms of records. In the plethora of paper
produced by supposedly paperless computers, companies are finding that they spend
more warehouse dollars on records than on product. I help them weed out the
unnecessary, cut down on the total, and establish criteria for routine control of
records."

He put his spoon down and to all appearances was genuinely enthusiastic.
"Now you have hit on a business angle that is really needed. Can you really do all
that in just six weeks?

"No. This trip was just for the initial survey to learn what records are kept
by each department. It will take a couple years to complete a company-wide
program that eliminates redundancy and obsolescence."

"You're exactly what I need. Are you still working with that chip maker?
When will you be available?"

I laughed. "I've just finished my job here, but I fly back to New York in
two days. With my schedule I might be available in about two years."

"Yeah, but you're already here in Costa Rica, and I am about two months
behind in getting my plant up and running, and nobody can find anything. When
they packed up the stateside plant, they were in such a hurry it was like an army
bug-out. That plant had been in place for fifty-five years and they sent everything.

It's a disaster. I don't care what you charge. I'm the boss. I can pay you a ten thousand dollar bonus on top of your usual fee."

I smiled and tried to look apologetic rather than gleeful. "I would love to help, but I have clients who have been waiting for me for months, I–"

"Look, I'm really under the gun here. There's going to be an international conference, and some of my guys have to get ready for a big presentation."

"Well, I don't know . . ."

"I'll tell you what. Now I'm hitting on you, but I hear that Escazu has some wonderful nightclubs, and I've been stuck in that damn compound in the middle of the rain forest ever since I got here. I don't even speak the language. My Spanish stops with *'uno mas cervesa, por favor.'* Let's bug out of this dinner early and take in some nightlife. Give me a chance to persuade you to clean up this shit-can of paper."

Now how could a girl resist such an appealingly worded invitation?

THIRTY-SIX

The minibus painted with the bright Blue Morpho butterfly picked me up at six a.m. James, who was already aboard, woke up enough to mumble a good morning and went back to snoring. He had drunk an amazing amount of booze last night and danced every dance, whether he knew the steps or not. Even when he was quite pickled, I didn't catch him stepping out of character. He was the Big Kahuna with a touch of Peter Pan's determination to never grow up. Why would Blue Morpho choose such a person to run a research facility that held secrets they would kill for? He didn't compute, and that's why he worried me.

With him snoring softly and the driver ignoring us completely, I opened my laptop and used the time for some last-minute study. My old laptop was stashed in the hotel safe along with my pistol. I was going to be living within the Blue Morpho compound and, as Sam had noted, if Woods or my new friend James decided to search me and my possessions, I didn't want them to find any reference to my real business on the hard drive. The new computer Sam sent down was a clean slate, loaded with an excellent records management working file to guide me through the process of doing the initial survey. There were also excellent maps of Costa Rica and I was able to follow our progress and get some idea where we were headed.

The van carried us into the foothills north of the city and treated me to spectacular panoramas of the central valley, as well as passing images of small villages, rural coffee *fincas,* an occasional waterfall, and green, green everywhere. After crossing the Cordillera Central between the looming peaks of the Poas and Barva Volcanoes, we dropped down into the northern lowlands. There the road followed the Rio Sarapiqui on its way to meet the Rio San Juan and flow into the Caribbean. Somewhere, far short of the Caribbean, we left both the Sarapiqui and the comfort of the paved highway and began to bounce along a pot-holed gravel road, following the winding path of a small tributary river. I checked the map but found no name on this tributary or any location name that looked to be Blue Morpho's plant. With the screen bouncing in front of my eyes, I shut the laptop, and put it away in its case.

The sky came down to meet the forest canopy, and the rain began to fall in a heavy, steady downpour. The unending green forest now glistened in the rain. The only sight that broke the monotony was at a fork in the road. As we took the southeast branch, a small wooden sign pointed toward the southwest branch, and to my great surprise it read "Enviro-Medic Research Facility." Well, Well! I had planned on looking up Ken and Judith Hoffman and Guillermo Jesus Montegro Y Monteblan but hadn't realized they would be lurking just off the flank of the new Blue Morpho site. How interesting.

I pulled out the computer again and checked the map. There on the southwest branch tributary was the a listing for a Medical Research Station and just a short distance away on the southeast tributary was a large compound with the innocent name of Misty Forest Resort. I would have bet a dollar to a donut that Misty Forest was where Blue Morpho had relocated. Perhaps I would find an opportunity to visit the good doctor and ask why they folded their tent and disappeared from that environmental expo so fast. Then again, maybe not. I had no idea whose side they were on.

Another twenty minutes of slow travel on bad road brought us to a quiet fenced compound that seemed to stretch for miles on both sides of the small river. The trip had taken hours. If I ever needed to get out of here in a hurry, I would be up the creek, literally and figuratively.

James woke up as the van bumped to a stop at a high security gate, his timing so perfect I wondered if he had feigned sleep to avoid questions. I had explained to him that before I could begin to build his records retention program, I would need to interview him and each of his department heads and learn what sort of business the plant did and what sort of records were necessary to each department. Other than telling me that the plant did research to produce better engines and better fuel, he had successfully avoided discussion of business, preferring to dance and drink.

He looked out at the rain and the blur of green that surrounded us and shook his head. "I come to a country with some of the best surfing beaches in the world, and the only water I see comes in the form of rain. God, I hate this place already."

A young guard with a buzzed hair cut, camouflage fatigues, and a hooded camouflage rain parka approached the van and signaled the driver to open the door. Though he looked too young to shave, he boarded the van with a sidearm strapped

to his hip and a rifle slung over his shoulder. Trying vainly to clamp down a
hardened scowl on his baby face, he looked around with the intensity of a Special
Forces veteran searching for terrorists. "Your security passes," he demanded.

His gloomy thoughts interrupted, James' mouth dropped open, and he
stared at the brash young man. "Son, I'm James Nolan. I'm plant manager here."

"Sir, yes sir. Company regulations require that all persons entering the
compound display security badges."

James stared at him a moment longer, then shrugged. "Well, I guess rules is
rules, huh." He dug out his wallet and displayed his photo ID. "OK now?"

"Thank you, sir." He turned to me. "Ma'am?"

"She doesn't have one. I just hired her. She'll get hers when she checks in
this morning."

The guard stepped back two paces, planted his feet, dropped the rifle from
its shoulder sling into his hands and held it at the ready across his chest. "Sir, no sir.
Company regulations state that no individual shall be allowed entrance to the
compound until their security clearance has been completed stateside or ordered by
Mr. Woods personally."

James was on his feet and over to the young man in a bound. He clutched
the rifle with both hands and wrenched it from the surprised guard. "Now you listen
to me you wind up GI Joe, I'm the man. I run this fuckin' plant. I sign your
paycheck." Still holding the rifle across the young man's chest, James punctuated
each sentence by shoving the guard back toward the van door. "Now you have seen
my ID: you have been told that this lady is here on my authority. Now get the fuck
off this bus and get that Goddamned gate open or I won't be signing any more
paychecks for you." As he stood there, his voice, stature, and posture were
completely changed. Suddenly my aging Kahuna looked more like a kick-ass
warrior.

Defiance played momentarily in the young guard's eyes, and I believe that
if he'd still had the rifle, he would have refused.

"I will have to write this up as a violation of security regulations, sir."

James poked pointedly at the name badge that read Sheppard. "Be sure to
write your name legibly so I'll know who the hell you are."

As the kid turned to go out the door, he hesitated. "Sir, my rifle?"

"You show up at my office later, buckaroo, and we'll have a little
discussion about your regulations and your toy soldier attitude, and then maybe
you'll get your play toy back."

James returned to his seat and, within sixty seconds, to his harmless surfer persona.

"Silly damn kid should know better than to mess with an old man with a hangover."

One of the members of my internal board of directors whispered, "Be very careful, Diana."

THIRTY-SEVEN

The afternoon was excruciating. James walked me to a two-woman personnel office, manned by Margaret and Polly: introduced me as a consultant who was going to straighten out the company files, and instructed the women to get me a security pass and guest room. For the next four hours I sat on a hard-backed wooden chair and waited for Blither and Dither to figure out what the hell to do with a consultant who had no prior security clearance. I wasn't even allowed to go to the restroom without an escort.

In my less lucid moments, I imagined James had made me right off, and this whole business of hiring me was a charade to lure me to the middle of the *Selva,* where I could be killed without anyone knowing. In my more analytical frame of mind, I decided he must be as ignorant of what he was into here as he appeared to be. It seemed to me that only complete naivete could account for the sack of wet brown stuff his actions exploded in this office. That would prove to be my naivete.

Margaret and Polly began with blank looks and hesitant questions regarding my credentials, progressed to whispered consultations in the back office, then to phone calls, faxes, and emails, and finally to one-at-a-time exits from the office for outside consultation. When Harriman Woods burst through the door, I knew all the brown chunks of indecision had found their way to the top. He spoke to no one, went straight to the phone, dialed, and barked into the receiver, "Nolan, get your ass down here to personnel. You obviously need some orientation regarding security protocol." He slammed down the phone, and we all waited in an unnatural and uncomfortable silence.

I continued the activity I had been employed at all afternoon, playing cards on my laptop. Woods had seen me once, briefly, when I was disguised as Clara Shimmerhorn and once from a distance as Tia Tillie. As I played solitaire and tried to look bored, I could feel his eyes on me and hoped his powers of observation didn't penetrate my current disguise.

In about ten minutes, we all heard footsteps in the hall, lots of footsteps, marching in cadence. Once again the door opened forcefully and in trooped four young guards, all armed. Among them was my young friend from the front gate. I noticed he had his rifle back. The unit came to a halt in front of Harriman Woods and the guard from the front gate spoke for the group.

"Sir, we have been directed to escort you, the personnel staff, and the new records management consultant to Mr. Nolan's office."

Woods's neck and face turned red. In a low, menacing growl he asked, "Just whose orders do you follow, Sheppard?"

"Sir, plant manager Nolan, sir." Then, in what was almost a whisper, he leaned in close and said, "Mr. Nolan spoke with me this morning and made corporate chain of command quite clear."

"We'll see about that." Woods marched out of the office as he had entered, in long, determined strides. I bagged the laptop, picked up my suitcase, and with the rest of them, followed Woods at a more leisurely pace.

By the time we reached Nolan's outer office, the shouting match could be heard thundering from his inner office. Few distinct words escaped the insulated inner sanctum, but the volume of combat rumbled through the walls like the echo of rams' horns from a mountain top.

Nolan's secretary acted busy and deaf while the rest of us once again waited in an uneasy silence. In the corner of the office I noticed Muscles from the airport, still wearing the same clothes and looking tired, unshaven, and rumpled. I wondered what he had been doing since I saw him last.

The inner office door opened and Woods strode out, barking an order at Muscles. Muscles rose tiredly. Woods paused at the door and gave me a long poisonous look. "Ms. Gomez, we will speak soon. I'll be handling your security background personally."

As Woods and Muscles left, Nolan stepped quietly to his office door. "Ms. Gomez, I am very sorry you have been put through such an unpleasant afternoon. Personnel staff, in my office."

They were not gone long, but by the time Nolan walked them back out, the short interview had left Polly flushed and Margaret teary-eyed. When Nolan excused the troops and told them to return to other duties, young Sheppard started to answer with a crisp military salute but saw the critical look on Nolan's face. He checked himself and switched from military to civilian protocol.

"Yes, si– ah, OK, Mr. Nolan."

Nolan turned to me and the women from personnel. Once again his personality had undergone radical change. He had straightened the shoulder slump and stood tall with a no-nonsense attitude and an unquestionable air of authority. His face and eyes had lost the bored stare, and his voice had taken on a new timbre. I wouldn't have looked twice at the guy I had gone dancing with last night, but this version radiated a potent, self-assured allure. Under the circumstances, however, any attraction I might have felt was arrested by the clear comprehension of how effectively he had used me.

Ass-kicking time over, he turned on all the charm. "Now, ladies, this was an unfortunate misunderstanding, but now that we are all playing on the same team, things will be much clearer and go much more smoothly. Please take Ms. Gomez directly to the best accommodations you can find, help her get settled in, then accompany her to dinner in the company diningroom."

They mumbled obedient, unquestioning responses and started toward the door, but I stood evaluating this third incarnation of James Nolan. With a new understanding of the true purpose of my employment, I had to both admire and dislike his methods. Nolan had said that I was just what he needed, but he hadn't been talking about records management. I was his pawn in a game of hardball with the big boys. He had arrived to find that though he was the titular head of the plant, Woods was covertly in charge. The son of a gun knew when he dropped me at personnel that I would just flatten my backside on a hard wooden chair until Woods took the bait. The verbal trouncing taken by the guards and the women from personnel was all part of his little game to wrest power from Woods and establish his command of this plant.

He turned his charm my direction, took both my hands, and said, "I am so sorry things got off to such a bad start, but I promise I'll make it up to you. By the time you have had breakfast in the morning, personnel will have everything straightened out and the heads of all the departments will have orders to cooperate with your survey. I want you to report to me each day and provide me with a complete outline of what you discover." Then, reverting to his boyish innocence, he added, "I guess if I'm going to run this plant, I better study up on what all my departments do. Have a good evening and a good night's rest."

I knew it was a mistake, but I couldn't help myself. He was so smug. Some childish part of me had to let him know I wasn't taken in by his performance. I pulled my hands from his, drew myself into heel-clicking attention, and said, "Sir, a good evening and a good night's rest." Then with a snappy salute I added, "Yes sir."

At first he gave me the same stern visual reprimand the gate guard had gotten, then a slight smile played on his lips. His eyes, however, remained hard and critical. In a voice so low only I could hear him, he said, "I can put him in his place, Ms. Gomez, but his place is Security and he's very good at it."

The deadly serious warning in his voice wiped the smart-ass smile from my face as I silently considered what he was saying. His intended use of me was not over. He wanted to know everything I learned about this plant, and he didn't want Woods to nail me. Why? Who was this guy and what was his agenda? What was the corporate agenda? Why would management employ two such combative men at this, their most secret plant? Was there a schism in Blue Morpho command?

To James I said, "OK, thanks for the warning."

THIRTY-EIGHT

Rested, showered, and dressed, I stepped onto the balcony of my cabana and took in the sounds and smells of the forest that surrounded me. The morning had brought clear sky and sunshine, and this place was so beautiful it looked like a Hollywood set for a jungle paradise rather than a research facility. Monkeys gathered their breakfast in the trees not a hundred yards from me. There were some bird sounds, though muted, as if they didn't wish to call attention to themselves. Flowers grew in greater profusion than I had seen in the forests on the way here, confirming my suspicion that this place must have been carefully cultivated as a resort before Blue Morpho moved in. The luxurious cabanas were definitely not company housing. They were well-appointed apartment duplexes set on stilts above the damp forest floor and connected to the main buildings by a network of elevated walkways.

I looked longingly at the hand-woven hammock that hung on my balcony, then reluctantly went back through the apartment, picked up my laptop and headed out the door. I was quickly jarred back to reality. Waiting just outside my door was my old friend Muscles, now clean-shaven, dressed in fresh camouflage fatigues, and looking much more rested than when I last saw him.

I forced a smile and eyed his name patch. "Good morning Mr., ah, Folger."

"Good morning, ma'am." Without another word, he simply fell into step behind me like Pan's attached shadow.

"Well, I must rate an honor guard. How nice."

When we entered the large diningroom, the buzz of conversation and the comforting clink of dishes and silverware came to a complete halt. As Folger took up a position just inside the door, I walked toward the cafeteria line. The only sound in the room was that of my heels hitting the beautiful hardwood floor.

Ah, yes. I understood that silence. Having lived in many small mining camps with my dad, I knew that no high tech communication system in the world could beat the speed of camp gossip. There was no doubt in my mind that news of the showdown between Nolan and Woods had been the main topic of discussion when I entered the room, and no doubt that everyone knew who I was.

I smiled at the young woman serving scrambled eggs and noticed that instead of a military-type name patch with her last name, she wore a pretty butterfly pin on her blouse that read "Bernice."

"Good morning, Bernice. Could I have a couple scoops of those eggs and a little fruit and yogurt, please?"

"Yes, Ms. Gomez."

Suspicions confirmed. I was the only one in the room who wasn't wearing a name tag.

As I sat down and started my breakfast, conversation slowly resumed, undoubtedly on a more innocuous subject. An older woman with short brown hair, a round pug-nosed face, and coke-bottle glasses stood up. Ignoring the sidelong glances she received from other employees, and the glare of hostility she got from Folger, she picked up her coffee cup and walked to my table.

"Ms. Gomez, I'm Lucille Owens. I was the company librarian for forty years, and Jim Nolan asked me to give you a little introduction to our company history. After you finish your breakfast, I'll to show you what I laughingly call the library."

"Thank you, Mrs. Owens. Won't you join me?"

She looked around the room and with a wry grin said, "I guess it can't hurt. I'm already retired anyhow."

I laughed. "If you're retired, why aren't you on the beach?"

"My plane leaves this afternoon."

As she sat across from me, I glanced around the room and chuckled. "Reminds me of that old stock-broker's commercial where everything in the room comes to a halt and all ears are tuned in one direction."

She smiled and sipped her coffee. "Yes, your arrival has certainly broken the monotony around here." By unspoken agreement we kept our conversation to small talk until I finished my breakfast. Then we bussed our dishes and got two coffees to go. I couldn't resist. Raising my voice to be heard across the room, I asked, "Hey, Folger, you want a coffee to go?"

A few giggles tittered around the room. He reddened with anger and answered, "No thank you, ma'am."

Lucille led me outside and down a winding path lined with flowers. In the distance we could see the monkeys climbing and swinging from limb to limb. I stopped to watch them. Folger came to a halt thirty paces behind us. Lucille followed my gaze toward the monkeys, then looked over her shoulder toward Folger. "They are cute little critters, but it really doesn't pay to tease them. They have ways of getting even."

I switched my gaze from the monkeys to Lucille's face. "Sometimes, Lucille, you have to rattle the cage to find out what's in there."

She smiled and started down the path. "I guess that works, unless it turns out you're the one in that cage."

We followed the path to a wide gravel road, and the road to a complex of three enormous Quonset huts. Each of the three buildings had both a large door for vehicular traffic and a small one for people. Lucille punched a number into the security box beside the people door. When she got a green light, she put a key in the lock and opened it.

"Once you get clearance, you will get your own security code. For now, you'll have to get someone to let you in. You will be able to work in buildings one and two, but three is for high-clearance science staff only."

As we stepped into the building, I saw a dozen or so cargo containers, all open. A couple containers were almost full, but most of the rest had been haphazardly emptied into messy unorganized piles around the building. I also noticed that Folger had joined us and stood just inside the door.

With the dismay only a librarian could understand, Lucille began explaining the mess contained in these buildings.

"The employees weren't allowed to pack their own stuff. In fact, we weren't even told the plant was moving. We went home on Thursday for a four-day weekend, and when we returned on Tuesday morning, the place had been empted out, except for the personnel office. Of course there had been rumors . . ."

She paused and eyed Folger. Her expression contained a mixture of distaste and knowledge I suspected she intended to keep to herself.

"No one would give us an explanation for the unannounced relocation of the plant. We were simply offered a choice of moving to Costa Rica, taking a generous severance, or an early retirement. Take it or leave it."

Now I understood why the container I had been locked in contained employment records. It wouldn't have been packed out until all the terminations and transfers had been completed. That was of little help now, but it was nice to be able to solve at least one of the little mysteries in this case.

Folger abandoned his military stance, turned his head to the side, and seemed to be straining to hear our conversation. Finally he took up a position closer to us.

"Movers stuffed anything and everything in boxes. The few boxes that were labeled were usually mislabeled; so, for the last two months, everyone has simply ripped through the containers. Once they had perfected the mix-master system of order, they called me back out of retirement to . . . how was it Jim put it? Oh, yes, to set up the new library. After a week here, I told him I'm just too old for this."

As we walked among the piles of boxes, she began to show me where she had started her organizing, and it became apparent that she expected me to take over the job. I hated to burst her bubble, but I had to explain my purpose here.

"I'm sorry, Lucille, I'm not here to take over the library. I'm just here to set up a records retention program so the departments will know what to keep, shred, and scan."

She studied me a moment, and I could imagine what her forty years of experience thought of an outsider waltzing in and instantly determining such basic organization. She took it well, with no more than a sigh and a shrug, then launched into an outline of company departments and a list of department heads.

During most of this, I listened quietly, taking notes while our shadow, Mr. Folger, made no attempt to hide his interest in what was said. It was when Lucille began to explain the company history that I saw his first nervous twitch.

Lucille explained, "You see you are really dealing with two companies here. Once upon a time there was a wonderful man named Macdonald Duffy. Mac owned a small petroleum company back east, and he gave it the name of Blue Morpho because the swirling colors in gasoline reminded him of the Blue Morpho butterfly. Mac refined his own gas and used ethanol as an anti knock instead of lead. That's what caused his downfall."

"I'm sorry, I don't understand."

Lucille was jarred from her monologue and took a moment to respond. "You know, the lead in gasoline."

"All I know about lead in gasoline is that they took it out a few years ago because it contributed to smog. What does that have to do with this plant?"

"Well, I can see I will have to go back and tell you the wonderful, secret history of lead."

Out of the corner of my eye I could see Folger reaching for his radio.

Lucille noticed it too and said under her breath, "There's a bit of paranoia around here on the subject of lead. I don't know if I can find them in this mess, but I have several books and articles you should read if you want to really understand this."

She picked her way through the sea of boxes with the unerring certainty of a spawning salmon, pulled the lid from a box and rummaged through the contents. "There you are," she declared. Librarians do amaze me. She handed me an article, "The Secret History of Lead," by Jamie Lincoln Kitman, from an old issue of *The Nation* magazine. "Here's a good short history to give you the overall picture.

Folger turned his face away from us and spoke quietly but urgently into his radio. Lead might be gone from gasoline, but paranoia seemed to still exist at Blue Morpho. As Lucille began her story, I wondered what response this was going to bring from Woods.

THIRTY-NINE

Under the hostile surveillance of our watchdog, Folger, Lucille began with a question that I knew she would soon answer. "How do you suppose lead got into gasoline in the first place?"

I shrugged. "Does it come out of the earth that way?"

"No. Lead, a known poison, was put into gasoline as an anti-knock fuel additive. It stopped knocking and raised the octane. "

Like the good student, I asked a leading question. "But back then they didn't know it was poison?"

She took a deep sigh and glanced sideways at Folger, then back to my face. For a brief moment I was afraid she would decide not to talk with me on this subject. Then she pointed toward the far end of the room.

"Over in that corner is where I've started piling material for the engine design and development department. They have promised to send someone down to collect it today."

As we walked toward the pile of boxes, she spoke in a normal tone of voice but low volume. "Of course they knew it was poison; in fact, it is one of the oldest known poisons. The Greeks and Romans wrote about its deadly effects over three thousand years ago. The particular form of lead they used in gasoline, tetraethyl was first identified in 1854, but it wasn't used commercially for sixty-some years, because science knew it was deadly."

"What does it do?"

She laughed. "You mean other than kill you? It's a potent neurotoxin, odorless, colorless and tasteless. Possible symptoms associated with lead poisoning include blindness, brain damage, kidney disease, convulsions, cancer, hypertension, strokes, heart attacks, and miscarriage. Children are the most quickly damaged, with lowered IQs, reading and learning disabilities, impaired hearing, reduced attention span, hyperactivity, and behavioral problems. I sometimes wonder if the increased incidence of attention deficit disorder isn't due to the increased amounts of lead."

'How much has lead increased?'

"During the leaded-gas era an estimated seven million tons of lead was burned in gasoline in the United States alone, and it's still in use in most of the Third World countries. This stuff doesn't go away. It doesn't break down over time. It doesn't vaporize. It never disappears. It's in our soil, our air, our water, our food supply, our bodies. It's estimated that modern man's exposure to lead is three hundred to five hundred times greater than natural pre-leaded-gasoline levels."

"If all this was known, how could the government allow it?

She smiled a mirthless smile and glanced at Folger who was again mumbling into his radio. Quietly she said, "Mr. Duffy's opinion was that it was due to what he called three sacred Ps: Profit, Power and Perpetuation. Supposedly, lead was added to gas because it stopped engine knock, but Duffy already had what he believed was an excellent anti-knock that wasn't so lethal. It was plain old ethyl alcohol, or ethanol. You know, like the grain alcohol they can make in stills. It was plentiful, renewable, easy to make, and it not only stopped engine knock, but could have been an alternative fuel. Before the Civil War alcohol lit our lamps, and later it powered two of the first internal combustion engines. It produced higher engine compression without smoke or disagreeable odors. Henry Ford even built his first car to run on it and predicted it would be the fuel of the future. Duffy figured there was just one little problem with ethanol: No one could patent alcohol and any idiot could make it in his back yard."

I laughed. "So you could fuel your car from the backyard still. That would have changed a few oil industry fortunes. Didn't health officials do anything?"

"In this country we make the manufacturers of a product responsible for the safety testing of their own product, you know, like tobacco companies, drug companies and food companies. Mr. Duffy thought that was like setting the fox to watch the hen house. But for seventy-five years those who claimed lead was a health hazard were ignored, and all attempts at independent testing, regulation, or oversight were defeated. Use of lead expanded until almost every gallon of gasoline sold in the world contained lead. The corporations that produced it made billions of dollars.

We heard the sputter of Folger's radio and realized he had crossed the room and was just on the other side of a container. We only caught a word or two before he either turned down the volume or moved off.

"Well, look at this. What's this box doing here? Give me a hand, Dolores. These records are from the emissions control research department. I have those piled over there."

We hoisted the box between us and headed across the end of the room. On the way we could see Folger walking back toward the door, radio to his ear. Lucille laughed quietly. In an undertone she said, "Did I mention the paranoia around here?" We set the box down and stood where we could keep an eye on Folger.

"I doubt that we will finish this story in much detail this morning. To make the story short, through the late twenties and early thirties Duffy's little company of Blue Morpho Petroleum tried to hold its own against Jim Marko's Marko Oil. They each had gas stations in the same major cities along the east coast. Marko used a lead formula and Blue Morpho was one of the last companies standing that still used ethanol. Lead interests were determined to wipe Duffy out.

"It was like urban war, and Marko used every trick imaginable. He fought Duffy at the banks and blocked his money supply; fought him in the courts with constant legal harassment that cost him millions; fought him in congress with legislation to make alcohol production either illegal or too expensive to be viable. He also fought him at the pump. If Marko couldn't drive Duffy's dealers out of business with low prices he strong armed them out. Marko, who drank like a fish, even became a strong supporter of Prohibition and lobbied for higher taxation on Duffy's alcohol distillery. During Prohibition he used to call federal enforcement regularly and report that Duffy was shipping his alcohol to the mob to make booze. He wasn't, but it cost him a small fortune to prove it each time."

"But Blue Morpho must have survived all these years?"

"Only in name. In 1933 there was an explosion at one of Duffy's gas stations in Laurel, Maryland, where he lived. It killed his wife and almost killed his son Douglas. Mac knew the explosion was set by Marko, but couldn't prove it. The death of his wife was the final blow. Duffy could fight no more and made Marko a deal. Marko could have Blue Morpho Petroleum if he just left Duffy alone. After Blue Morpho in Maryland sold to Marko, Duffy moved to California and set up his new firm of California Automobile Research Facility. He spent the rest of his life trying to develop and patent a fuel that would replace gasoline."

All of a sudden I was very alert. "A fuel that would replace gasoline?"

She hesitated for some moments, then looked right in my eyes and said each word with a deliberate pause for precise delivery of both words and message.

"He could have succeeded too, but he had a conscience. He wouldn't produce a fuel that would damage health or environment."

Zing! It was like all the extraneous bits of information, all the people I had met in this weird case, all the seemingly unconnected ideas, suddenly slipped into place like puzzle pieces locking into a finished picture. At that moment I knew, no mater how incredible it might seem, that Evelyn Lilac's Red 19 was real. Did that give credence to the diary? No, I couldn't go that far. It didn't matter whether her information came from Martians or from someone inside the Blue Morpho. Red 19 was real, and Duffy had discarded it as deadly.

"Holy Shit!" I whispered. Then asked, "Duffy's dead?"

She nodded again. "For many years. His daughter, Catherine ran the plant until she died in 1999."

"Who owns the research plant now?"

"The stockholders of Marko's Blue Morpho Petroleum bought it after Catherine died. They didn't care about the research, of course, but Duffy had branched out to keep enough money coming in to continue his research. Other departments in the company are quite lucrative. We provide design, development and testing services for engine, vehicle and component manufacturers. After the California Automobile Research Facility was sold and once again became part of Blue Morpho Petroleum, we added several government contracts with the army and air force for fuels and lubricants research."

"When we started getting into government contracts, the toy solders and wannabe James Bonds started showing up in the company." With a slight nod of her head, she indicated Folger. "Speaking of which, I think someone must have wound his spring. Story time is over."

I looked up to see Folger marching toward us. His face held a hint of a sneer as he stopped in front of me. "Ms. Gomez, Mr. Woods has ordered you to cease your inquiries regarding this company until after your security clearance has been completed. You are to accompany me to his office immediately."

I turned to Lucille. "More wasted time, and I have clients waiting in New York. I am going to have to tell James that this is not working out."

Lucille picked up my call for help. "I'm heading that way. I'll let him know you need to speak with him."

Folger stepped in front of her blocking her path. "I'm afraid not, Mrs. Owens. You are to accompany me to Mr. Woods office also. He wishes to speak with you regarding security protocol."

Lucille removed her thick glasses, polished them with the edge of her long blouse, and replaced them.

"Sonny Boy, you tell Harry Woods that I won't be needing his security lecture for two reasons. First, I have already retired and am returning to the States this afternoon. If he wants this mess picked up, he will have to find someone else to do it. Maybe some of his young toy soldiers, if he can find any of you who can read. And, second, tell Harry that I have a long memory for security matters, memory that goes all the way back to 1989 and a certain young congressman's wife."

Then she carefully unpinned her security pass, opened Folger' hand and thrust the badge into his palm, pin first.

He jumped back, his aggressive expression changing to one of confusion. "Hey, God damn it! Watch it."

Lucille turned to me. "Good luck, Dolores." Then she turned and walked out of the building, leaving Folger sputtering and me almost choking as I tried not to laugh.

FORTY

Any compulsion I might have had to laugh disappeared when I entered the office of Harriman Woods. He was about six feet tall and, despite the paunch, in better physical condition than I had noticed in our previous brief encounters. His face was bony and hard with age lines that drew a permanently grim expression. His small, dull brown eyes were rimmed with red, reminding me of my uncle's old Yorkshire sow. She was the meanest animal I have ever met . . . and the smartest. Here in his office, under his control, I should have had the good sense to feel afraid, but I remembered the story Sam had told me of how he had butchered those children, and all I could feel was rage that such an evil person should be allowed to live.

Without looking up he growled out, "Sit down, Gomez."

I studied him a minute, steadying myself to gain voice control. "And good morning to you, Mr. Woods. How kind of you to offer me a chair."

He looked up from the papers on his desk. The expression in his eyes was hollow, as if there were no soul behind them.

"We won't waste any time on pleasantries or verbal banter, Ms. Gomez, if that's your name. I've checked your CV. It all checks out, as I expected. It would probably get by most investigations; but you see, I have planted enough phony covers to recognize one when I see it. Yours has no depth. Some places I can find a computer record or a personnel clerk who can verify your employment, but not one employee who remembers meeting you."

"Since I am an outside consultant, that should hardly be surprising."

"Uh huh. You're an outside consultant here, too, and I believe you have been here less than twenty-four hours, but every employee in the plant could identify you and tell me what your job is supposed to be."

"Right. In a tiny compound in a foreign jungle. Try the same thing in New York or Dallas. Look, I don't know what your problem is, but your boss yanked me away from other jobs to come here as a favor to him and help with your records. Now if you have a problem with that, talk with him."

"I have, and as soon as I get through with my job, you can get on with yours."

He opened the bottom drawer of his desk and pulled out a box and opened it on the desk top. It was a fingerprint kit, one of the old-fashioned ones with nasty, real ink.

"So let's just run your fingerprints, and if your ID checks out, you will be allowed to work with non classified records."

"I don't believe this. You want to fingerprint me like some sort of criminal?"

"No, Gomez, like every other employee in this plant. It's standard security protocol. You should have no objection, unless of course you have something to hide."

My brain was scrambling for an out. If he just checked the states where my CV said I had worked, he would find no record, but there was no doubt in my mind that he would run it through the FBI repository. There he would nail me. I had been fingerprinted in California for both my PI license and my guard card. The only question was, how long would it take? The FBI's new automated fingerprint identification system can kick back an answer on a criminal search in two hours. That wouldn't even be time for me to get to the main road, unless I could snag a car. But he would have to run me as a civilian request, and that would take at least twenty-four hours. That was time enough to get away, but I would leave empty-handed.

"Let me get this straight, you want to fingerprint me and run some sort of check on me before I can go to work. How long will that take, and what am I supposed to do in the meantime?"

"About three days, and frankly I don't give a fuck what you do as long as you stay away from our company records until I've cleared you."

"And then what else? Will you find some other way to–"

There was a soft knock at the door.

"Who the hell is it?"

The door opened and James Nolan stuck his head in and gave us a smile.

"Hi. Understand there's a slight misunderstanding down here."

"Nolan, you try to interfere in security and I will have your nuts."

James came in and put his hands up submissively. "Oh, hell no, Mr. Woods. I wouldn't think of it. I just realized that Mrs. Gomez here may not have worked for a company with security clearance needs like ours, and she might think you're picking on her. Now, Dolores, I know this seems a little severe, but we have a lot of military contracts here, and I'm afraid it is necessary. Now just go on and cooperate with Mr. Woods, and then we can get on with business."

I hesitated wondering if James had any idea what he was doing. By the time those prints came back, I intended to be out of here. But what would happen to the guy who brought me in?

"Go on, it's got to be done."

I walked over to Woods and surrendered my hands, allowing him to roll each fingertip through the damned ink, then roll them onto the print cards. When he finished, I stood there waiting for him to supply me with something to clean my hands. Noticing the omission, James pulled out his handkerchief and offered it to me.

"Here, you can wipe the worst off with this, then we can walk back over to the commissary. You can clean up, and we can have lunch."

We walked silently out of the building, then James left the elevated pathway and guided me down a lovely garden path lined with brilliantly colored flowers.

Once clear of the building, I asked in what I hoped was a jocular tone, "James, what if he discovers I'm really something terrible like a serial killer or something? What will that do to your position, since you brought me in?"

He stopped on the path just in front of me, picked a flower, and as he handed it to me said, "Or something like a private investigator? Game time's over, Diana."

At the sound of my real name, my heart started pounding faster. I looked from the flower to his eyes and saw that the Kahuna was gone and the warrior was back.

"He'll deliver that card to the embassy in San Jose within three hours and get a report back twenty-eight hours after that. Now we are going to take a pleasant little walk around the grounds and have a little talk, and we don't have time to waste. I'll start, then I need to have some very straight answers from you."

He spoke quietly as we continued walking up the path. "In one week, scientists from this company are going to release the first of two information bombs that will cause more economic, political, and diplomatic havoc than a full-scale war. Some of us in the company would like to believe we are doing the right thing and that the disruption we are going to cause is the lesser of two evils.

"A lady named Evelyn Lilac claimed to have information that could be crucial to a responsible decision, but the board of Blue Morpho hadn't heard of her until just a few weeks ago. When I started checking I found that Woods and his bunch had been searching the world for Lilac, which gave credence to a report we had received. Now Woods is putting the same effort into finding one Diana Hunter."

To my amazement, James began to chuckle. How could he find anything to laugh at?

"I would love to see that bastard's face when those prints come back and he learns that you were standing two feet from him."

My anger flared, and I grabbed his arm and pulled him around to face me. "Oh, yeah, that will be just hilarious. Does your company know that son of a bitch killed Evelyn and, so far, five other people that I know of?"

"We do now. What the hell do you think I've been doing down here, soaking up the sunshine? I have enough information to put him and several of his lackeys away, but I have to give him rope until I learn what the hell it is that Evelyn had. So give."

"What's next week's information bomb?"

He studied me for several seconds before answering. "It's a series of scientific studies by us and other petroleum companies confirming the worst predictions of global warming and proving that fossil fuels are the chief cause. It also contains papers proving conspiracy to deny and discredit these facts."

"Wow! Like the tobacco industry admitting they knew nicotine was addictive."

"Much worse. You can always quit smoking. The engine that drives the entire modern civilization is oil. Without oil, none of our factories will produce, none of our modes of heat and transportation will work, all of our economies worldwide will collapse. None of our home heaters or refrigerators will run. Do you suppose this modern civilization could turn around in a week and learn to string bows and chip arrowheads, go back to bringing home the bacon the old-fashioned way?"

"But that dismal picture is not exactly what Blue Morpho has in mind, is it? What is the second information bomb the company has planned?"

"We've developed a new fuel to gradually replace fossil fuel. It's inexpensive to produce, clean burning, environmentally safe."

"I suppose that news flash is timed to ride to the rescue after your first release has been checked by world scientists and everyone is nicely desperate about the future. But it won't be free, will it? Your replacement fuel is patented by Blue

Morpho, right?"

He nodded, and I found myself laughing and realized it was as inappropriate as his laugh had been.

"No wonder there is so much security and paranoia around this plant. You guys are planning to cut down the richest, most powerful people in the world and replace them with yourselves. Mr. Duffy's dream comes true. Good luck. You're going to need more than Woods's toy soldier brigade to pull this off."

"That's not my problem. My problem is Evelyn Lilac's information. If she has proof that the new fuel is actually more harmful to the environment than petroleum, our company will not proceed with next week's release. I think you know what she had and where it is. I need you to tell me."

Suspicion and cynicism truly are occupational hazards for both reporters and investigators. It's not that you start out that way. It's that time after time you learn through experience that nothing is ever what it appears to be . . . nothing. Suddenly I felt as though I had been manipulated ever since I got here in an elaborate game of good cop, bad cop. I wanted to ask how he knew my name and when he knew it, but this was not the time. Now I could reveal no suspicion of James Nolan. Now I had to play his game.

FORTY-ONE

"Well, James, as you put it, that's not my problem, and not the reason I came down here. The FBI agent who is investigating Evelyn's murder called me to identify her body. I held out on him because the story Evelyn told me about Martians colonizing Earth was so ridiculous, I figured he'd think I was as loony as she was. Now he wants to take my license and toss me in federal prison. I came down here looking for her murderer in the hopes that if I help him he will back off on me. Now you tell me a new whopper of international oil intrigue that sounds as crazy as Martians. If you really have hard evidence regarding Evelyn's murder, I'll take it to the FBI for you, and they can take care of Woods."

He smiled. "I'll bet you would. We might arrange something like that, but first I need you to give me the data Evelyn had."

"Data? All she gave me was a chapter of a science fiction book."

"No, I know all about her Martian book. She had something else, some old experiments that Duffy had done on an alternative fuel code-named 'Hyacinth Red'."

"She wrote about Red 19 in the *Martian Diary*, but she never mentioned any real experiments or anything to do with Blue Morpho."

He stopped walking, grabbed me by the shoulders, and turned me toward him. "Think. She must have told you something, a hiding place, a contact, a friend, a plan of some sort."

My mind raced ahead, checking the parts of the story I could tell and what I could not. I wanted to appear cooperative and trusting and give him lots of detail, but none of it involving anyone else they could find and kill.

It's tricky when you begin to lie extemporaneously and very easy to trip yourself up; so I stuck with the facts, except that I substituted Evelyn as the person who sent me the *Martian Diary* chapter. I told him the whole story of Antia's escape from the subterranean Martian city and her narrow escape from Red 19. I told him about my encounter with Evelyn and her would-be kidnappers on the river and her hasty departure and disappearance. I left out the receipt of the second chapter, but told him in painful detail about my embarrassing interview with Agent Camas, my subsequent search for the boat, and my entombment in the ocean-going container. I avoided mentioning my side trip to the desert where I met Jim, and left out any mention of Sam's special assistance, Richard's disguise mastery, and my friend Barbara's reluctant assistance with Customs and the LAPD.

As I talked, his expression became more and more grim. If I hadn't seen what a wonderful actor he was, I would have been sure that he believed every word and was totally discouraged by my lack of useful information. He let out a big sigh and shook his head.

"When I learned you were the last one to talk to Evelyn, I hoped—"

I interrupted. I didn't want him to ask questions that might poke holes in my story. "James, I was far from the last person to talk with her. Our meeting was two weeks before her body was found. I have been in over my head since this whole thing started. If I stick around and those prints get back, Woods will have me killed too. I need to get out of here."

The look he gave me was so different from the friendly, boyish face he had presented at the ambassador's dinner that he seemed like a different person. "Evelyn got out. He still killed her. I warned you he's very good at what he does."

He was quiet for a long moment, then shook his head again. "I was foolish to bring you in here, but now that you're here, your only chance is with me. Listen carefully. We are going to have lunch, then you're going to take a dinner back to your room and stay there until dark. At nine o'clock you will meet me over there at the High Security Building."

"Why?"

"Old man Duffy discovered and quietly patented Hyacinth Red, but he never used it. His formula turned up after Blue Morpho took over his research facility in California. It is the fuel from that formula that will be announced by the corporation next week unless I can find the original studies that proved Hyacinth poses a worse environmental hazard than petroleum. Needless to say there is not a large group of us in the company who are looking too hard for the downside of this fuel. If you really don't have Evelyn's copies of his studies, our only chance is to find the original reports. I have been looking each night, but now that Woods has your prints, this will be our last night to search. And Diana, don't come out your door. It will be watched."

FORTY-TWO

After our lunch, I headed down the elevated walkway toward my cabana and found that Folger was back, playing shadow. When I went inside, he took up his post out front. I locked the door and stepped out onto the balcony to survey the area and make my plans.

The mosquitoes buzzed around me, and I knew they would be worse at night. I took my quinine, stripped, slathered my whole body with mosquito repellent, and wrapped myself in my Tahitian pareau., basically a piece of hemmed yardage you simply tie around your body. They were invented by European missionaries to cover the heathen nakedness of the Pacific islanders. Now the missionaries' granddaughters wear thong bikinis and the tourists buy pareaus. Cool and comfortable, it rolls into a small ball, travels well, and can be everything from a sun dress to a nightgown. Like my Amex card, I never leave home without it. This particular one is covered with bright tropical flowers and is highly visible from a distance.

I laid out my green hiking shirt, pants with cargo pockets, and small daypack, then stuffed the pants pockets and the pack with things my prospector great-grandfather would have called *possibles*. That meant anything you might possibly need. My hiking shoes went into the pack.

At five o'clock I ate the light supper I had brought from the diningroom, then took two pillows and went out on the balcony, leaving the cabin door open. I stretched out in the hammock and both slept and feigned sleep until eight. By then it was quite dark.

Folger's movements had been routine all afternoon and evening and were not hard to follow, because his heavy boots were not exactly designed for stealth. He had maintained his guard outside my front door, doing one tour of inspection around the building each hour on the hour, and had just returned from his eight p.m. inspection.

In case there was a second guard who was not so noisy, I moved carefully, untying the pareau and laying the loose edge over the top of the pillows at my side.

With gymnastic control I didn't know I still possessed, I moved to the deck, leaving my pareau behind and causing little rocking of the hammock. Lying in the darker shadow between the hammock and the wall, I listened to all the night sounds of the rain forest, trying to discern any that might belong to the human jungle. After several minutes of careful listening, I crouched behind the hammock, arranged the pareau carefully over the pillows, then crept inside the room.

I put on the shirt and pants and shrugged into the daypack, then slipped back out onto the balcony. Crouching down and moving slowly in the shadow of the wall, I reached the end of my balcony, folded myself over the top of the stucco wall, and slithered to the floor of the next balcony.

Moving slowly and silently, I reached the far end of that balcony and climbed down the trellis, feeling carefully for each hand and foothold. At the bottom I stepped to the cool, wet ground, then slipped behind the trellis and under the balcony. An overcast obscured the stars and moonlight, making it a dark night. I stood there for several minutes, listening, watching, giving all my senses time to adapt to the night: eyes, ears, nose, taste, skin, and that sixth sense that is harder to define. I could smell Folger's cigarette smoke, the rotting foliage on the damp forest floor, the dank green river at the edge of camp, the resin used to treat the wood in the balcony, a faint sweet perfume from some night-blooming flower, the musky odor of some nearby rodent nest. My sixth sense told me there was more. I waited.

I could faintly hear a radio playing in the next duplex, frogs croaking near the river, an occasional bird or animal cry, and over all the constant buzzing and humming of the insects. No cars. A slight, damp, balmy breeze kissed my cheeks.

Then it came. The crack of a twig, the crushing of leaves, sounds that did not belong to the forest. My second watcher was on a small hill about thirty-five yards west, between me and the river. From his vantage point he would have a clear view of the back of my cabin, as well as the elevated walkway to the diningroom and the garden path that led around the encampment to the front road. Training my senses in his direction, I prayed whoever was there was not equipped with infrared goggles.

The sound of his urine splattering against the leaves on the ground reached my ears a few seconds before the breeze carried its strong smell to my nose. My brain does work in strange ways. While one member of my internal board of directors debated whether Nolan or Woods posted this guy up there, the mother in me was noting that he should take water with him on watch because his urine had that strong stink of dehydration. Some rational voice on the board suggested that neither thought was truly useful at the moment.

The building where I was to rendezvous with James was farther south and west, across the main bridge and on the other side of the river. If I moved to the south, I would be in the watcher's line of sight and be back-lit by the lights of camp. If I went around in front, I would be spotted by Folger. The only route open was to head first north, then west to the river and follow the river south, past the back side of the hill.

I crouched to the ground, moving out from under the balcony, feeling carefully before I put weight on either my hands or my bare feet, making sure I made no sound. Just three feet from the balcony I reached the cover of tall heavy foliage and could stand almost upright and still be hidden from the view of the guard on the hill. Moving as quickly as I safely could, I made my way past the end of the hill and down to the river.

There I met my first real obstacle. To the south, there was no path or open ground of any sort. Deep thick undergrowth grew all the way to the water's edge. There was no way to move through that stuff silently. In fact, there was no way through it without a machete. With the main road out of the question, crossing the river would require back-tracking to the long swinging foot bridge. It would be impossible to move across that bridge without setting up vibrations that would make the bridge swing.

Going into the river would be my last choice. Though my childhood trained me pretty well for surviving in the wilderness, the wilderness I knew best was the Southwest desert and the High Sierras. My experience with tropical rivers was just sufficient to make me wary. I had no idea what could live in this one. Whether this river held schools of paranha like the Rio Caroni in Venezuela or tiny parasitic critters that entered various bodily openings, like the Amazon, or large crocodiles, like the Sarapiqui, I had no desire to go swimming.

Hoping to find another route toward the rendezvous point, I backtracked to the path. I was debating my chances of making it across the swinging bridge unseen when my ears picked up a familiar sound, water slapping against wood. I headed to the river and there found two boats tied under the bridge, one a rowboat with oars and the other a small motorboat.

The river here flowed north to meet the Sarapiqui, but it was slow moving and the current was not too strong. The motorboat was out of the question but I thought I could get the rowboat across the river without losing too much ground to the north. Once on the other side, the water would mask my sounds.

I untied the rowboat, pushed off, and rowed as silently as possible. Beaching the boat just down river from the swinging bridge, I found a good path running parallel to the shore. In most places there was enough shadow and cover to hide me should my watcher on the hill look in this direction. No longer needing stealth, I sat down and put on my hiking shoes, then followed the path south to the High Security Quonset hut. Positioning myself behind some foliage, I waited for James to show.

FORTY-THREE

On the road to the south I heard footsteps and saw James, alone. He didn't
walk in front of the Quonset hut, where the night-light was, but turned at the other
side and made his way around the back of the building, along the north wall, and
right past my hiding spot. He peered around the front of the building, looked
worriedly toward camp, then searched for a place to get out of sight. He headed
directly toward me.

I stood up. "Sorry, this bush is taken."

He flinched. "Jesus, Diana, you scared the shit out of me. Come on." He
moved to the door and punched in a code, inserted his security pass, opened the
door, and motioned me in.

He shut the door and flicked on the light. "I've searched those boxes by the
front wall. Start with this bunch over here. We have until morning to find the
Hyacinth Red research. With or without it we have to get out of here in the morning
before Woods learns you're AWOL."

"OK, enough games, James. You're the plant manager. Do you really
expect me to believe you have to sneak around like this to look in your own files?"

"Do you really believe Woods would let me out of here alive if he knew I
had the file?"

I stared at him, not knowing what to believe.

"You're supposed to be smart, but you don't get it yet, do you? This fuel
that old man Duffy developed and called Hyacinth Red is now going to be used by
Blue Morpho and is intended to totally replace petroleum-based fuel. Some people
see it as a way of saving the world environment. Others see it as a means to absolute
power. No more oil competitors, no troublesome problems with Middle East oil
production, no more problems with any of the puny little countries of the world. I
work for the good guys, the ones who want to use Hyacinth in a responsible way.
Now, on the brink of introducing it to the world, we hear it might be a worse
ecological disaster than we already face. A few people in my corporation would like
to know the truth before it's too late. Other people in the corporation and in the

military don't care."

"How could they not care? What good is absolute power if the Earth becomes as barren as Mars?"

He shrugged. "Did they care about mass atomic weapons? Did they care about lead poisoning? Do they care about global warming?"

"People tried to fight all of those things, too. Did it do them any good?"

I wished I hadn't said that. The look on his face was so close to defeat I knew I had hit too close to home. He turned away without answering and began searching through the nearest file box. I stood still for a moment, wondering if there was anything else I could say. Finding nothing brilliant, I looked around at the nearby file boxes. I opened the first one. "Oh, cripes. I could be looking right at it and not know it. I don't know what this stuff means."

"Just look in the upper left corner for the department. Any files generated by the fuel research division, bring to me. If they say engine performance or lubricant or any other department, set them over by the door with the others.

Out of the first four boxes, I found one for James and three for the door. The fifth box I opened was a surprise. "James, there's a personnel file here."

"Just put it by the door."

I picked it up and headed for the door but something seemed very wrong. As I set it down on the growing stack I asked, "How many personnel files have you found in here?"

"None. Ignore it. Someone just misfiled it–"

"No, it can't be just misfiled. The personnel records were in the can they locked me up in. They wouldn't even be here yet."

I began looking through the box. James shook his head and went back to his own search. What I found was so fascinating that I took two file folders out. Sitting on the floor between the pile of file boxes and a pile of iron pipe that was stacked against the front wall, I rapidly scanned the contents.

The door burst open and Woods strode in, pointing a nine millimeter at James, who was in plain sight in the middle of the room. He stopped, slightly in front and to the left of the pile of boxes that shielded me from view.

"Hello, Jimbo. You been having fun in here playing with the files at night?" He laughed. "You think you're so damn smart, and you are really so fucking dumb. Every time anyone slides a pass card through that security slot it registers a nice big red light in my office and gives me the user's ID."

James stood. "What do you think you're doing, Woods?"

"Following orders. Keeping you occupied and out of trouble until it's time to put you away."

With no warning, he adjusted his aim and prepared to fire. As soon as Woods's hand tensed around the weapon, James dived behind a nearby container, but Woods followed his moving target and fired. I heard James yell. Woods started moving to the right, trying to see around the container and determine if he had killed James.

"Oh, that hurt, Jimbo? I hope so, you interfering prick. The funny part is that what you want isn't even here. We purged the whole Hyacinth safety research file."

He laughed again and moved farther to the right, which brought him almost in front of my pile of boxes.

"It wouldn't do you any good to find it anyway. The whole project is now out of civilian hands and locked down in a military special projects division where it belongs. Hyacinth Red will rule the whole fucking world and those sand rats in the Middle East can stick their oil right back down their little black holes."

He took two more steps to the right and was standing directly in front of me. If he turned around, I would be in plain view, but he was concentrating on James, trying to figure out how badly he was hit, where he was, and if he was armed.

I eyed the pile of iron pipe. One of those would make a great weapon, but trying to pick one up without making noise would be like playing pickup sticks with wind chimes.

Woods brought his left hand up to support his right wrist as he spotted his prey. I wrapped my hands around the pipe that was on top of the pile, but I could see that when I raised it another pipe would be freed and would clatter down the pile. I would have to be very fast.

Woods's body tensed as he took aim. In one fluid motion, I rose, swinging the pipe with all my weight and power. Distracted by the sound of the pipe, Woods started to turn toward the noise as he squeezed the trigger, pulling his shot and sending the bullet whizzing high above the target. The pipe connected with the back of his skull and his gun fired again, but the bullet went into the roof. Woods sprawled on the floor unconscious or dead, I wasn't sure which.

"Get his gun."

I grabbed the nine millimeter and searched Woods for other weapons, retrieving a knife from his sleeve and a small .22 from his boot. I stuffed the weapons, Woods's radio, and the two personnel files I had been reading into my pack, then ran to James. He was on his feet, leaning against the container, trying to tie a large bandana around the bleeding wound in his thigh.

"Not bleeding enough for a vein. Did it get the bone?"

"No, muscle."

I finished the makeshift bandage. "Come on, lean on me. We have to get out of here before some of Woods's playmates show up."

"No, I can hardly walk, much less run. You get out of here and don't quit running until you get back to California."

I stepped under his arm so he could use me as a crutch. "As you already pointed out, that didn't do much good for Evelyn. Besides I've got us a ride."

FORTY-FOUR

As we hobbled down the road like a team in a three legged sack race, we listened anxiously for sounds of alarm from the camp, but all remained quiet. Leaving James beside the river, I ran to the spot where I had left the rowboat. Stumbling along the water's edge, I towed the boat upstream to James and helped him into it. We pushed off, using both the oars and the river current to carry us across the river to where the motorboat waited.

James managed to move to the motorboat without help while I tied the rowboat to the back and pushed our small flotilla out into the current. I was climbing into the boat when the woop, woop woop sound of the camp alarm blasted the quiet night. Soon lights lit the camp and guards could be heard relaying orders and reports.

James and I used one oar each like paddles and punting poles, as needed, to make our way down the far side of the river. The search was still limited to camp and we were a good half mile downstream before we saw the first spotlights trained on the river in back of us.

"Diana, they'll see the boats are missing and send someone down the road to the bridge."

"We're not going as far as the bridge."

He said nothing else for a while and we let ourselves drift for two or three miles without the engine.

"James, untie the row boat. We can let it drift down to meet them at the bridge and give them a new puzzle."

James grimaced and said, "You better cut me loose too. I'll never make it through the forest."

"Don't have to. There's a doctor over on the next tributary and if and if my hearing is accurate, we are about to the confluence of the two rivers."

He stared at me blankly. "How could you know that?"

"Long story." I started the outboard engine, turned on headlights, and powered us through the rushing water at the forks. Then cutting the lights, I headed upstream toward the Enviro-Medic Research station and what I hoped would be medical and transportation assistance.

There was not a light on anywhere and the station was little more than a slightly darker shadow against the blackness of the forest. If it hadn't been for the protrusion of a small dock on the river, we might have missed it. I tied up at the dock and climbed the steps to peer through the windows into the combination house and medical office. Unable to wait for my report, James had hobbled up beside me, causing his wound to start bleeding again.

I knocked for the third time and got no response. I tried the door and both windows but found them all locked.

"It doesn't look deserted. There's stuff inside, but the doc doesn't seem to be home. Maybe we better break a window and get some disinfectant and decent bandages for your leg."

James nodded and sat down on the step as I picked up a club-sized piece of wood and prepared to smash the glass.

"Please don't break the glass. It is very expensive to replace out here."

Startled by the voice, we both turned toward the shadows at the edge of the clearing. Even without seeing him, I knew who was there. The soft mellifluous voice, with its slight Spanish accent and cultured English tones, could only belong to one person. The question was, would he be friend or foe?

He walked into the clearing, and I could see that he was even wearing the same distinctive leather hat he had worn when he followed me around the environmental expo in Long Beach.

"I am Guillermo Jesus Montegro y Monteblan. At your service. Sir, you seem to be in need of medical aid."

"Yes, I'm afraid so. I'm James Nolan, and I've had a bit of an accident. We heard there was a doctor here, but he doesn't seem to be in. This is . . . "

"Dolores Gomez. Happy to meet you. Could you help us get in here for some disinfectant and bandages?"

Gill pulled out a set of keys and opened the door. "Certainly, please come in. Unfortunately the doctor and her husband have returned to the United States, but they still have some supplies here. Our local people became quite dependent upon them for medical assistance. We miss them."

The only light in the place was a Coleman lantern. Gill lit and set on the table. While he collected first-aid materials, James untied the handkerchief and took off his pants. As Gill began to clean the wound, he asked, "Who shot you, Mr.

Nolan?"

"Me, I'm afraid. One of those stupid things, trying to clean my gun and the damn thing went off."

"Hmm, you must have very long arms. No powder burns. Why would you have a gun anyway?"

"Self protection. Snakes, crocodiles, you know."

"Oh, of course."

I wasn't sure where this nonsense interrogation was going, but our previous meeting had convinced me that Gill was a professional investigator of some sort. To keep him from notifying the authorities, we would probably have to tie him up or lay out our credentials and see where he stood. With one hand inside my pack in case I needed a gun, I asked a little question of my own.

"Gill, I need to know one thing. Why did you and Ken and Judith Hoffman disappear so quickly from the environmental expo in Long Beach?"

He stopped, frozen for a moment while he processed that one. Then he turned around and studied me, raising the lantern to direct the light to my face.

"Well, well. Diana Hunter. Very good. I truly did not recognize you."

"Answer the question, please."

"Certainly." He set the lantern back on the table and continued wrapping the wound. "Because we were all afraid, both for our own lives and the life of our friend Evelyn. We didn't know then who had sent you. I stayed in California long enough to learn who you were, while Ken and Judith came back here."

"What happened to them?"

"Oh, they are quite all right, but when they returned to the station and learned that Blue Morpho had moved into the lodge next door, they were terrified it was more than unfortunate coincidence. They were back in the United States before I had time to get down here. They won't be coming back, I am afraid."

"Why are you here?"

"I live here. I am retired to a small *finca* not far from here, and I still keep an eye on this place. Once in a while, I am able to give some small first aid to local people who were used to seeking medical assistance here. And why are you here, and how did this man really get wounded?"

Before I decided on truth or lie, James asked, "Retired from what?"

"I was an employee of my country's government, in law enforcement."

"I'm afraid your fears for Evelyn were justified," I said. "She was found in a dry wash in Arizona, murdered. Since my card was found on her, the FBI called me to identify the body."

Gill nodded. "A friend of mine in Interpol notified me. I assume your arrival here has something to do with her death, but I am still curious about Mr. Nolan and his wound."

James looked at Gill sharply and asked, "Did this friend of yours in Interpol have anything to do with a report sent to Blue Morpho regarding Woods and the local research facility?"

There was silence while we all looked at each other and waited for Gill's answer. Instead he countered with a question of his own. "Could you tell me, please, how you know about the report?"

"I read it just before my boss at Blue Morpho sent me down here to look into it."

"Ah, so your assignment to the research facility was in response to our report. I see. I would have hoped that our report contained sufficient merit to warrant more than one man."

"It was a good report. If it hadn't been, you wouldn't even have gotten me. So you did write it?"

"No, but I supplied information for it. I prevailed upon my old comrade at Interpol to see that a report got to the proper persons. We had hoped it would generate a full investigation."

"Yeah, well, the 'proper persons' decided the first step was to check the situation out, quietly."

"I see. So you are an intelligence officer for Morpho?"

"No. I was a plant manager in Santa Barbara."

Gil's look was frankly incredulous.

James shrugged. "Yeah, that's what I thought too. But you see, Woods knew everyone in investigations. Since I, at the tender age of nineteen, had worked in army intelligence, I'm what you got."

Gill studied him a moment, then nodded. "Perhaps you two should come to my house for something to eat and drink. It seems we have some common interests to discuss."

FORTY-FIVE

It rained all the way to San Jose, and I was glad Gill had convinced us to wait for daylight to travel the rutted back roads that challenged even his rugged four-wheel drive. Though long and uncomfortable, his route provided us with a safe and uneventful trip into the capital.

Before we left the Enviro-Medic Research compound, we had untied the motorboat and allowed it to drift down the river, knowing it would come out at the same bridge the rowboat had. We hoped that would keep our pursuers beating the bushes and searching the river for us or our remains.

Conversation en route was minimal for we had said most of it the night before at Gill's house. As we'd shared information, we'd learned how the three of us happened to arrive at the same point in time and space. For each of us the catalyst had been, directly or indirectly, a frail, determined activist named Evelyn Lilac. She was the single pebble plopped into still waters, and we were swept along with the ripples.

As we bumped along the road to the city, I had just one last thing I needed to know from James.

"James, why can't your boss at Blue Morpho just tell the world the truth about Hyacinth Red?"

"What truth, Diana? That's what I was sent here to discover. We had the rumored existence of an old study that Duffy did, God knows when. I didn't get it. You heard Woods. They purged the entire file."

"But haven't you learned enough to justify a moratorium on Hyacinth until it can be fully researched?"

He looked grim. "I hope so. I'm just not sure what I will find when I get back. As he was trying to kill me, Woods said that Blue Morpho's civilian board had lost control of the Hyacinth fuel project. We don't have any idea what sort of environmental problem Hyacinth might have or what sort of tests Duffy did. Without the scientific report . . ."

Gill spoke up. "Evelyn had a copy. I saw it."

"You don't happen to know what she did with it, do you?"

"No, I assumed that whoever killed her took it."

James shook his head. "No, that's my one hope. If they had it, they wouldn't still be searching so hard."

I reached into my pack and pulled out two thick folders and handed them to James. "They might have purged the Hyacinth Red test file, but not the personnel file. I read these after you went to sleep last night. There was a young chemical engineer at the Blue Morpho facility in Paso Nuevo by the name of Todd Summers. Todd discovered Duffy's material and ran his own tests. He confirmed Duffy's conclusions, told his superiors, and tried to stop the development of Hyacinth Red. When they wouldn't listen to him, he slipped his girlfriend a copy of the test results. The girlfriend was Evelyn Lilac. After her protest at the Blue Morpho gate, the in-house security accused Todd of industrial espionage. The next week he died, supposedly of exposure while hiking alone in the Sierras."

The pen James took out of his pocket had a blue streak along the side that appeared to be a window to see how much ink was left. When he touched his thumb to the top of the pen, the blue streak lit up. He laid the pen on the top of the first page and pulled it to the bottom.

"I saw a scanner like that once, and only once. Where did you get that?"

He looked sideways at me and smiled with genuine good humor. "Probably in the same place you saw it. Sam's house."

"You know Sam?"

"Do you really think you would have foxed your way into Blue Morpho if Sam hadn't vouched for you?"

For a moment I sat there stunned, then I laughed. "And I thought it was my expertise with pejibaye soup. You guys and your dumb little games. It would have been so much easier to trust you if you had just told me."

He continued to scan the data in the file. "Would it? Sam should have taught you better than that."

"I'm a private investigator, not one of Sam's agents."

"That explains it, I guess."

I decided to ignore the taunting comment and change the subject. "What are you going to do with this information? Will it help?"

He shrugged. "Maybe. I don't know. At least it gives us one more murder we can probably add to Woods's case. The paperwork is done and the warrants ready on four other murders, Evelyn's and the three in the house in San Jose. With this lead, the law enforcement teams may be able to find evidence for the murders of Todd, that Costa Rican reporter, and his girlfriend."

Gill turned his eyes from the road momentarily to look at James. "So there is more than one man working on this?"

James smiled and nodded. "Teams are ready in three countries. We will be picking up Woods and four of his men shortly. But, Diana, this file doesn't change the fact that we don't have the scientific tests and have no idea how they were done or what they found."

"What if we did?"

He looked up, an almost hopeless expression on his face. "Best-case scenario, we would stop the production of Hyacinth Red and it would be forever banned from use in a peaceful and unified world. Worst-case scenario, they'll kill us. Hell, they'll probably kill us anyway."

"What if every country leader and every scientist knew the truth. Couldn't that prevent them from using Hyacinth? And wouldn't that give us a little life insurance?"

"Did Lucille tell you about old man Duffy's three Ps: Profit, Power, and Perpetuation. Lead was one of the oldest know poisons, but it took health activists seventy five years before they finally got the word out on leaded gas. Hell, lobbyist are still trying to put lead back in gas. It's still sold in any Third World country too small and poor to argue. How many years did it take to get to the truth about tobacco and asbestos? How many more years will it take before people quit buying into petroleum propaganda and accept the truth about global warming? The world must have petroleum. If Hyacinth Red can replace petroleum, it is nothing short of world domination. How do you get around that to tell all these people your truth?"

Silently I wondered how much I could trust these two. Finally I said, "I believe I know where Evelyn hid the Hyacinth test report, and I believe I know what she intended to do with it. I would like to finish her work. Would you two like to help me?"

FORTY-SIX

Back in San Jose, our first task was to reclaim my belongings, which I had left in the Hotel Aurora Holiday Inn. It was doubtful that Woods's people would be watching here, but we took no chances. With James and Gill hanging out in the lobby like bodyguards, I went to the desk, presented my Dolores Gomez identification, and requested my belongings. I collected my original laptop, my Walther, and the virus-like program disk that Patricia had given me the night before she was killed.

We had agreed that I would leave the hotel by myself, take a cab to the San Pedro Mall, switch cabs, and take the second cab back to the Gran Hotel. James and Gill would each follow me in separate cabs and make sure my appearance at the Aurora Hotel didn't pick up any tail.

The exercise went almost without incident. That is, no one tried to tail me from the Aurora. However, when I jumped into the cab that was at the head of the line at the mall, I got a small shock. When the driver turned around to ask where I wanted to go, I saw it was Roberto. Surprise registered on my face before I could control it. Roberto noticed that something was wrong but didn't recognize me, and I decided it was best to keep it that way.

"The Gran Hotel, please, driver."

Now he looked surprised, and he studied me closer.

"I know that voice, but, Tia Tillie?"

I couldn't help a slight smile but didn't say anything.

"I knew you were too spry to be so old."

"Sorry, Roberto. I promised never to bother you again and if I had known it was you I would have gotten into another taxi."

He shoved the car in gear and laughed. "Oh, I am glad you did. It is nice to know you are all right. Have you found the killer yet?"

"Sorry. Can't talk about that. What happened to the Green Machine sign on your taxi?"

"My wife. She was afraid and made me paint it. She say it made me stand out too much."

"Sounds like a smart woman, but I am sorry that something I got you into made you change it. You were so proud of it."

He gave me his characteristic shrug, and we made small talk the rest of the way to the Gran. As he dropped me at the hotel he said, "Tia Tillie, please, I know you can't talk about the investigation, but you can tell me if my family will need to worry about danger for much longer."

"I have a flight back to the States tomorrow afternoon. Pick me up at the Gran at 2:30. I may be able to tell you more then. OK?"

"Sure, thanks."

Three hours later, when I emerged from my room at the Gran, I was blond, blue-eyed, fair-skinned, with full makeup, and attired in "Hollywood Safari" like an overdressed tourist. My passport now said Jillian Morgan.

I joined my two companions on the hotel patio and was gratified to receive a double-take from Gill and a long admiring smile from James. All those years of watching Richard do my makeup had taught me something. A waiter set a latte in front of me almost immediately. James explained.

"We ordered your latte to be served at 11:00 a.m. sharp and have been betting on whether you would be on time to drink it hot."

"Ah. Who won?"

Gill shrugged. "James did, but he had an unfair advantage. He had worked with you. I had only my vast experience with women to go on. How was I to know you would be an exception?"

"Serves you right for harboring sexist stereotypes. Now, how about you? Did you get the equipment we need?"

"Yes. GPS was no problem. The satellite phone cost a bit more than anticipated, but it works in all atmospheric conditions and the dish zeros in on the satellite all by itself, so we won't have to fool around with compasses and levels and so forth."

"Good. James, were you able to send all the evidence you have collected on the murders?"

"Yeah. Used the secure link at the consulate to download all my information to Shanley at Blue Morpho, and he will be coordinating efforts by a number of agencies. They'll begin making arrests here in Costa Rica and elsewhere this afternoon. One of the agencies involved will, of course, be the FBI, and so I called your friend Agent Camas personally. Told him what a fine job he and the

Bureau had done on the case and how much we appreciated his efforts."

"Somehow, I doubt that flattery will deter him from nailing my ass as soon as I get home."

"Well, he might have somehow gotten the impression that you were working undercover with Interpol at the time he interviewed you and had not been at liberty to speak freely."

"Did he buy that?"

"I am not sure, but I know he got the point when I said we were drafting a letter to his superior, commending him for his cooperation with you."

"I owe you one, James."

"No, that just makes us even for that home run you hit on Woods's skull."

"Speaking of Woods, do you know if I– if he's alive?"

Surprisingly, the answer came from Gill. "Oh, he's alive all right, very angry, and marshaling forces to have you both killed on sight."

A slight suspicion creeping into his voice, James asked, "How do you know that?"

Gill smiled. "I have a friend who works at Blue Morpho."

The two men stared at each other as James calculated the significance of Gill having a spy at Morpho. I didn't want my little partnership to blow up just yet, so I called James back to the present project with a question.

"Did you get the dissertation?

From a plastic bag, James pulled an inch-thick set of papers bound in cardboard covers with brads. "Yeah, I dug it out of the library at the University of Costa Rica this morning and made you this copy, but I really don't see anything in it about fuel. Are you sure this is the right paper? And what are the GPS and the phone for?"

I hadn't told either of them what my hunches were or exactly what I intended to do. I wanted to check my theory first. They watched with curiosity while I opened the dissertation written by archeologist, Paul Hamerstat, the late husband of Sophia Hamerstat. I searched through the index and then turned to one of the maps showing locations in Costa Rica dotted with tiny circles. Each circle or group of circles was labeled with the name of a planet, star, or constellation followed by numerical coordinates for a position of latitude and longitude. First I verified that there was no sphere for Earth, and then I found the circle I was looking for and turned the paper for Gill to see.

"Here, Gill, do you know where this location is? Is it far from here?"

"This is in the Diquis Delta, a few hours from here by car." He looked more closely at the writing and I saw his eyes widen. "What is this?"

"An acquaintance in the States told me that her husband had written a doctorate on the great spheres of Costa Rica. These granite balls were carved with such precision that they are perfect spheres, having the same diameter and circumference when measured from any point, a trick modern technicians would have difficulty duplicating. They range in size from a few centimeters to over nine feet in diameter and weigh as much as twenty tons. Thousands of them have been found in Costa Rica, miles from quarries, not only on the flat but up in the coastal mountains, and out on an island as well. None are found anywhere else in the world. Since none of the civilizations known to have lived in Costa Rica had ever displayed the technology to build them, much less transport them up mountains and across water, most archeologists have simply ignored them as an unsolvable enigma.

"Hamerstat believed the spheres were the archeological remains of an unknown and ancient navigational society that had created a three-dimensional map of the heavens. He believed that this great map served as a university of astronomy, mathematics, and navigation. He made calculations verifying that certain spheres were mathematically in perfect distance and ratio from other spheres to represent specific stars, planets, and constellations. Though many of the smaller spheres had been moved, Hamerstat mapped enough of the larger ones in original position to support his theory."

Gill turned to the title page, back to the map I had shown him, and then looked up at me with far too much understanding in his expression. In almost a whisper, he asked, "These calculations can really identify specific spheres as specific planets?"

I nodded.

James expression indicated he hadn't a clue what this meant or why it was important. I had to keep in mind, however, that this was the man who did such a good job of playing it dumb on the night I met him.

Gill's reaction however made me realize he had to have read more of Evelyn's documents than just the Blue Morpho file. As Gill knowingly examined the document before us, I was sure he had read the *Martian Diary* and had now guessed, as I had, where Evelyn had hidden the file. That should have forewarned me of what was to come.

FORTY-SEVEN

As soon as Gill understood where we were going and why, he said the drive over the Cordillera de Talamanca and down the Pacific side would take too long. He went off to make calls and came back with SANSA Air tickets from San Jose to Palmar Sur and a reservation in Palmar Sur for a four-wheel-drive rental car.

For such a small country, Costa Rica has amazing climatic changes in surprisingly few miles. When we stepped onto the plane in San Jose, it was seventy degrees, with scattered clouds and a pleasant light breeze. When we stepped off in Palmar Sur, the humidity and mosquito factors were way up, and a torrential downpour started before we finished renting the car.

At the Palmar airport, we loaded our equipment and rain gear into the Range Rover, and Gill drove south through banana plantations toward the river port town of Sierpe. To my dismay, we left the paved road almost immediately. We bumped down a muddy dirt road, through cattle pastures and forests and over a one-lane suspension bridge so narrow I would have sworn the Rover was too wide to cross it. Though San Jose had been perpetual spring since I arrived, rain had been falling on the Diquis Delta for days. In addition, the area is circled by rivers and mangrove swamps, washed by the Pacific, and receives runoff from the mountains to the east.

As we left the better maintained roads near the banana plantations, the mud became several inches thick, and we passed two cars that had landed in the ditch and were abandoned with mud up to the doors. Traveling under a heavy blanket of clouds, on roads that were not on the map, I guided Gill by relying on our GPS receiver. I had programmed it to guide us to the coordinates that Hamerstat's calculations identified as a sphere representing the planet Mars.

Almost an hour later we reached a spot where the only track going in the direction we needed to go was a footpath through the forest.

"Stop here, Gill. This looks like it will be as far as we go by car, but we are within one kilometer of the site."

Gill brought the Rover to a slushy, skidding stop. We put on our bright blue rain parkas and grabbed the folding shovels. As a precaution, I programmed the current location of our Rover into the GPS memory.

James watched me and smiled. "That gadget beats the hell out of bread crumbs."

We stepped carefully along the slippery path that ran under a claustrophobic ceiling of tangled forest and followed the GPS steering arrow toward the coordinates for our Mars sphere,

The granite globe, about five feet in diameter, was set on a slight rise on the eastern side of a small clearing. In the light of the clearing, with the rain pounding on its polished surface, the sphere seemed almost luminescent.

They both watched as I surveyed the ground around the sphere. On high ground on the north east side, I saw it. It might not have been obvious to the casual glance, but to someone looking for it, it was as plain as a doorway. There was a circle, about two feet across, where a shovel had cut into the ground. The Earth and plants had been carefully removed and carefully replaced, but roots had been cut so that dead plant material made a brown outline just beneath the green grass and vines. It was slightly sunken as it had resettled into less firmly packed soil.

I unfolded the shovel and began to dig, first removing the same section of ground that had been taken out before. Three shovels full of soil down I found the case buried partially under the sphere. As I tried to dislodge the case and pull it out, James appeared at my side to help. As the case came out of the ground, I had hold of the handle but James did not let go of the far edge.

"I'll be damned," said James. "How did you know?"

By his question I knew that James had never read the *Martian Diary*. To answer I would have to tell him the story of Antia and how she had hidden the final documents under a similar monolith on Mars. The one Antia had chosen represented Earth. Evelyn chose Mars.

Many things made sense now, like my card, still in Evelyn's bra so long after I had given it to her. She had put it there when she knew her death was near. She knew I would be called and come to Arizona. The note to High Pockets that she had left in Jim's house would mean nothing to anyone who hadn't read the diary. But what a chance she took. She gambled that I would come, that Jim would give me the note and that, against all odds, that note would bring me here. All of that was a part of the story James didn't need to know, and telling it seemed like a betrayal to Evelyn.

"Oh, just something Evelyn said to me finally clicked into place," I lied. As

I finished speaking, I happened to catch Gill looking at me intently. His face held a hint of a smile, but I couldn't read his expression.

James was not really interested in how I had done it. He was concentrating on the case we held between us. "OK, Diana, good work. I'll take it from here."

He tried to take the case and my anger flared. I clung to the handle and grabbed the other side with my free hand.

"So you really are with Woods after all."

He looked surprised. "How can you say that? My people are arresting Woods and his men as we speak."

"Your people? You mean the people that Woods said are no longer making the decisions about Hyacinth Red?"

"Look, Woods may have his little military clique, but we have people who can go directly to the President of the United States.

"Remember Duffy's three P's, James. Hyacinth Red is the ultimate ring of power. You take this back to them and they will bury us and anyone else who objects to using it."

He took a firmer hold on the case and prepared to yank it from me. "What do you think you can do with it? You going to chain yourself to the gate and wait for the press to plead your case? Evelyn tried that. You going to try to publish these papers? If you succeeded, and you would probably be killed before you did, but if you succeeded, all you would do is give away the formula. If this stuff will really destroy the atmosphere, it would be like publishing instructions on how to build a hydrogen bomb."

The distinctive clicking of semiautomatics chambering bullets came from three sides and effectively ended both our wrestling match for the case and our debate on the fate of its contents. We looked up to see Gill and two other men who had appeared from God knows where, all pointing guns at us.

"Ms. Hunter, Mr. Nolan—kindly set the case down on the ground and back away from it."

With no real option to do otherwise, we did as we were ordered. Gill walked over and picked up the case.

"Now, kindly place your hands on Mars."

As we leaned over the sphere, Gill instructed his friends to search us for weapons. I had slipped my little Walther into the cargo pocket of my pants. James was packing a nine millimeter, for what good weapons did either of us.

"Thank you. Now, shall we go back to the car where we can get out of this rain?"

As we started to walk toward the car, James asked, "You working with Woods?"

"If you recall, I am the one who urged Interpol to bring Woods to your attention, Mr. Nolan."

"Who, then? Russians, Chinese, French, Israel? Who is trying to get control of this?"

"I work for no foreign power. I am simply trying to reclaim something that Evelyn had taken from my friends."

"What? The Morpho files?"

Gill did not answer and I didn't need him to. I had finally figured him out, just a little late.

FORTY-EIGHT

When we got back to the road we found a second car there. Obviously, when Gill made our travel arrangements he had also managed to have his companions follow us. In Spanish, Gill asked his friends to take James to the second car, then changing to English, he instructed me to get into the back seat of our Rover. He put his gun away in its holster and climbed in beside me.

"Now shall we see what we have here?" He opened the watertight case and found several paper files and two compact discs. The first disc was labeled:

15643-9-23

(47th language translation-English)

(Copy 2,783) (Caretaker-Nosha)

This one he placed in his coat pocket and I asked the obvious question to which I already knew the answer.

"You're one of the Caretakers of the diary, aren't you?"

"Yes."

"Did Evelyn know that?"

"Not at first, but by her last visit, yes."

"So you didn't just accidentally get acquainted with her, did you? You were keeping an eye on someone who might betray the cause."

He hesitated a moment, but made no answer. Then he handed me the second, unlabeled disc. "I believe that if you put this in your laptop and pull it up you will find it contains the data that Evelyn wanted to submit to world opinion. Am I correct in assuming that you have the transmission program she had created for this task?"

I nodded.

"Then I'll set up the satellite phone, and you get ready to transmit."

He reached into the cargo space behind us, handed me my laptop case, and put the case with the satellite phone in his lap. I sat watching as he opened the case and began to set up. He looked at me, his expression curious.

"You have another concern?" he asked.

"What if James is right? What if it is like publishing instructions for a hydrogen bomb?"

He shook his head. "The formula for Hyacinth Red is not in here. It never was. Todd didn't give her that part. What is in this file is pure science, showing the electrical and chemical reactions of certain elements with the upper atmosphere and demonstrating why the release of these elements in quantity into the atmosphere would result in the depletion of the atmospheric envelope around our globe. This disc also lacks the copy of the *Martian Diary*, which Evelyn wanted to publish. We convinced her that the world was not yet ready for that revelation."

"I see."

I loaded the transmission program that would send data to every government, every university, every environmentalist, and every scientific institution, newspaper, and journal that Evelyn's German programmer had been able to find. It would then raid their mailing lists and also send copies to all of their correspondents. Then I inserted the Hyacinth Red data into the transmission program, and Gill connected the laptop to the phone. The phone found the satellite, and we connected to the web. Hand on the send button, I hesitated.

"Gill, you are a bright, trained investigator, experienced in looking empirically at evidence. Do you really believe the *Martian Diary* is a true history?"

"Which part of that story do you find unbelievable, the fact that mankind could travel across space and colonize a nearby planet or the fact that mankind could be so stupid, greedy, and short sighted as to completely destroy the planetary environment?"

Bewildered by the thoughts his question raised, I sat silently and he answered for me.

"There are scientists, right now, in your country associated in an enterprise to colonize Mars. They believe they can make an inhabitable colony within one to two hundred years by a process that I believe they call *terraforming*. They believe they can create the water, air, plant life, shelter, and fuel necessary to survive on this now barren planet. Do you believe that?"

He waited for my answer. I nodded. "I have read about it, and I even know one person who is working on it."

"Why is it so much harder to believe that mankind could have colonized a lush and abundant planet like Earth?"

I found no answer.

"As to environmental destruction, just look around you. Right now our

Earth is experiencing the greatest rate of extinction since the death of the dinosaurs, and this time it cannot be blamed on a great cataclysm. It is due directly to human overpopulation, pollution, and wanton destruction."

"OK, I grant you that both ideas are possible, but if a society advanced enough for space flight had been on Earth at some time in the past, wouldn't there be some evidence of it left around for us to discover?"

He began to laugh.

"My question wasn't intended as a joke."

"I am sorry. But the real question is, would we recognize such evidence if we laid our hands upon it? About a half an hour ago you placed both of your hands on a sphere which none of the sciences of our great modern world can satisfactorily explain. They know of no people who could have made them, have found no tools to carve them, and have only recently begun to find clues as to their possible astronomical significance. What has establishment science said of these mysteries? They have simply dismissed them as 'out of context' with known civilization. They have simply shrugged and ignored them."

The unpleasant sound of ridicule flavored my next question. "So you think the Martians made these spheres?"

He studied me for a moment then answered quite seriously. "These stones are not all our science ignores. Man's history is far older than our current beliefs allow for. You ask for evidence? The world is littered with marvelous mysteries and empirical evidence of a great, seafaring, scientifically advanced society, composed of many peoples and many races, a society that was wiped out about twelve to fifteen thousand years ago. There are megaliths and structures, each demonstrating a knowledge of global geography and heavenly astronomy that has not been duplicated by modern man until the last one hundred years. Ignorant Europeans inaccurately attributed these works to primitive civilizations that could not possibly have constructed them. Then these barbarian conquerors burned ancient Mayan libraries, thousands of books, that might have educated mankind not only in the sciences, but in their own prehistory.

"Do I believe this ancient society, now lost and forgotten, owed some of its knowledge to Martian colonizers?"

He smiled and paused for effect. "It doesn't matter because that is not really what you are asking. What you are asking is, can the *Martian Diary* provide you with justification for sending the data that rests at your fingertip? The answer is *no.* You do not need the *Martian Diary* for that purpose. Just look around at what you know is happening to Earth's environment, every day. That is all the justification you need. Do it."

I clicked Send, and in the twinkling of an eye, the world was given new scientific knowledge. The question was, what would they do with it?

EPILOGUE

Gill and I had talked all the way back to San Jose, much of our conversation being about those stone mysteries that dot our globe. He refused to speak about the *Martian Diary*. When he dropped me off at the Gran Hotel, he reached back and grabbed my laptop.

"You have been quite true to Evelyn in the face of many dangers and have been of great assistance to the Caretakers. I want to leave you with a small gift of thanks. It is our way of showing our appreciation. In the coming years of doubt, it may help you to feel justified in what you have done."

He then put the *Martian Diary* CD in my computer, pulled up a single file, copied it to my hard drive, and retrieved the CD.

I held my curiosity in check until I was back home and safely out on Sam's boat in the harbor. Then I opened it and read the final chapter of the *Martian Diary*.

*   *   *

Paus Tak, Southern Laboratory

For a moment the sound that drew me from slumber had made my heart leap for joy, but once fully awake I knew it to be just the wind. Then the stabbing sadness of loneliness overwhelmed me. I wished I could sleep or could die. Perhaps today I would have the courage to do it, to bring a final end.

Then I heard it again, sounding so like a human voice. She often fools me like that, the wind. Sometimes she whistles from the sky and makes me believe that by some miracle a great Taner still lives and flies the skies. Sometimes I even look up, not because I really believe any of the great birds escaped extinction, but because, for a brief moment, I can pretend I will see one.

Sometimes she scuttles along the ground sounding like a Mitmox following at my heels, waiting to be fed. On those occasions I do talk to her like she was a small pet. Of course, I am going mad. I actually did see a live Mitmox once when I was a child. One of the geneticists bred it, quite against the rules of course, but he was lonely for some companion critter. He made me promise never to tell.

Then I heard the sound again, and this time I also heard footsteps in the outer cave. I began to hope that there really could be another human being alive and here at Paus Tak.

It's been two and a half years since I heard the last human voice. I preserved Klal Matak's remains in the old science way, placing his stem cells, tissue, and all organs cells in the frozen zoology calesets along with the rest of the extinct flora and fauna of our sad, dead planet. This I had promised him, though for what purpose I cannot foresee, for I, Klal Tslak, am the last of the preservers at Paus Tak. When I die, there will be no one to perform this task for me; in fact, there will be no one at all, for I am the only living creature here. I could, of course, clone a new companion, but even if it were not forbidden by my vows, I would never be so cruel as to create another to sit in our solar-powered island and await the last morsel of food and final silence of our world.

But the voice. Somehow there was a voice. At last I knew it was real. I tried to answer but it had been so long since I had spoken aloud my voice failed me. I ran toward the caller trying to yell out. When I met him I threw my arms about him and cried until the poor man passed out in my arms, for he had arrived more dead than alive.

He is a Nomad called Choam who now eats and rests in my solar chamber after a harrowing journey from burrocity Zed. His mission was to bring news of the final rebellions and to request a written history and detailed scientific data regarding the purpose and product of the Preservers. He says the Hidden Ones wish to take this information with them on the last ship across the skies to Atland.

I do not believe there is any purpose to this because to my knowledge there is no one capable of biological preservation, much less capable of the biological restoration of all the species we have preserved at the cellular level. It took only two generations of withholding biology from the burro curriculum to turn science into superstition. The only remnant left is some sort of religious ceremony in which the organs are removed from the body and the whole saved in impure mummification. Deprived of true knowledge, they believe this *ritual will bring life after death somewhere out in the heavens. Men descend to barbarity far faster than they ascend to science.*

As to the rebellions, it is no more than I expected. The tunnels of the burrocities ran ankle deep in human blood, and all cities are by now airless, frigid, and lifeless. That leaves myself, Choam, perhaps a few isolated Nomads, and a small handful of scientists at the tiny outpost burrocity of Zed. We are the only living organisms on this planet that was once a lush garden of life.

The only news that surprised me was the cause of the outbreak. It wasn't the tragic, inhuman condition of life in the burrocities. It wasn't even the knowledge that only a privileged few would secure transportation to the new planet. It was the dissemination of an old environmental visual recording of the once living planet, its lush flora and fauna, its oceans and free-running rivers of water. It was the knowledge of what had been lost.

The extinction records Choam needs are ready; in fact, a list of extinct species was begun ages ago, even before the genetic preservation program was begun. The scientific methods of preservation are also well documented and detailed and have only awaited the call to be carried to the new world. It is the final thing he requested that I am helpless to supply. The Hidden Ones want a brief history of extinction. A brief history. How does one briefly recite the history of the destruction of an entire planetary ecosystem? If I could find the words, they would break my heart.

Choam returns in the morning to Zed, where the final ship waits to carry the Hidden Ones, the Caretakers of our people's history. He takes this note from Klal Tslak, the last of the Preservers, who lived a life of hope for a hopeless cause. I pray someone comes back to the ice caves of Paus Tak and restores these bits of genetic patterns of the living flora and fauna that once graced this land.

If Choam can survive another round trip to Zed and back, he will join me here to await the final silence of all save the wind.

The End

Joan Francis is a licensed private investigator and owner of Francis Pacific Investigations. She has also worked as a newspaper reporter and is the author of a new Diana Hunter thriller, Silent Coup. She spent her childhood in small mining towns and camps in the western United States and in South America with her family and mining engineer father. Moving from place to place as her father opened up new mine sites, she attended fifteen schools before graduating with a B.A. in history from the University of Washington in Seattle. Married with three grown children, she and her husband now live in a secluded valley of the Tehachapi Mountains. Her website is www.joanfrancis.net and her email is diana@joanfrancis.net.

www.ingramcontent.com/pod-product-compliance
Lightning Source LLC
Chambersburg PA
CBHW030245130626

46549CB00002B/401